Mike Ripley

is the author of eight novels in the award-winning 'Angel' series and co-edits (with Maxim Jakubowski) the **Fresh Blood** anthologies promoting new British crime writing. He is crime critic for the *Daily Telegraph* and *Publishing News* but never gave up the day job in the brewing industry. He is currently adapting *Angel in Arms* for television and vows that *That Angel Look* will be his last novel.

That
Angel
Look

Mike Ripley

BLOODLINES

First Published in Great Britain in 1997 by
The Do-Not Press
PO Box 4215
London SE23 2QD

A Paperback Original

ISBN 1 899344 23 3

British Library Cataloguing in Publication Data. A catalogue record for
this book is available from the British Library.

Printed and bound in Great Britain by The Guernsey Press Co Ltd.

The writing of this one involved a lot of people one way and another and this, in no particular order, is not so much a roll of honour, as a sharing of blame.

For technical help: my wife Alyson, Naseem Khawaja, my former editor Elizabeth Walter, Caroline Roberts, Jim Driver at The Do-Not Press and various policemen who put up with idiot questions and prefer not to be named.

For support and the chance to try out a few jokes: Michael Dibden, KK Beck, Ian Rankin, Philip Oakes, Maxim Jakubowski and Bill Carmichael, and John Jarman and the rest of the Thursday Club.

– M D R

1.

Then

I was sitting in the foyer of a Mexican restaurant looking up the atrium of the Canary Wharf building, having my shoes shined and drinking a pint of Margarita. It was such a perfect moment I just had to ring somebody on my mobile phone and tell them about it.

I pulled the Motorola out of my jacket and flipped it open. The guy cleaning my shoes looked surprised, then suddenly very smug.

'Hey, they still use those things?' he chirped.

'Long as somebody else is paying the bills,' I said.

'Wow. I thought those were museum pieces. Never see them nowadays. You want one of these.'

He shot back the cuff of his red shirt and waved his wrist at me. He was wearing a bright red Swatch bleeper watch, which even in the January sales had cost three times as much as the phone I was holding.

'Can't use that to call a cab,' I said airily and punched a number in the memory.

Twenty-five floors above me, a phone rang and The Sarge answered with an irritable, 'Yeah, what?'

'Sarge, it's Angel. You still working?'

'On the last set-up. Where are you?' he growled. He always put an unlit cigar in his mouth when he answered the phone. Made him sound tough.

'Below you, in the Tex-Mex restaurant, having my shoes shined and drinking Margaritas.'

'Did you say shoeshine?'

'Yep. It's policy. If you have to wait for a table, you get a free shoe-shine.'

'You booked a table?'

'No, you did. Lunch was part of the deal.'

I knew he wouldn't mind and almost certainly had forgotten to book anywhere himself, but he let me hang there for a while as if considering it.

'Margaritas, eh?'

'By the frosted pint mug,' I tempted.

'Good drink, Margarita. Contains all known food groups.'

'Yeah, salt and tequila,' I said, robbing him of his standard line.

'Right,' he said, recovering. 'So get some more lined up. We'll be down in fifteen minutes.'

'You got my girls up there, Sarge?'

'Course I have and I've been the perfect gentleman. Haven't even hinted that they might like to get their kit off.'

'Good man. I know it must be a strain.'

'Tell me about it. Hey, you don't suppose they would, do you?'

He had dropped his voice. The girls must have been close.

'I'm at the bar, Sarge, and your tab is running,' I said and snapped the phone closed.

The guy cleaning my shoes sighed at the naffness of it all, but thought he had better make conversation if he was going to get a tip.

'And what sort of music does sir like?' he smarmed, just like a hairdresser asks where you have been on holiday.

'Jazz, actually,' I said, moving my feet to make life more difficult for him.

'That John Coltrane, he was the business, eh?' he said without looking up, but I could hear him thinking maybe Coltrane was too modern for someone my age.

'Gimme Armstrong every time,' I said, playing along.

'Louis Armstrong?' he looked tip at me, genuine surprise in his eyes. 'Hey, that *We Have all the Time in the World* – that was a great song. What a voice. He done anything since?'

That did it. His tip was history.

He probably thought I was.

The Sarge got his nickname back in the eighties when he wore an old army combat jacket with three bars on one sleeve whenever he was on assignment. The jacket had enough pockets to store all the film he needed, spare lenses, two back-up Olympus Trips and his mobile phone. The camouflage design even came in handy when he was covering Animal Liberation protests and sit-ins aimed at stopping motorway building. But in more urban settings – the Poll Tax riots, the odd student protest, Gay Rights or militant disabled marches – he found himself confused with the protesters and, after a while, found it difficult to get private medical insurance. Then, on his way to a friend's wedding, he stopped off to cover a Lesbian Avengers rally in Whitehall and, because he was wearing a suit, didn't get truncheoned or trampled by a police horse. Since then, he had always worn a suit. The suits got better and now he wouldn't carry a mobile phone in case it spoiled the cut. He had someone else to carry his cameras.

'So how you doing, Angel?' he asked, sitting down opposite me.

I had claimed a free table for two, thus depriving The Sarge of his complimentary shoeshine.

'Not as well as you if you can afford this place,' I said. 'I've ordered chilli.'

'Cool,' he said.

'I hope not.' The Sarge liked his food hot and spicy. If it didn't hurt, he rated it nutritionally lacking.

'It's OK. Food's good here.' He waved limply at a passing waitress. 'Beers, love. Make 'em Dos Equis.'

The waitress smiled and said, 'Sure thing, right with you,' and hurried off to cater to his every whim. I'd been kept waiting for half an hour. My shoes were like mirrors. If I'd have stood near the waitress's skirt, I could have been arrested.

'You driving?' he asked.

'Nope. Knew I'd be meeting you.' And talking money, I added mentally. 'So I left the wheels back in Hackney and jumped the Light Railway.'

'Wise move, me old mate,' he nodded wisely. 'There's a coupla good pubs I want to show you. And anyway, security's as tight as a duck's arse round here. They're frightened of car bombs but I reckon it's not terrorists, it's people with a down on the fashion editor. They even stop the black cabs here and ask the drivers for their names. The dumb fuckers at the gate got five Hugh Grants in one day last month and didn't notice a thing.'

'That was probably a record,' I agreed.

'You still driving that black taxi of yours?'

'A new one. Well, a new old one, if you see what I mean.'

'What happened to the old old one?'

'It died on me,' I said, not wanting to elaborate. 'So how did things go?'

'Ace. Your girlies got on like a house on fire with that fag-hag of a fashion editor. She was over them like a rash. I think it's safe to say they passed the audition.'

'Audition?' I asked, saluting him with a beer bottle as my order arrived.

'That's what I call it. Our beloved Associate Editor (Fashion) does not have meetings any more; she auditions people to see if they will perform to her liking, if and when they're allowed to grace *her* pages in the paper.'

'So what exactly does this audition involve?' I asked between sucks on my bottle. Mexican restaurants were about the only places you could get Mexican beer now the fashion had faded and I hadn't been able to say, 'Buddy, can you spare a lime?' to a barman for months.

'It's all about presentational skills,' said The Sarge, adding a spoonful of raw onion to his chilli and stifling a belch. The Ass Ed (Fash) has her eye on multi-media opportunities, if you know what I mean.'

'No I don't, Sarge. I'm just the talent-spotter in all this.'

'Yeah, yeah, and you'll get your cut.' He waved his spoon at me. 'But it's like a police reward these days, you don't get the cash unless you get a conviction. There was a time when you could spot a pair of jugs bouncing down Tottenham Court Road, whip out the old Nikon and snap, flash, there was a portfolio. Slip it into the News Editor round the pub and wallop – you 'ad a commission for the next Page Three girl and a star was born.'

'Assuming you could persuade them to get their kit off,' I noted dryly.

'That was never a problem,' The Sarge said, straight-faced. 'But nowadays, we've got to go for the joint deal. It's not enough to find a new face any more – the bleedin' primary schools are full of wannabe models. You've got to get the face that goes with the clothes that goes with a story that can be put over in the style magazines and then on daytime television and then into mail order premium offers.'

'So it's a business. Wasn't it ever thus?'

'Naw, it used to be two businesses, maybe three. You had the big name designers who went over the top at the big fashion shows to shock their way on to the fashion pages. You ever see anyone wearing some of that stuff? Bin-liners, arses hanging out, more tinfoil than a turkey farm, skirts for men, cod-pieces for women; it's all bollocks, designed to hype the designer's name and the supermodels on the catwalk.'

'Ah, come off it, Sarge. People like you might photograph the outrageous bits, but the big catwalk shows are meant to provoke, spark off ideas, get people talking. That's where the fashion biz can experiment with new materials, colours, ways of cutting cloth.'

He narrowed his eyes at me, both barrels.

'You shagging a fashion PR lady?'

'Not exactly. But I'm learning a lot through the girls.'

'I'll bet you are,' he smirked, wiping his chilli bowl with the last of the garlic bread. 'Which one?'

'That's for me to know and you to wonder. You said there were two or three fashion businesses.'

'Fashion photography, I meant. The old Fash Flash. Yeah, there's the catwalk crap – the season – the shows. Most of the good shows are London now, actually. But then there's the standard, bread-and-butter stuff, which you can set your watch by.

'It's spring and it's going to be a riot of pastel shades and bright neon, day-glow colours for the young at heart with hemlines up.' The

Sarge had placed both hands on his hips and was turning his head like a swan watching tennis. 'Lime green could be a lucky colour this year too. Then, suddenly it's summer and we're shrieking bright prints, with hemlines up again, or down if there's a gypsy look. If it's a leap year, throw in some natural calico or linen. But before you know it, those autumn leaves are falling: reds, purples, browns and mustard yellows and – *yes* – the *coat* is coming back. Hemlines down and if the year ends in an even number, chuck in a velvet revival.

'And that's it. Year in, year bloody out. That's the business That's what women wear.'

'What about winter?'

'Doesn't exist except in the fur trade, which is so incorrect it's a sin to even suggest a photo spread on it. Throw on an extra layer of thermal undies and keep the skirts short. It's true. You'll see more short skirts in London when it snows than you ever do in the summer. It must be a femme thing. You know, like those macho bastards up north who go out drinking in shirtsleeves even though their nuts are frozen solid, just to prove how hard they are.'

'So, the third part of the business?' I prompted, scoping anxiously for a waitress – for more beer, not fashion tips.

'What the trade calls NBBWs.'

The Sarge went into Smug Mode, picking his moment.

'Not Bought By Wearer. Undies. Naughty knickers. Basques, boob-enhancing bustiers, matching suspender belts. One-piece satin things with no release valve. The memory lingeries on – geddit? Any colour you like as long as it's black or red.'

A waitress – short, black, pretty and world-weary – had materialised at our table.

'Two more beers?' I nodded meekly. 'I'll make them cold ones,' she said.

'Mostly bought by men, always good value for the Christmas and Valentine's Day markets and the number of times I've flogged the story that suspenders and stocking tops are coming back, you wouldn't believe.'

'I think I just might. You still freelance?'

'Too right, but I keep my contacts from the old Fleet Street days. That's why I thought of this place.' He jerked a thumb skyward to the newspaper offices above us.

'But the girls had to do this audition thing first, right?'

'Yeah, like I said. Once over for the frocks themselves, then see how they look on the one that's the model and then the pitch from the one who looks after the business. That's Amy isn't it?'

'No. Amy's the designer. Lyn does the business,' I said, before I had a chance to regret it.

'I'll bet she does,' he leered. 'Is she the one you're… ?'

'And Thalia is the model. And don't forget to pronounce it with a "th", not a "t". She's very sensitive.'

'And in all the wrong places, knowing my luck,' he sighed, but I didn't encourage him. 'What sort of a name is that anyway?'

'I think it's Finnish,' I said to throw him off the scent.

'So, it's Thalia, Amy and Lyn, eh? Quite a backing group.' He stared thoughtfully at the beer bottle in his hand, then realised it was empty. A spark jumped a gap in his brain. 'So, how did you come to meet them – and which one are you screwing?'

I waved at the waitress for more beer and took a deep breath. Most people didn't believe the story. The trouble was, The Sarge would.

'I was in a pub,' I said as I had a hundred times, 'minding my own business, nursing a pint and working on the meaning of life…'

'Yeah, yeah. Fast forward please.'

'Well, the three of them were in there, at a table on round six or maybe seven of Moscow Mules and looking like they'd be out of order by closing time, so, naturally, I had them clocked. Then they started this argument about who had the best legs.'

'You're kidding,' breathed The Sarge.

'I don't have to, but you can jump the plot. Longest, best shape, years of ballet school, born with long ones, always my best feature, that sort of stuff. Then it got on to muscle power and who had the most tension just here.'

I stood up and dug the fingers of both hands into the back of my thighs.

'All three of them, standing up by now, hitching their skirts up and feeling each other's thigh muscles.'

'And your eyeballs have gone telephoto, right?'

'I may have glanced their way,' I conceded. 'I must have done, because one of them called me over and asked me to judge which one had the best thigh muscles.'

Now I had his attention.

'You mean they asked you to feel them?'

'Of course. How else can you judge a muscle?'

'In the middle of a pub?'

'It was a girlies' night out. The pub had seen worse.'

'All three of them?'

'Well, six, actually. Legs, that is.'

'And you had the final call?'

'Absolutely. Independent Adjudicator they called me.'

'And I bet you got off with the winner.'

I just smiled at that one but The Sarge wouldn't let it lie. 'But how did you decide who had the best thighs?'

'I lied.'

2.

Later

'And that was the last time you saw Eugene Sargeant alive, was it?'

'Eugene?' I played dumb, to gain thinking time. 'Oh… The Sarge… Yeah, it would have been.' Playing dumb wasn't that difficult.

'You're sure about that are you, Mr Angel?'

This was a nightmare.

'Yes, course I'm sure. I said so, didn't I?'

'And that was when, exactly?'

'A month ago, something like that.'

'You can't be more specific?'

'Probably not.'

They didn't like that; not specific enough.

'But you definitely haven't seen him since that meeting at Canary Wharf?'

'No.'

There was no point in denying that one. There were other people there. And then there were security cameras, restaurant bills, The Sarge's claim for expenses and all the other ways there are of tracking you these days. Not to mention what happened in the pub that afternoon.

There was no way they wouldn't find someone who remembered that.

'Have you heard from him since then?'

'No.'

That was true. Of him, yes, but not from him.

'So you weren't big mates then?'

'Not that close. I knew he liked his beer and his Friday night vindaloo. He spent good money on good suits, had a collection of the first fifty CDs ever made – kept them in the freezer. Supposed to be good at his job. That's about it.'

'But you'd been to his place, had you?'

This from the quieter one who hadn't spoken much so far and who didn't look old enough to drink, let alone be a career detective.

Still, it was the one part of the economy still booming. If you could buy shares in crime, I'd get a broker.

'No, I never said that,' I said slowly, like I was helping him with the last crossword clue.

'You haven't actually said very much at all,' said the other one. 'But you knew about Sargeant's CD collection in the fridge.'

'He talked about it. It's a laddish sort of thing to talk about. He bought the first fifty CDs ever released in this country. It was his nest egg. He didn't listen to them, just wanted to keep them until they became antiques. He kept them in the freezer because that way they keep longer. Well, that's what they used to say. Is this relevant to anything?'

'Probably not,' said the younger one. Then he changed tack, proving that he'd read the detective's almanac more recently than his partner.

'We've got you down as living in Hackney, Mr Angel. At number nine, Stuart Street. Is that correct?'

'Yes,' I said pleasantly. If he wanted to play Nice Cop, I could play Nice Suspect and resist the temptation to ask how they had placed me so quickly. I certainly hadn't volunteered my address.

'Do you own the house?'

'No, I rent part of it.'

I wasn't driving when they picked me up, so they couldn't have traced me through vehicle registrations.

'And you live alone?'

'Yes, apart from the cat.' The flatmate from hell, I added silently.

'That's not far away,' said one of them.

'Far from what?' I said, distracted by the thought that I hadn't fed Springsteen for two days.

'Far from Whitechapel,' said the younger one. I blanked him so he had to add, 'Hackney – not that far from Whitechapel.'

'That's not the sort of thing they'll put on the Borough signs, is it? I mean, "Welcome To Hackney, it's not far from Whitechapel" isn't exactly going to draw the punters, is it?'

I was rabbiting inanely, just to buy time. (My Rule of Life Number 74 says that you can work your way out of most situations if you can give yourself enough thinking time.)

'Mind you,' I gabbled on, 'Whitechapel does get the tourists, doesn't it? I mean, there are all those Jack the Ripper tours, aren't there? Meet outside a pub, troll around for two hours in the freezing cold and come away with a certificate in disembowelling. There's supposed to be forty or more tours a week in the season—'

'Are you taking the piss?' growled the older one.

'No, I just don't understand the question. Hackney is close to Whitechapel in what way? Ethnically? Culturally? Property values?'

It was a blag and it was mostly rubbish, but only mostly. I knew the Metropolitan Police no longer recruited exclusively from outside London, but even the newest incoming beat copper, let alone a detective, should have picked up that distances in the East End are not measured in miles. Race, religion and family redraw the map faster and more accurately than the guys at the Ordnance Survey ever could.

'Whitechapel is where Eugene Sargeant lived,' the younger one offered. 'It's not very far from Hackney.'

'I didn't know that. I mean, I know where Whitechapel is, of course, and you're right, looking at it that way, it's not that far.'

'Are you on something?' snapped the older one, the fingers of his right hand making a show of strangling his pencil. Still, that was a good sign; we were still at the pencil and notebook stage, not yet into the taped interview.

'Some sort of medication?' he went on, looking more interested in me all of a sudden.

'Sorry,' I said, 'I was wandering. There's a syndrome called Attention Deficit Disorder.'

'There is?' said the detective quietly and I nodded.

There was. I didn't have it but there really was.

'What was the question?'

'More of a point, really,' the younger one sighed wearily. 'You live near where Sargeant lived and you knew about his CD collection. You went drinking with him and put some work his way. Are you telling us you never went round to his gaff? You really didn't know where he lived?'

'That's exactly what I'm telling you. I didn't even know his first name was Eugene until you said it. Look—' I opened my hands so they could see the empty palms, just like they tell you to in the body language manuals. 'I used to see The Sarge around, that was all. Just around.'

That seemed to satisfy them for all of half a minute, then the younger one said again, 'So that was the last time you saw him? When he bought you lunch at Canary Wharf?'

'Yeah. Well, in the pub later that afternoon, to be really accurate.'

3.

Then

The girls came into the pub like a dust devil, the crowd of after-noon drinkers, almost totally male, moving aside and nursing their glasses to let them through. It didn't go quiet, like it would have in a Western when the pale rider checked into town; it was more that a low animal hum was added to the general soundtrack of background noise.

I knew them and I was impressed.

They, of course, were oblivious of the impact they made, busy chattering to each other so much that they reached the bar before remembering that they were there to meet us. They stopped and looked around and by this time The Sarge was on his feet, striding towards them with his arms open, saying, 'Ladies—'

If that was his best shot at a chat-up line, he was in for another night at home filing his CD collection.

Thalia, the tallest of the three, spotted him first and switched her face on to automatic pilot: full smile, head dipping slightly to the right, an oh-so-carefully-trained hank of her long, straight hair flopping down over her face.

Lyn jerked a weak smile in his direction and then said something in Thalia's right ear. At that distance my lip-reading was far from precise, but I felt sure I saw the word 'toad' in there. Amy, mean-while, was taking a bottle of wine and three glasses from a barman and pointing at The Sarge to make it clear who was paying. By the time he reached the bar he had had an air-kiss on both cheeks from Thalia, a pat on the shoulder from Lyn, a nod from Amy, and he was eight quid worse off.

Leaving The Sarge to pay the barman, Amy led them in triangle formation over to the table where I was sitting. Thirty pairs of male eyes followed them, most of them glued to Thalia's catwalk prowl which could have set new standards of precision for Swiss watch-makers. There was also the fact that whilst her hemline wasn't exactly too high, a cynic might say that her belt-line was a little too low. And for about the millionth time, I told myself that black opaque Lycra tights really did have a lot to answer for.

Then Amy was shoving me along the bench seat with her thigh and plonking down the bottle and glasses on the table and saying:

'What a piece of work he is. Who told him he was cool?'

'Another man,' Lyn and I said together. Then we gave each other a quiet high five.

'Never mind him, though,' I said, 'he's just a drone. What about the Queen Bee? How did you get on with her?'

'She's a sweetie, darling,' gushed Thalia, leaning over to kiss me on the cheek. I could imagine the view she was giving the bar as she did so. There were now forty pairs of eyes on us.

'She loved us, Angel, simply loved us. Loved the ideas, loved the clothes, loved the marketing strategy.' Thalia paused only to sink half a glass of wine in one. 'And she's promised us the moon.'

'Which is just about as sterile and pock-marked as she is,' hissed Amy.

'Oooh, you bitch,' Thalia giggled.

'Oh, come on, Big T,' Lyn joined in. 'You know she's kidding herself if she thinks she's still got time for babies. That's one biological clock running on double summer time if ever I saw one.'

'If I said any of this – or he did –' I pointed my glass at the returning Sarge, 'you'd knife us.'

'Of course we would.' Lyn smiled and gripped my right knee under the table; not enough to hurt, but not casual enough for me to take my eyes of her. 'But we're women, so it's allowed.'

'Well now, have all my lovely ladies got a drink, then?'

The Sarge pulled up a chair so close to Thalia's that there wasn't room for an extra coat of varnish. She smiled her smile at him and raised her glass, not seeming to mind in the slightest that his arm had snaked accidentally around her waist.

'You forgot me,' I said to cover the sound of air hissing over both Amy's and Lyn's teeth.

'No I didn't. It's your shout and I'll have a lager while you're up. Now, ladies, how did you get on with the absolutely fabulous Ass Fash?'

'Fabulously,' gushed Thalia. 'She said we were innovative and streetwise without being in-your-face. That's good isn't it?'

'Let's just say she was very interested,' said Amy.

'Very interested in Thalia, anyway,' Lyn said into her glass.

'She wants to see a portfolio with pictures, fabric samples and some prices,' Amy pressed on.

'Pictures?' The Sarge grinned. 'Then I'm your man, right?'

'She said we could use you.'

'Unless we could find somebody cheaper,' interrupted Lyn.

The Sarge fiddled with the knot of his tie and looked over the top of his glasses at her.

'Plenty do it cheaper, nobody does it better.'

Thalia leaned forward and planted her elbows on the table so that she interposed her breasts, straining under a shiny silk scoop-necked top, between The Sarge and Lyn.

'Are we just talking photography here?' she said huskily.

'Oh leave the poor man alone, Thalia,' said Amy, trying to save The Sarge's blushes. She knew he was out of his league with Thalia. So did I, but I would have liked to watch.

'Hey, I can handle it,' laughed The Sarge with only a hint of hysteria.

I heard Lyn mutter something which included the words 'pond life' and decided it was time to get another drink. I picked up my glass and the wine bottle, both of which were empty and nudged Amy's thigh with mine until she stood to let me make a run for the bar. She didn't stop talking business as I squeezed by. So much for my ego.

'Just get it clear that whatever you take is not for syndication. This paper gets a first hit, that's all. Then maybe we can negotiate. You take what I want taken and you use them when I say so. OK?'

'*We*, darling,' said Lyn, 'not "I".'

'Yeah, sure. I meant "we".'

'Amy was just using the Royal "I". She does that a lot,' said Thalia, not helping matters.

I drifted to the bar and out of earshot. I'd heard it all before and though if it was an act, it was a good one, especially played on lone men. No matter how much they bickered among themselves, or seemed to, it was all part of their campaign strategy. Find a man you needed or wanted something from and let him try and divide the three of them, holding out the promise that he might actually conquer one. I had seen it work on better men than The Sarge. It had worked on me.

And it was fair enough as long as you remembered that if the chips ever went down, the triumvirate reformed like globules of mercury rolling downhill. Whatever the odds appeared to be, they were always three-to-one.

I eased into the bar through a crowd of young suits who were either carrying on from a long lunch or settling in for an early evening. At least two of them were already over-lagered and all of them were casting glances over towards Thalia, Amy and Lyn. I didn't think any of them were interested in The Sarge.

They made no attempt to lower their voices as I gently shouldered my way into the barman's eyeline.

'...not many of them to the pound...'

'I've 'ad a rush of blood straight to the groin...'

'I could really abuse that...'

I tried to ignore them but they were not going to let me.

"Ere, they with you?' One of them nudged me with an elbow.

'Sort of,' I said out of the corner of my mouth while offering a five pound note for two pints of lager.

'Which one's yours?' Another one of them breathed in my ear.

'All three.' I pocketed my change, not turning round. Eye contact is what leads to trouble.

'All three?'gasped the first voice.

'He's lying,' drawled somebody else.

'Or greedy.'

'No, straight up,' I said picking up the beers and turning away, still not facing any of them off. 'When the agency booked me they never said anything about there being three of them. 'Scuse me.'

'Agency… ?'

'What did he say… ?'

'What's he on about… ?'

'The Escort Agency I work for. Didn't tell me it was a trio. Still, it's a way of keeping the cost down for them, isn't it? And they don't have much dosh. I mean I'm having to buy my own drinks, aren't I?'

This stream of drivel got me out of the crush and on a clear run back to the table.

From behind me, one of the young suits asked, 'Any jobs going at this agency?'

'Form an orderly queue,' I said over my shoulder.

'What were they laughing at?' snarled Lyn as I sat down with them.

'Me, probably,' I said. 'Have I missed anything?'

'Thalia here was breaking new ground,' said Amy, 'telling your mate that he couldn't have her body.'

'We were stunned, too,' Lyn muttered into her glass.

'Now, now, you old tarts,' Thalia laughed, 'I was telling The Sarge that he couldn't have me for the body.'

'You've got to have A Body,' said The Sarge, not taking his eyes from Thalia's cleavage. 'If you launch a new make-up you have A Face. If we're selling a new look in clothes, we need A Body. You're the model of this mob aren't you? Somebody's got to be in front of the lens.'

'No, sweetie, you just don't understand.' Thalia patted his knee and from his expression I would have bet those trousers would never be dry cleaned again. 'We all wear the clothes. The punters see me first and say to themselves: Sure, but I couldn't wear that. Then Lyn and Amy show them they can.'

The Sarge cringed at that, half-expecting one of the others to take the bottle to Thalia's blonde head.

'And I'm *not* being bitchy.' Thalia patted his knee some more.

'That's the whole trick of TAL and our range. You don't have to have a naturally good body to look good.'

'Or a load of money,' added Amy.

'Or implants,' said Lyn, straightfaced.

'You've got me marked down as the model,' said Thalia, and her expression wasn't giving anything away either, 'not just because I happen to be the one with the most experience—'

'Modelling experience,' Amy chipped in.

'… but because I'm the tallest. Models have to be tall. It's what Angel would call a Rule of Life. But the truth is if you are tall, you've got to have top of the range quality to look good. If you're Lyn's height, say, or even average height for a woman, then you can get away with so much more. The smaller and thinner you are, the more expensive your clothes look, even if they're not. If you know what you're doing, that is.'

The Sarge looked at me over the top of his beer. 'Do they know what they're doing?' he asked.

'Oh yes,' I said.

I meant it. As soon as I heard the idea from the girls themselves, I knew it had the potential to do gangbuster business.

They had met originally at college doing art and design and then some time later, at a party or window-shopping in Mayfair on a Saturday morning, or wherever, depending on who was telling the story. Thalia and Lyn had both dropped out of college. Thalia had gone on a crash secretarial course and signed up with a firm of temps rather than go for a regular nine-to-five, so she could scout the model agencies for jobs. She didn't get many. She had the height, the hair, the skin and the legs, but not, unfortunately, the necessary vacuous expression in the eyes which means the lights are on but no one is home. Her problem was that if she was expected to look sexy, she did. And she enjoyed it. If a guy hit on her with the 'God, but you look fantastic in that' line, she would come back with, 'You think so? Like to see me out of it?'

Lyn found her niche in a market research and public opinion polling company, learning not only that business but the business of running a business within a couple of years. It was while she was running the results of an in-store survey for a major High Street chain that she got the idea that was at the core of the TAL concept.

But no rag trade concept is worth a double stitch if you haven't got the rags, and that was where Amy came in. She had stuck it out at design college, although so unspectacularly that she didn't so much graduate as they forgot to fail her. 'Breathtakingly ordinary,' 'Uninspired beyond her years,' and 'Who?' were just some of the comments on her final college report, if she was to be believed. However, that did not stop her getting into the business, albeit as a third or fourth string designer for a mail-order firm, where creativity was measured in terms of ripping-off chain store designs without being accused of ripping-off.

So, those were the component parts of TAL: a designer with a track record striving towards the mediocre, a market researcher with an attitude and a part-time model with legs and an attitude. But just as a perfect omelette can be more than the sum of its constituent parts, and a frozen paella TV dinner-for-one never can be, TAL worked superbly when all the ingredients were blended together.

The concept, first explained to me over a pub table groaning under the weight of more empty Moscow Mule bottles than the average bottle bank sees in a fortnight, had an almost nineteenth-century industrial revolution ring to it. Find out what they want, tell 'em you're going to give it to them, give it to them, then tell 'em you've given it to them.

Lyn had a database of places which employed more than thirty women aged over twenty-one but under twenty-eight, mainly in secretarial or accounts office jobs. She would hit them with questionnaires and even Focus Group discussions – in the office if it was allowed, round the local wine bar if it wasn't – and then analyse the results. Amy would adapt her existing range of designs to tie in with the results and have samples run up. Thalia would wear them, again at an informal gathering with the women who had been surveyed, usually after office hours in the wine bar or a nearby pub. And when they said, as they did, that it was OK for Thalia, she'd look good in anything, then all three girls went to work.

They told the customers how to mix and match, how to accessorise, how to stand, what size heel to wear, how to get the most fashion bang for their buck. And all the time it was practical stuff, because these were clothes by working girls for working girls. The budget was always a factor but not always the prime directive. What could be worn as both office smart and afterwork chic was, naturally, doubly popular. But the fabrics which went the longest without dry cleaning were also important. So too was the adaptability of anything that went with the ubiquitous, industrial-strength black lycra tights which were worth their premium price because they were tough and lasted longer. Though even they gave the appearance of being welded on after too many late nights down the cafe bar.

Stuff like that. That's what TAL did, and they did it well.

They were on to a winner with a philosophy of democracy in fashion.

And as soon as they got well enough known, some big company would come along and buy them out. Then they'd be rich democrats.

'Well, I know what they do for me – 'specially that Thalia – but what do you do for them?' asked The Sarge.

The girls were over by the juke box arguing about a music selection. They were standing in line, ranged by height from left to right: Amy, Lyn and then Thalia, the tallest.

'That Thalia's got a fine pair of pins,' The Sarge said before I could answer. He was fiddling with the knot of his tie, a nervous tic he seemed to have developed in the presence of the girls.

'They all have,' I said. 'You just notice Thalia's more because they're longer. Watch the other two.'

Sure enough, after a few seconds of standing in line, Amy and Lyn put into practice what they preached to their office-working customers when being ogled by men from behind. Without any apparent collusion and at no particular given signal, Amy and Lyn moved the position of their feet. From standing straight, with feet at twelve o'clock, Amy moved her left foot to ten o'clock and Lyn her right to roughly two o'clock, redistributing the weight from their hips.

It was a small movement which would have gone unnoticed had you not been looking at their legs, which of course we were, as were most of the men in the pub. It suddenly gave the two shorter women a curvier, sexier outline, distracting the eye from Thalia's longer, but straighter legs.

'I see what you mean,' said The Sarge, looking with his photographer's eye for once, rather than just following his hormones. 'That was bloody clever. Do they know they're doing it?'

'Of course they do, they're female. Someone like Thalia is always going to be seen as competition, so you compete by making the most of what you've got.'

'Still, that Thalia really is well saucy,' he breathed. 'Where does that name come from? Did you say it was Finnish?'

'Danish,' I said, not remembering.

'So what was it you said you did for them?' He didn't look at me; his eyeline tracking slowly across three hemlines.

'I drive them between gigs – shows, seminars, meetings with their customers. Sometimes they do three an evening, usually straight after work when the offices chuck out. It's nearly always rush hour when they do their thing, so a taxi comes in handy. And there's room in the back for them to get changed between shows.'

That got his attention. 'Changed? They change clothes in the back of that old banger of yours?'

I decided not to correct him by pointing out that I now had a *new* old banger of a black London taxi.

'Sure. Saves so much time and it means they can go straight into their routine when they get to a venue without having to take over the Ladies for the first fifteen minutes.'

'I bet you drive with one eye on the mirror,' he leered.

'Nah, the novelty soon wore off,' I lied. 'It's just a job and it's not even regular work, though they are getting busier. It's only fifty quid a week but—'

'That's all you could afford,' The Sarge completed smugly.

'I wasn't going to stoop to such an old joke,' I retorted and I meant it, as I had used that line at least a dozen times. 'I was going to say that it covers the cost of the diesel and it gets me out of the house.'

'Yeah, yeah,' he said dismissively.

The girls returned as the first of their CDs rapped out of the speakers. Thalia leaned over The Sarge to get to the remains of her glass of wine. The view she gave him down the scoop neck of her black silk top transfixed him more effectively than a butterfly on a knitting needle.

'Whose round is it?' As she leaned over she moved her weight from one leg to the other then back again, giving the young suits at the bar an object lesson in juggling.

'Er… mine,' said The Sarge, having difficulty with his words.

'Here, get 'em in, Roy.'

He handed over a £20 note, which I held up to the light. It looked genuine enough, though I wasn't really sure what I was looking for. I did it out of habit as most shopkeepers and barmen did it nowadays. The £10 note had been the easiest to forge, so it was said, and there were so few £5 notes in circulation in London that one had to suspect the worst. The current rumour was that there was a forged £50 note around which could fool even the ultra-violet detector machines.

I picked up the empty bottle and said, 'More white swine?' to Lyn.

'Why not?' She smiled sweetly; always a bad sign. 'And another pint of Prozac for your friend,' she added.

I knew there was going to be trouble before I was halfway to the bar and I should have seen it coming.

Three of the young suits broke from the bar and headed for the juke box as soon as I stood up. That would put them within ten feet of the girls and give them the opportunity to use the, 'Who put this crap on?' line. They were hardly subtle and I knew the girls could take care of themselves, but the suits were young and by the look of them, had been on the lager for a few hours and they had mates still at the bar they had to impress.

It was only happening because Thalia, Amy and Lyn were the last females left in the place. Where were all the other women who worked at Canary Wharf? Females supposedly outnumbered males by four or five to one here. Sadly, they all seemed to be taking their jobs rather more seriously and were actually doing them rather than wasting the afternoon getting reckless in the pub.

I was still waiting to be served when I heard Thalia's laugh, far too loud, above the music, but I resisted the temptation to turn around and look. Then I heard a, 'Oh come on, darling,' followed by more shrieks and then Lyn's voice, quite clearly saying, 'Go play with yourselves, lads, we're busy.' At that point, two of the suits still at the bar just to my left turned to each other and one said:

'I told you the redhead was a lesbian.'

I ordered my round with a sigh. The barman looked over my shoulder towards the table and he had the expression of someone who thinks they've left the gas on back home. His expression cracked into one of pain, almost as if he had stomach cramps, when we heard Thalia say, 'Some other time, guys, this is a business meeting.'

Neither the barman nor I actually had to hear what sort of a response that got; we just knew.

Thalia's response was swift and sure.

'You'd like some too, would you? Would you?'

I turned around, picking up the bottle of wine I had bought just in case. As I could have predicted, she'd picked on the smallest suit who had made the fatal mistake of drawing up a chair and sitting next to her.

Thalia jumped to her feet and towered over him.

'OK then, you look like a tit man,' she shouted.

The jukebox track ended right on cue, or maybe the barman had pulled the plug so we could all hear better. Certainly the whole pub was listening.

'You've been looking at mine for the last half hour, so you must be,' Thalia blitzed on. 'You want 'em?'

Before any of the suits could move or say a word, Thalia crossed her arms and whipped off her black silk top, scrunching it up into a fist like a magician doing sleight of hand. Underneath she was wearing a white sports bra, the sort which, from behind, looks like a double shoulder holster.

'This is a half-wired, uplift and separate, reinforced sports bra. It is the Mercedes of sports bras. In fact, it's got more roll bars than the average Mercedes. And if you can get it off–' she cupped both hands to her breasts and leaned towards the guy's face '–you can have 'em.'

4.

Later

'We have a file on you, Mr Angel, but it seems a bit thin in places…'

The first pair of detectives had gone. Maybe they had homework to do. They had been replaced after a gap of ten very long minutes by two more. Older, sharper-suited, even more clean-cut, totally laid back and in control. Dangerous buggers.

On the plus side, I'd had a cup of tea and was keeping my statutory toilet break in the bank for the moment. Also, the two new boys didn't seem in a hurry to plug in the tape-recorder or the cattle prod just yet. Surely a good sign.

'Maybe you can fill in a few gaps for us? Just so we have things straight in our minds.'

'Do I need a brief?'

'You're not being charged with anything,' said one.

'Yet,' said the other.

Fair enough. They were being honest and upfront, so I could do no less than be helpful.

'I've absolutely no idea what's going on,' I flannelled. 'I've told the other two officers everything I know.'

'You haven't actually told them very much at all, Mr Angel,' said one with a faint Geordie lilt.

'We've seen their notes,' said the other. 'A bit thin.'

He tested the back of a chair with both hands. He was either gauging whether it would take his weight or he was sussing it as a weapon.

'So, you're looking to put flesh on the bone, pad things out, paint in the background, fill in all those boring blue sky bits of the jigsaw.'

They looked at each other.

'Terry was right,' said one, 'he is on something.'

'Nah,' said the other confidently, 'just fancies himself. Let's start with a few names, shall we?'

'OK, you tell me yours and I'll tell you mine,' I smiled.

'Us? Oh, we're the SAS.'

'Don't look so worried, Mr Angel, I'm only joking.'

He produced a warrant card and waved it in front of me, quicker than you would flash a dodgy bus pass.

'I'm Detective Sergeant Stokoe and this is DC Sell. Stokoe and Sell, geddit? The SAS. Just a nickname.'

'So you're The Sarge in charge?' I said before I could stop myself, and then went one worse. 'The Sarge in charge of the case of The Sarge.'

'Gosh, what a thought,' said Stokoe doing the wide-eyed act. 'D'you think I could get a pound for every time somebody says that? If I did I could be as rich as DC Sell here. He gets a fiver every time some wag says they don't want to spend a night in the cells.' He turned to his partner. 'And, you know, Steve, if we ever pulled a case where a Colonel Mustard got knocked off in a library with a piece of lead piping, I reckon we could clean up.'

'Too right, Sarge. That would be a triple-word score, no question. You don't mind me calling you Sarge, do you, Sarge? It doesn't confuse things, like, does it?'

'No, I think I'm still following the plot. How about you, Mr Angel?'

There was nothing else for it. Nice policeman/nasty policeman I could handle, but these two weren't partners, they were a double act.

'What do you want to know?' I asked wearily.

'We want to know *you*,' they said together. And then they smiled. They'd rehearsed that, too.

Yes, my name really was Fitzroy Maclean Angel, and yes it was after the late Sir Fitzroy whose book, *Eastern Approaches*, my father had been reading the week I was born. Was it a lucky break that he hadn't been reading *David Copperfield*? Gosh, I'd never thought of that. I was just relieved that he didn't get round to *Mein Kampf* until my sister was born. Ha, ha.

Yes, I lived in Stuart Street in Hackney and I had told the other two (sane) policemen that. No, I didn't own the house, I just rented a small flat in it. The house was owned by a very nice Pakistani called Nassim Nassim, if they really had to know. Yes, a Pakistani and 'Nassim Nassim' because he had a way of repeating it when you asked his name and his other name was probably impossible to pronounce. And, no, I'd never had any trouble with him. True, he hadn't liked the way I had cut a cat-flap in the front door, and he hadn't been too keen the week me and a couple of mates had rehearsed our film noir set to accompany the Robert Ryan retrospective at the Stoke Newington festival.

But I didn't tell the SAS any of this as I didn't see that it was any of their business.

Did I live alone? Sure, not counting the cat, which you did at your peril. Neighbours? Of course I had some, but I didn't offer any details. Why did they need to know about Inverness Doogie, hotel chef and football hooligan, and Welsh Miranda in the flat above? Or Lisabeth and Fenella in the flat below, who really would have liked to go on that Lesbian Avengers march but they had cushions to plump, or lentils to soak, and anyway, that day's horoscope wasn't quite right. Or even the mysterious Mr Goodson from the ground-floor flat, who was something in local government, but not much, and who kept to himself and tolerated the rest of us.

And how long had I lived there? Five or six years, though why that mattered as much as a hill of beans was beyond me as well.

But I was the owner of a delicensed Austin Fairway taxi, wasn't I? Yessss…

And I had been previously the owner of an Austin FX4S cab? Possibly…

Would the name Roy Maclean and the address 23 Redcross Place, Southwark ring any bells?

Ding dong.

'I don't live there any more,' I said and it sounded lame even to me.

'No one lives there any more,' said DI Sell. 'It doesn't, well, sort of, exist any more.'

'It blew up,' I said quietly.

'In the war? Terrorist suicide mission? Spontaneous combustion?' Stokoe suggested helpfully.

'Gas leak.'

'I see,' he said, nodding his head with the conviction that only policemen and school teachers can summon up so quickly and so fleetingly.

'And the FX4S?' Sell was consulting his notes.

'Pardon?'

'You used to own a delicensed black cab, an Austin FX4S, registration number—'

'Yeah, yeah. I used to own an FX. Now I have a Fairway. They're both delicensed, private use only, not for hire. That's not illegal.'

'No, but it is unusual in London,' Stokoe ruminated. 'Mostly they're sold off outside the Metropolitan area. Can't do much for your street-cred.'

'Oh, I don't know. Easy to park, doesn't get nicked. And I hear some of you guys have been issued with Volvo estate cars. Dead tasty in a high-speed chase they are, I'll bet.'

'That's the City Police, not us, if you must know, and I wouldn't give them any lip about it if you know what's good for you.'

I had no such plans, but I had worked out that these weren't City of London Police. They weren't tall enough. You know when you're in a City nick; you can't reach the hat pegs.

'So what happened to it?' Sell persisted. 'To the FX4?'

'Oh, you know, the usual. It must have had three hundred thousand on the clock when I got him.'

'We heard that that sort of blew up as well.'

Caught fire would have been a more accurate description, but I wasn't going to argue the point.

'Now where did you hear that?' I tried.

They both smiled and Stokoe said, 'Computers are wonderful things.'

'So people keep telling me,' I said.

I was still having trouble putting it together.

I hadn't been driving when they pulled me, yet they knew about the two black cabs I had owned and a previous address. That, they could have got from the Driver and Vehicle Licensing Centre down in Swansea, but only if they'd known what they were looking for. And there must have been another connection to have made them ask. I wasn't convinced that one set of computers talked to another.

If they did, none of us would get away with anything.

'We came across some notes, you see,' Sell, the junior one, was saying. 'About you. They'd been put on the computer after the event, so to speak. Made us think you might be interested in talking to us.'

What the hell had they got? I hadn't lived at the old Southwark address for ages, although that was where I was when I'd registered Armstrong I – the FX4S. My new wheels – a black Fairway – had been registered to me at the Stuart Street, Hackney address. But so what? If you don't sell a vehicle on to somebody, there was no pressure on you to tell the DVLC computer that it no longer existed. And in the case of Armstrong I, there had been nothing left to drive. Even the local scrap merchant had turned his nose up at the wreckage.

'Notes?' I went vague on them again. 'About my car?'

'No, no, no,' said Stokoe, scratching the underside of his chin. 'Police notes.'

'You mean like on the PNC?'

'No, just internal stuff. You can check the Police National Computer yourself now, you know. Under the Freedom of Information Act or whatever it's called.'

I knew. And I had.

'So, what sort of internal notes?'

I could well believe there were some, although I had been promised that nothing more would be said about the incident that had resulted in Armstrong I going up in smoke.

'Expenses claims,' said Sell, and you could have knocked me down with a feather, let alone a rubber truncheon.

'What?'

'Claims for cash,' he explained slowly, like I was a moron or something.

'Cash for what?' I asked, moronically.

'Does it matter this far down the line?' This from Stokoe. 'We are talking a few years back. Water under the bridge and all that. Unless you think it relevant, of course.'

'I have honestly no idea what you're talking about.' I took a deep breath. 'Look, I'll admit I have a bale of marijuana in my bedroom. It's stashed behind the case of Romanian AK-47s which I bought with some of the bullion from the Brinks-Mat heist and I won *that* for nobbling one of the Queen Mother's horses at Ascot last year. All this I confess without you even having to throw me downstairs, but I have not got clue one about any fucking expenses claims. Who am I supposed to have claimed from?'

Stokoe looked at Sell and they both shook their heads slowly.

'Well, that clears up the case of the Queen Mum's horse, don't it, Sarge?' said Sell, deadpan.

'I think we can class that as a result, DC Sell.' Stokoe took a pen from his jacket and clicked it. 'Get a bit of paper, will you, so we can get a confession.'

'Right away, Sarge.'

Neither of them moved.

'OK, OK.' I held up my hands in surrender. 'You do the funnies.'

'Correct, Mr Angel. Glad we see eye to eye on that.' Stokoe put the pen away, patting his jacket after he had done so. Maybe he was worried about pickpockets.

'The expenses my colleague referred to were not made *by* you, but *for* you.'

'Still not with you, I'm afraid. Give me a hint.'

'Come on. It may have been a couple of years, but surely you remember working for Detective Inspector Malpass?'

Malpass! Where the bloody hell had they dug that up from?

'Er… yes. Mr Malpass. Of course I remember him, but I haven't seen him for… ooh… er… ?'

'No, you won't have,' said Sell, 'unless he's holding reunions. He was rasp— I mean invalided out of The Job three years ago.'

Sell had been about to say *raspberried* which was Met slang for *raspberry-rippled* or *crippled*. It didn't surprise me. He'd been in a pretty bad state the last time I'd seen him.

But the last time I had seen DI Malpass had been six years ago at least, not three.

'What do you mean "working for" Malpass?' I asked carefully.

'Relax, Mr Angel,' beamed Stokoe. 'The police force couldn't do its job without informers. There's nothing to be ashamed of, or worried about. Your secret is safe with us.'

Secrets? Who had any secrets? These guys probably knew my inside leg measurement. And if one of them had read my mind and suddenly said, 'Thirty-one inches,' out loud, I wouldn't have been at all surprised. But maybe that was just paranoia. There was a lot of it about.

Keep cool.

'Look, I helped out Mr Malpass when he was after a bad guy called Jack Scamp.' A very bad guy, actually, and I didn't have all that much choice in the matter. 'But it was ages ago. I mean I don't make a regular habit of helping the police, if you get my drift.'

'Drift well and truly got, Mr Angel.' Stokoe interlocked his fingers and flexed outward with a satisfying crack. 'Nobody likes to admit to helping us if they have an image to keep up. And we do realise that it is over three years since you were on DI Malpass' books. But, like the Catholic Church, you might get excommunicated but you're not allowed to resign, so we thought you might consider being reactivated.'

I did some arithmetic. I hadn't seen the mad Malpass for six years yet these guys were talking about three years ago, when Malpass was invalided out of the force.

Then the penny dropped. Malpass had been claiming slush money for me as an informer. Not only had I not seen a penny when I knew him, he had kept me on the books as an informant for a further three years. I had always known he was a bastard, now I knew he was a mean one.

Stokoe and Sell would hardly have raised the matter if there was a danger of dropping a colleague, even a retired one, in it. So maybe they were just scrabbling around, putting two and two together and making one. They didn't really have anything on me at all.

'How can I help?' I smiled.

Stokoe and Sell looked at each other, then Stokoe turned back to me.

'Tell us about these girls in this fashion business, TAL. How did you get involved with them?'

5.

Before

I was in the basement bar of The Hog in the Pound, one of the biggest pubs off Oxford Street. (There aren't any pubs actually *on* Oxford Street until you get to Tottenham Court Road.) And I was on my own.

I was supposed to have been meeting a man about a band. The man was a friend of a friend of mine, Danny Boot. So, OK, that was pushing it a bit. Danny Boot didn't have friends, certainly not me, but he did own a recording studio down Curtain Road and occasionally gave work to musicians who really could play their instruments. The work was invariably fill-in riffs and background feel or *atmos* and usually uncredited, but it allowed Boot to boast that he was doing his bit towards keeping music live and unplugged and helping to create his trademark studio sound. The sceptics among us pointed out that the session musicians didn't do anything a computer couldn't replicate these days, but we were cheaper.

According to Boot, his friend Topher (a diminutive of Christopher for people who have difficulty with all the syllables in *Chris*) had just returned mind-blown from the World Of Music, Arts and Dance festival at Reading. Hit of WOMAD, with a bullet, Boot said, had been a Macedonian brass band and a resurgence of the electric Scottish folk/rock style which the critics in the music papers had dubbed 'Acid Croft'. This Topher guy wanted to combine the two styles and produce an album, and he had enough of a private income to pay for the demo. So Boot had given him my name – because I played the trumpet, not because I was an expert on Macedonian brass bands and not because I knew where Macedonia was and he didn't. I had agreed to the meet because I always trusted Boot's instincts on things like this. After all, he'd been right about Punjabi Rap and I'd laughed at that.

But by eight o'clock it looked as if I would have to miss out on the great tartan/Greek fusion, because Topher was a no-show. He'd probably discovered a Zimbabwean thumb piano orchestra busking at Bond Street tube station and signed them up instead.

So, there I was, nursing the same pint of lager I'd gone in with.

Not that I had to keep a clear head or anything, but I had my new set of wheels parked very illegally round on James Street and it was a Thursday. That meant payday for a lot of people, late night shopping and cross-dressing night down in Soho, so there would be more than the average number of cops on patrol. And while the Met. police don't usually prosecute if you breathalyse under 42 microgrammes (the limit being 35), it's still not worth the hassle.

I was bored, getting hungry and wishing I'd brought something to read, not that the Hog was the sort of pub which encouraged customers to curl up with a good book. In fact, the only thing to read in the place was the blurb on the condom machine in the toilet. It said, 'Double Action Condoms. Stimulation Outside, Delay Inside,' and sounded like most of the females I'd met recently.

I noticed them first when the couple at the table next to me got up and went. No, to be honest, I had noticed the tall blonde one when she had gone to bar and returned with a fistful of bottles of Moscow Mule. I may have been bored but I wasn't blind.

I could now see there were three of them and I was able to over-hear most of what they were saying, helped in no small part by the increase in volume that comes in a direct ratio with the amount of alcohol consumed. And even if I had been trying and not worried about driving, they would have been ahead of me. The table they had taken over was covered with bottles of the vodka-based Mules. It looked like a drunk's bowling alley.

I leaned back in my seat and slouched to my right so I could over-hear better, running through the routine scenarios in my mind.

A hen party? Nah, too few of them and anyway, they were still in what appeared to be their office clothes. Girls on a hen night usually made an effort to seriously party, and the Hog was an unlikely rendezvous even if they were going on somewhere else. No, a hen party would have gone for one of the piano bars in Soho or the All Bar One type of pub, which have more windows than the average cathedral and which are spotlessly clean. Real Men don't go there because there's no pub atmosphere, but I quite like them. They're always full of women.

Maybe they were girls on an office night out, celebrating pay day. Any of the beggars on the Central Line will tell you that Thursday evening is prime time as far as they are concerned, the most generous donors being secretaries who have just been paid.

But that wasn't it. I didn't know why but it was again something to do with what they were wearing.

They were dressed alike; not identically, but very alike. Far too similarly to be dressed like that, work in the same office and be friends enough to go for a drink after work. All three wore short, hound's-tooth check skirts and black tights. And all three had black jackets, the tall blonde one having thrown hers casually across the back of her chair.

So far, so what? Given the time of year, they were dressed in fairly standard working girl uniform for office London.

Uniform.

That was it; yet it wasn't. They were all wearing the same clothes but somehow they were different and not just physically. There was the blonde, much taller than the other two, with hair down to her shoulder blades and probably the small of her back, if she ironed out the crinkle curls. The other two wore their hair short. One cropped severely into a light brown stubble, the other more relaxed and of similar colour but with fading blonde highlights.

Whatever it was, it niggled me and I decided that the problem required some more detailed observation. But that would have to wait, because their conversation had taken an interesting turn, so serious earwigging was called for.

'Short skirts never failed…'

'Depends what you've got on show…'

'Crap. You could have matchsticks and still pull a fellah if your hem is round your bum…'

'My mother has – and does. The older the bloke the easier they are.'

'So you're saying, never mind the shape, flash the length?'

'In one, sister, though that's what Thalia usually says to blokes.'

The tall blonde one roared with laughter.

'Well, I will from now on!'

More hilarity, more Moscow Mules supped from the bottles.

'I'm sticking to what we tell the punters,' said the one with the blonde highlights.

Punters? I couldn't be that wrong, could I?

'I work on my legs and I'll tell the punters to. It can give you the edge. I'm proud of my muscle tone.'

'So you should be, sweetie, having to wear all that purple lycra in the gym.'

'Gym? I thought it was a disused church hall. Anyway, what is this week – box-aerobics?'

'Step-aerobics, if you must know. Three times a week.'

'So that's where you keep disappearing off to. Why not move to Marble Arch? The escalators on the tube haven't worked in my lifetime. You could run up and down there and have the legs of a shot-putter inside a month.'

'Thank you, partners, thank you very much. I have to work on my legs and if it gives me more self-confidence, what's wrong with that?'

'Nothing, sweetie, if all you want to do is pick up men.'

'You're in the wrong business to start getting politically correct.

We make women feel good. Most want to feel good to pull a bloke. Get real.'

'So you wiggle your arse stepping on and off a milk crate three days a week just to please men?'

'No way. I do it to keep fit and improve my—'

'Muscle tone?'

'Yeah, that's right, and you could both do with some yourselves. Neither of you could run for a bus.'

'Darling, I never have to run for a bus.'

'There's nothing wrong with my muscles. Get a grip on them. Go on, real nut-crushers…'

'I've heard it said…'

'Watch it, you lippy cow…'

'Stand up, then, and tense yourself.'

'She should be so lucky!'

More hilarity.

'Can't feel a thing. Look, feel here, at the back.'

They were all three standing now, their short skirts hitched up even higher. I scoped the pub but nobody except me seemed to be taking the slightest bit of notice. Except for the tall blonde one, who had certainly noticed me; noticed me watching and listening.

'Let's call in the independent adjudicator on this,' she said.

The one with the close-cropped hair looked down at me and, with full eye contact, said, 'Who? Dickhead?'

She pulled her skirt up another inch, hands on her hips.

'They call me Mister Dickhead,' I said, wondering if I dare risk another beer as my mouth had suddenly gone dry.

The three of them went, 'Ooooh', as if they were impressed, then the one with the blonde highlights took a step towards me and turned around.

She turned her right foot out at an angle and bent her knee slightly, her hands sliding her skirt up to the curve of her buttocks.

'Come on,' she said over her shoulder. 'We want you to decide. Who's got the best thigh muscles?'

I put my glass down and automatically wiped the palms of my hands on my jeans before I stood up.

All three were standing in line now, backs to me, looking over their shoulders at me as I went into a slight crouch.

'It's a dirty job,' I said, 'but I suppose *somebody's* got to do it.'

6.

Later

'By my reckoning,' said Stokoe, in measured tones, 'that set you up for one shag and two slaps. Minimum. Steve?'

Detective Constable Sell considered this as if it counted towards promotion.

'A clever lad could have strung it out, gone to a re-match, then a penalty shoot-out and maybe ended up with three shags and no slaps.'

'Or…' said Stokoe, holding up a finger like he was testing the wind, 'the whole thing could really be Fantasy Football. A load of total porkies. Made up to impress the lads down the pub of a Sunday lunchtime.'

'You told that story before, Roy?' asked Sell.

I had, but not more than twenty times. Usually down the pub, but not necessarily on Sundays.

'You asked me how I got involved with them. I told you.'

'You've told us how you met them, not how you were involved with them.' This from Stokoe.

'And he hasn't told us which one he shagged,' Sell pointed out.

'Maybe he did score with all of them,' Stokoe said to him, as if I wasn't there.

'Then I think he should tell us in which order. It'd only be fair. He is supposed to be cooperating with us, isn't he, Sarge?'

'It doesn't jump out and grab you, does it?'

I was beginning to suspect that they didn't have Off Duty any more; they'd renamed it Rehearsal. I showed them the palms of my hands in surrender.

'Give me a break, hey?'

Sell, the younger one, looked genuinely surprised.

'Give *you* a break? You're the one getting a free feel of thighs, more than you'd get in a kosher butcher's and now you want sympathy as well? Walk on, sunshine, walk on. Let's have a few more details.'

Stokoe came in right on cue.

'I think DC Sell is requesting more details of your business relationship with TAL. Isn't that right, DC Sell?'

He raised an eyebrow and Sell produced a fake sigh. 'If you say so, Sarge,' he said, casting his eyes to the floor.

'So what happened, Mr Angel?' Stokoe returned to me, deadpan.

'They offered me a job,' I said, waiting for it.

'As what? Physiotherapist?'

I'd heard them all before.

'Look… er… officers… what's all this about? You're not charging me with anything and I can't help you if I don't know what's going on, can I? So, why don't you tell me?'

'Not yet, Mr Angel,' said Stokoe, almost formally. 'You show us a bit more of yours, then we might show you ours.'

7.

Before

'Did you know there's a panther in your kitchen?' said Amy casually, putting down a mug of coffee and climbing over me and back into bed.

'Ah, yes, sorry about that,' I muttered, rubbing sleep from my eyes. 'I'll get the First Aid kit.'

'What for? He was perfectly friendly. What's he called?'

I reached for the coffee she'd brought me, badly in need of the caffeine.

'He didn't bite, scratch, wound, lacerate or attempt open heart surgery?' She shook her head. 'Then it can't be Springsteen.'

'Springsteen? What sort of a name is that for a cat?'

'He's never objected to it. I think it came with his pedigree. Springsteen by Chuck Berry out of Slim Gaillard.'

'Who?'

'Never mind. He didn't draw blood, then?'

'Course not. Cats like me.' I'd heard that before, usually just before the screaming started. 'Anyway, I've had every rabies and tetanus shot going. You have to in my business.'

Maybe, but had Springsteen?

'Get a lot of trouble from your models, then?' I feigned mild interest. 'Biting and scratching in the dressing room before prodding them down the catwalk? Is that why they call it a catwalk?'

'I told you, we don't use professional models. That's our USP. I did tell you, didn't I? How much did I have to drink last night?'

'Yes, you did, come to think of it.' Several times. 'But you didn't admit to having a USP. I think you should have warned me. Is that why you have to have all those shots?'

She pressed her empty but still hot mug on to my chest and I yelped.

'Unique Selling Point. We deal in fashion but we don't use models, that's our USP.'

'Would you like—?'

'No, I would *not* like to see your USP. I've seen it, it was nice – while it lasted – but I've got work to do.'

'I was going to say *breakfast*,' I said, thinking quickly.

'Oh. Sorry,' she said meekly, placing her right index finger on my lips. 'I'd love a slice of toast or something, but I couldn't find anything in your kitchen. There's a ton of French beer in your fridge but no food.'

'Bit late on the shopping this week,' I said, flipping my feet on to the floor.

As I sat on the edge of the bed, she scratched me lightly with her nails, right between the shoulder blades. I twisted my neck muscles in appreciation.

'Your cat – Springsteen? – he likes that too.'

I stiffened. 'He let you touch him?'

'Once I'd fed him.'

'Fed him? What with?'

'Cat food. That stuff in the plastic box.'

The only thing in the fridge in a plastic box had been the remains of a killer chilli cooked by Inverness Doogie, my upstairs neighbour. Now Doogie is a chef, a professional one at a West End hotel, so he knows what he's doing. The only trouble is that apart from cooking and his Welsh wife Miranda, his only leisure interests are football hooliganism and cooking chilli for a bet. Whenever he won a bet, I got to eat the leftovers and that week he'd won a lot of money from a visiting Texan businessman who had made the near fatal mistake of saying there was no such thing as a really hot chilli north of the Rio Grande. I had been looking forward to trying it. That's why all that French beer was chilling down.

'Did I do something wrong?' asked Amy.

'No, no,' I said, 'that was his favourite.'

*

'It's not like you won me as a prize or anything,' she had said, slurring her words. 'But you made the right choice.'

'I know that. It was easy. No competition.'

I had turned and spoken to her through the open glass partition of Armstrong II. She was sitting in the back, nearside, with her winning legs stretched out on the rumble seat and crossed at the ankle.

'Then why did it take you so long?'

'Judging legs is a serious business. It requires years of training and a constant honing of technique. If Leg Judging is ever going to be taken seriously as an Olympic event, then we have to maintain professional standards. And I have to say that the recent allegations of drug-taking have not helped. It'll be a sad day when Leg Judges have to go through compulsory dope tests. I mean, the sport'd be a laughing stock, a bit like synchronised swimming.'

She roared with laughter; a good, clean, dirty laugh.

'Ever thought of being a Leg Judge at synchronised swimming?'

'I tried it, and damn near drowned.'

She laughed again and said, 'You're funny.'

As they had staggered out of the Hog, they'd all thought it funny that I drove a black Fairway, no matter how many times I had said it was delicensed and not a working cab.

'If that's a fashion statement, I'm taking the night bus,' Lyn had said.

The tall blonde one, introduced as Thalia, had stood in the middle of the street where I had parked, and hiked up her skirt again, put a hand in the air and yelled 'Taxi!' as loudly as she could. Then she collapsed into giggles, saying, 'Just looking for a second opinion.'

As it happened, a real black cab came around the corner and she flagged it down, asking if anyone wanted Notting Hill.

The cabbie, a black guy built like a wrestler, eyed me – and Armstrong II – suspiciously. I palmed the ignition keys back into my pocket and pretended the parked Fairway was nothing to do with me.

'I told you, I'll take the night bus, you flash cow,' Lyn said heavily.

'Suit yerself,' Thalia chirped, climbing in. 'What about the Queen of Thighs? Booked yourself a late exercise session, sweetie?'

'Apparently I don't need the exercise, sweetie,' Amy shot back. 'But you never know. See you tomorrow. Don't forget it's a work day.'

'Yeah, yeah, yeah.'

Thalia slammed the door and the cabbie set off, shooting me a final glare and snapping the clutch so that Thalia bounced back in her seat.

'Can I give anyone a lift?' I had offered, producing my keys again.

'Where are you heading?' asked Amy. She was doing it again; standing with her leg bent slightly.

'Hackney. Anyone going east?'

'You can drop me off in Stoke Newington,' she said like she was doing me a favour.

'Sure.'

'I'm on the night bus,' said Lyn. 'You meet a much more discriminating sort of person, I've found. And you'd better watch it, Amy, I think his meter's running.'

'I told you,' I had said, 'the cab's delicensed.'

'I didn't mean the cab,' Lyn said over her shoulder as she turned back into Oxford Street.

I had looked at Amy and she had nodded her head towards Armstrong's door and said something like, 'Let's go then.' She had smiled to herself as she climbed in, the sort of smile she would not explain but which I was supposed to notice.

And so she had settled down in the back, with her feet up on the drop-down seat, something a real cabbie would never have allowed. And I had made her laugh, so that was probably another first for the back of a London cab.

We had yet to make Islington, when she said, 'Look, my place is a mess. It really is. How about yours?'

I had considered this long and hard as we waited at a red light. These matters were not to be taken lightly these days.

'My place is always a mess,' I had said.

'I don't mind,' she had said.

'OK, then. But I thought you said there were no prizes for judging the leg competition.'

I was watching her in the mirror and she turned from looking out of the window so that we made eye contact in the shiny rectangle on the dashboard.

'I lied,' she had said.

The lights changed to red and amber.

*

And now she wanted breakfast and it was the least I could do for a woman who had walked naked in front of Springsteen and survived.

But she was right about the state of my larder, so I pulled on a pair of fresh boxer's and a pair of less fresh jeans, and trotted down half a flight of stairs to Flat Two.

Lisabeth and Fenella would have bread and if Fenella answered my knock, I would get some. If Lisabeth answered the door, I would have to go to Plan B and fight Springsteen for what was left of the chilli; but then, Lisabeth never opened the door, especially not to me. And if she was awake and out of her pit, she would have heard me padding down the stairs.

'Good morning, Lisabeth,' I said, rather too loudly. Fear does that to me.

'Is it?'

How the hell would I know? I hadn't looked.

She was blinking furiously and I suspected she had just jammed her contact lenses in.

'I wondered if I could scrounge some bread,' I said, pitching it over her shoulder in the hope that Fenella would hear me inside the flat. 'It's just that I haven't had a chance to do any shopping yet this week and the old cupboard is a bit bare…'

I tailed off as I realised she was looking over my shoulder, just as I was trying to shout over hers. On the video security cameras (if we'd had any), we must have looked like a couple of old headbangers miming to Freddie Mercury.

We caught each other doing it and she scowled and turned back into the flat yelling, 'Fenella, it's the Angel person. Deal with him would you, some of us have got to get to work.'

Fenella appeared wearing striped flannel pyjamas, the jacket tucked into the trousers which were fastened with a white cord with tassels on the ends. She had her hair up, sleep in her eyes and furry nylon slippers shaped like roadkill frogs on her feet. In other circumstances, I would have said she looked not half sexy, but then Lisabeth was still in the northern hemisphere.

'What's up with her indoors?' I whispered.

'She's a grouch in the mornings,' Fenella said through a yawn, 'when she has to go to work and I don't.'

'Day off?'

'Permanently. Again.'

'Oh dear. Sorry. The travel agent job didn't work out, then?'

'Not really. Do you know how many countries there are now where Russia used to be?'

'Hmmm. Tough one. Look, have you got any bread?' Suddenly she was awake.

'You told me never to lend you money. You were quite specific at the time, though Lisabeth said you were drunk and—'

'No, bread as in loaves. You know, for toast, like for breakfast.' Or maybe lunch at this rate.

'Bread? Oh yeah. Yes, of course. We're into bread. I've got granary, wholemeal, poppy-seed, pugliese and ciabatta.'

She ticked them off on five fingers.

'Add a couple of sardines and you could feed a multitude,' I said cheerily.

'You want fish as well?'

'No, just bread. White, sliced, stale, anything. It's just for toast.'

She waved a finger at me, indicating for me to stay where I was, took two paces into the flat and turned back to me.

'Is it for your guest?'

'Yes,' I said irritably. 'You can't get anything past the *blockleiter*, can you?'

'Oh, no problem if it is. I mean Lisabeth knows her.'

'What?'

'Well, I think *know* is being too forward. She recognised her when you got out of Armstrong last night. Knew her straightaway. "That's Amy May," she said, "the fashion designer I told you about." Just like that. Knew her instantly.'

'Lisabeth knows somebody?' I said before I could stop myself.

'Well, like I say, I don't know if she knows her to talk to, but she knew who she was. She'd told me about it, actually. Their travelling fashion show with the funny name – just initials – came round the office where she works and asked all the girls for their input on fashion.'

Ask Lisabeth about fashion? I wondered what TAL had done for the other fifty-nine minutes of the lunch hour.

'Lisabeth was very favourably impressed with Amy's designs and how they could be tailored to a secretary's budget,' Fenella went on as if she had learned it as a mantra. 'I think she wanted to see what she was wearing, not that she bought anything off her.'

Her mind switched gears. You could see it happen.

'You're not wearing a shirt.'

'To show you my empty stomach, Fenella darling.' I slapped my gut to emphasise the point. 'You were getting me some bread.'

'Was I? What sort?'

'Wholemeal will do, thanks.'

'I've got poppy-seed,' she said helpfully.

'They explode in the toaster,' I said patiently. 'Oh, and some honey, some butter and do you have any jam?'

*

Amy was dressed, all bar one shoe, and sitting on the edge of the bed, when I brought her a slice of toast and organic, vegan honey. (Do they ask the bees if they are vegans?)

'Any idea where my other shoe is?' she asked, taking the plate I offered.

'Through there,' I said, indicating the one and only other room in the flat.

I followed her as she limped into the living room to see how long it would take her to spot it. Not long.

'Sorry,' she said through a fine spray of toast crumbs. 'I must have been pissed.'

'Or just accurate.'

She retrieved the shoe from where it had been slotted over the mouthpiece of my ancient B-flat trumpet which was balanced on its bell-end on one of the hi-fi speakers. She dropped the shoe on the floor and pushed her foot in, sticking the toast in her mouth and using both hands to straighten and pull her tights up each leg.

'God, but I hate going to work in the same clothes the next day,' she mumbled. 'It's such a giveaway.'

Then it hit me.

'But you're not. You've changed.'

She had but she hadn't. She was wearing the same shoes, same tights, same skirt, but the top was different. It was what had bugged me in the pub the night before. All three of them had been dressed the same, but different. A uniform, yet individual.

'It's the same top, but you're wearing it in a different way,' I said slowly. 'The others had the same top on, but not the same. Right?'

She finished her toast and sucked the ends of her fingers. For a moment I forgot entirely what I had been talking about.

'Very good,' she said, smiling. 'Men don't normally notice such things. Come to think of it, men don't normally notice anything much. Nothing important, anyway.'

I tried to remember how she had looked before with clothes on.

'Last night… it was a V-neck.'

'You could see my tits.'

'Well, yes. But now it's a polo-neck.'

'Tits covered to give a hint of mystery.' She put her hands on her hips and turned to the side, bending the leg again. It was as if she was giving a sales pitch.

'You've put it on backwards,' I tried, knowing I was on a loser.

'So where did the sleeves come from? Watch.'

She reached up and fumbled behind her neck and suddenly the material of her top drew in like a curtain opening to reveal her cleavage. Then she did something with her cuffs, folded the sleeves once and reached behind her elbows. She did a 'Ta-Da' fanfare and there she was, as she had been last night.

'Or, if you're feeling brave… '

She pulled the top out of her skirt, scrunched up the hem until she was showing four inches of bare midriff and reached behind her back. Then she reached up behind her neck, released something and with a flick of something at the throat, the neckline changed from a V to a circle.

She did a twirl to show off her exposed stomach and back.

'The crop-top. Mind you, you need good boobs and a flat gut to carry it off.'

'Would you like a professional judgement?' I asked, my hands straying automatically towards her.

'Too slow,' she grinned, releasing something behind her back so that the top fell down. She began to tuck it into the waist of her skirt. 'A couple of hidden popper fasteners and drawstrings in neck, sleeves and hem and you have three tops for the price of one. Add you own accessories and the permutations are endless.'

'Your design?'

'Yes. We call it the TALtop – until we can think of a better name. We always wear them when we're doing a show.'

'Sell many?'

'A few. We're still working on it, trying out new fabrics and colours. To keep the cost down we're using cheap stuff which means it doesn't survive too many trips to the launderette and it's not exactly warm and the stitching— What are you looking for?'

'Just admiring the engineering.'

She slapped my hands away.

'There isn't time. I've got to get to work.'

'Now you know it makes sense always to offer the judges a bit of bribery and corruption,' I tried.

'Behave yourself,' she said, twisting out of my arms and reaching for her jacket which was draped over the television. 'I've nothing to bribe you with and you've had your corruption.'

She thought for a moment, then she said, 'You could give me a lift to work if you wanted to.'

'OK,' I said. I had nothing else to do. 'Where's work?'

'Seven Dials, edge of Covent Garden. You'll put a shirt on, though, won't you?'

'If you insist. Got any fashion tips for me?'

'I've seen your wardrobe. It's not that long a journey.'

Sitting in the back of Armstrong II, she applied a minimal amount of eye make-up and orange-red lipstick while giving me directions to Covent Garden, as if I didn't know.

'This really is your cab?' she asked once she had convinced herself I was heading in roughly the right direction.

'Yeah, it's mine, it's paid for and you're getting a free ride. Got any problems with that?'

'Why a taxi?'

I didn't have to think about that, I just wished I had a fiver for every time it had been asked.

'London cab, in London? Who notices it? When have you seen a cab with a parking ticket? Who'd pinch one as a get-away car or for a joyride? When has a cab driver ever been hit by a Rolex bandit?'

'What's a Rolex bandit?'

'Kids on motorbikes who pull up alongside Porsches at traffic lights and rip off the driver's watch.'

'They should shut their windows,' she said primly.

'The bandits carry lump hammers.' It was true. 'But they never bother me.'

'Because of the taxi?'

'No. I don't have a Rolex.'

She laughed at that. 'Have you got a job?'

'Several, none regular and none with any prospects. None during the hours of daylight, come to think of it. Why? You offering?

She moved to the drop seat behind me and put her face close up to my shoulder.

'When we do our shows, you know, like we told you last night, we get the girls from an office together after work, we sometimes have to do three or four a night. It can be a pain trying to hop a cab, especially if it's rush hour and it usually is. It'd be good if we had a cab on tap, so to speak. We can easily get all our stuff in here and there's even room to change if we have to, between shows.'

'Change in the back of the cab, huh?' I said, mainly to myself.

I swerved to avoid a big, red, double-decker bus I had somehow not noticed.

'Let me think about it,' I said.

8.

Later

'Is that it, then?' asked Stokoe. He seemed genuinely disappointed. 'You just gave one of them a lift home and they gave you a job?'

'Yeah, more or less.'

'He still hasn't let on which one he boffed,' Sell muttered.

OK, so I hadn't told them *everything*.

'Then so far it's been a fair exchange,' I said, hoping that I sounded more confident than I felt. 'I've been here over an hour and no one's told me how The Sarge died, or where, or if I'm in any way suspected of anything, or if I need a solicitor.'

They looked at each other, cueing-in their bloody double act again.

'Did you get that, Sarge? He said "solicitor".'

'So he did, DC Sell, so he did.'

Stokoe pretended to look impressed at the significance of this. I knew it was just to get me rattled.

'So what?'

Stokoe looked at Sell, who raised his eyebrows and pouted his lips to make a breathy 'pfui' sound, then back to me.

'Most people ask for a *lawyer* or a *brief*, because that's what they've heard on television. You said, "solicitor", which says to us that you're not a man to be trifled with. I think in that case, we ought to cooperate as fully with you as you have with us. Do you agree, DC Sell?'

'Absolutely, Sergeant. It's only fair.'

Stokoe sat down opposite me across the plywood table. Sell scraped his chair nearer until they were side by side. They both rested their forearms on the table and intertwined the fingers of their hands. Then they both smiled at me.

Tweedles bleeding Dum and Dee.

'Now what?' I said, when they said nothing.

'Fire away,' said Stokoe.

'Feel free,' said Sell.

'To do what exactly?'

'To ask us questions.'

'It's your turn now.'

'Me… interview… you?'

They nodded happily, a couple of big kids. It was ridiculous. It was a farce. It was making me nervous. It was working.

'Who are you?'

'We, 'said Stokoe dramatically, 'are policemen.'

'I'm getting one of my headaches,' I muttered to myself, pinching the bridge of my nose. 'Yes, I gathered that,' I said slowly. 'The police station… the cheap furniture… the men in uniform at the desk outside. It was a bit of a giveaway. But what sort of policemen are you?'

'It's a trick question, Sarge,' Sell jumped in. 'He wants us to say "corrupt ones".'

'Well, we are not going to fall for it, are we, Constable?'

I had to admit that Stokoe could do a half-decent Oliver Hardy when he set what was left of his mind to it.

'What sort of honest policemen are you?' I tried patiently. 'And if you say "tall ones" then I'll scream police brutality.'

'Ooh, can't have that, sir,' mocked Stokoe through pursed lips. 'We're with AMIP – that's the Area Major Incident Pool.'

I knew what it stood for. When something major, like a murder, happened in London the cops would pool resources in certain designated areas, the theory being that the investigating team could call on local and specialist knowledge and expertise. To cover this area of London, it would be 2 Area AMIP based at Edmonton, to the north of Hackney and Tottenham. In fact, until it moved recently, it had been the nearest cop shop to the Tottenham Hotspur ground at White Hart Lane. It's call sign was Yankee Echo, but I wasn't going to tell these comedians I knew that either.

'What's that?' I asked, playing dumb but not certain that I was convincing them.

'It's a sort of task force set up to investigate serious crimes,' said Sell.

'In this case, the murder of your mate Eugene Sargeant.' This from Stokoe.

'Not very catchy, is it?' I said, and they blanked me. 'I mean. what are you going to call the TV series? *AMIP: Life on the Streets*. It sounds like something out of *The Muppets*.'

'He's not taking this seriously, is he, boss?' said Sell, not taking his eyes off me.

'OK, OK. You're sure it was murder?' I said reasonably.

'Oh, yes. Quite sure.'

'It's more than our jobs are worth not to recognise a murder when one stares us in the face.'

'In fact, we're quite good at it.'

'And, to be fair, boss, this one wasn't exactly difficult.'

'That's true. All that blood and brains all over the carpet… What was it you said a minute ago, Mr Angel? Oh yes; a bit of a giveaway.'

'No, it certainly didn't take us long to work that one out.'

'Couple of hours – tops.'

I ground my teeth, but did it quietly. If they kept this up through the afternoon, I would confess to anything, even once owning a pair of white Chinos.

'So The Sarge gets his head blown off,' I pushed on, 'and I'm very sorry for him, but I don't see—'

'Excuse us?' they said, well-rehearsed.

'I don't see what I've got to—'

'Who said he had his head blown off?'

'You did.'

'No I didn't.'

'You said—'

'I know what I said, Mr Angel, and it wasn't that.'

'You implied… OK, so I *assumed* from what you said that The Sarge had been shot in the head.'

'Then you're jumping to conclusions. Eugene Sargeant was, as a matter of fact, stabbed in the head.'

'Stabbed? *In the head*?'

'Yes,' said Stokoe. 'It's not something you see every day.'

Actually, it probably was something some people saw every day – or at least maybe Friday and Saturday nights – if you worked on a casualty ward. I didn't know what the odds were on getting murdered by a knife these days, but they must be shorter than the chances of dying from eating peanuts – which they reckon are ten-million-to-one and pretty good odds unless you're the one with the fatal allergy to peanuts. It's always amused me the way the newspapers and the experts will say ten-million-to-one, it'll never happen. Then they try and get you to buy a Lottery ticket, where the odds are fourteen-million-to-one and they say, *it could be you.*

It certainly seemed that The Sarge's number had come up, and knowing the *how* didn't really help me. Knowing the *when* might help clear me. The *who* and the *why* were problems I was quite happy to leave to the two jokers opposite.

But would they tell me anything? Anything worth knowing, that is. They hadn't even told me why they had dragged me out of the pub and round to Bishopsgate nick to go through this pantomime.

Come to think of it, how had they known I was going to be in Dirty Dick's that lunchtime?

'When did it happen?'

Stokoe put his head on one side at that, then looked quizzically at Sell.

'Interesting, eh? Most people would have asked how it happened. but our Mr Angel is right in there with a specific *when*? Now what does that tell us?'

'Guilty conscience, Boss? Sniffing for an alibi?'

'You might—'

'Look, let's cut the crap, eh?' I interrupted. 'Tell me what's going on, tell me you're charging me with something or tell me goodbye.'

'Mmmm. Tough guy,' Sell muttered quietly and Stokoe raised a hand – I knew they must have some form of body language code – and he went quiet.

'Very well, Mr Angel,' said Stokoe, 'let's get serious. Eugene Vincent Sargeant was killed—'

I burst out laughing.

'I'm sorry,' I said, biting my lip. 'But *Eugene Vincent*? Per–lease! You are pulling my plonker again, aren't you?'

'I'm afraid not. That was his full name. And you didn't know, did you?'

'No, I didn't and trust me, I couldn't have resisted that. But that's no reason for killing him,' I added quickly.

His parents, maybe, but not him.

'No, it isn't, though I've come across dafter reasons,' said Stokoe, and he said it like it meant something. 'So let's be seriously serious, shall we?'

I shrugged an after-you gesture which is something like Body Language manoeuvre number 68: The Grovel.

'Mr Sargeant was found yesterday afternoon by the cleaning lady who comes in for a couple of hours every Wednesday. We think he was killed some time on Friday night.'

'Friday night?' I said aloud. 'Jesus, that's terrible.'

'I know, Mr Angel, it is sad – but not by any means unusual – for someone to go unmissed and unloved for that length of time. Not in London, anyway.'

'Oh... er... yes,' I said. What I had meant was: that was terrible because I didn't have an alibi for Friday.

'So, of course, we've been trying to piece together his work patterns, contacts, friends, social life. Anything, really. We've no real idea as to what he might have done to upset somebody enough to get himself killed.

'Frankly,' Stokoe leaned back and scratched his head, 'we're clutching at straws to get a picture of what he did for a life. You're one of the straws, so we're clutching.'

'But why me? How on earth did you dig me up?'

'You were identified from the photographs,' said Sell cheerfully.

'Straightaway, no question about it. Nice lady. Told us you'd be in Dirty Dick's this morning.'

I didn't have to ask.

'Lady called Amy May,' said Sell.

9.

Before

The TAL office was on the second floor of a warehouse in a building on Earlham Street, which bisects Seven Dials like an arrow through an apple.

In any other European capital, Seven Dials would be at least a curio on the tourist trail, but in London, on the border badlands between Covent Garden and Soho, it goes mostly unnoticed. The narrow streets and the racetrack which is the Seven Dials round-about make parking almost impossible, and the street market doesn't help, though you can buy cheap CDs and tapes as well as fruit and vegetables. The pubs are scruffy and attract more than their fair share of weirdos, especially in the afternoon. On the other side of the coin, there are some world-famous fashion names based there, as well as top hairdressers, and some high class restaurants catering for all tastes, ranging from mushroom freaks to people who like their oysters washed down with cloudy wheat beer, served by Australian students dressed as Belgian monks. There is always music in the air, whether seeping from one of the tiny dubbing studios, fashion shops or second and third floors where most of the office space is infested with the music-playing computers of graphic designers who always have the windows open because they can't afford to run the air-conditioning.

Apart from that, the area doesn't have much going for it.

I parked illegally and inconveniently for at least two of the street market traders and though I got some filthy looks, nobody said anything. After all, I was a black cab driver and if I didn't actually own the streets, I could give a damn good impression of doing so. I noticed Amy noticing the fact and storing it away for future use.

She led me to an arched doorway guarded by an intercom from which two broken wires dangled forlornly, and into a hallway ankle deep in junk mail. The postman didn't even ring once here. He couldn't; the bell didn't work.

On the wall by a wide metal staircase were handmade signs saying which company was on which floor. TAL was on the second, along with a graphics company. Something called Sager Intergalactic

Advertising and a company called WEB 18 seemed to share the third. There didn't appear to be a first floor, nor a lift.

Amy took the stairs at a cracking pace. I followed, half concentrating on Amy's legs and half wondering where they stashed the emergency oxygen. She didn't pause on the first floor landing, which was really just a turn in the staircase. There was a door there, unmarked and sealed at the bottom by a drift of dirt, dust, cigarette packets, McDonald's cartons and scrunched-up yellowing pages of newsprint.

She beat me to the red metal door on the second floor and was pressing numbers into a keypad lock as I drew level, the sound of her heels on the stairs still ringing in my ears.

'Welcome to Mission Control,' she said as the door clicked open.

Inside was an airlock system with two doors leading from it. One had a business card for the graphic design company glued to it, the other had the letters TAL stencilled on in black paint. Amy opened this one with a Yale key.

It was basically one high-ceilinged room with a partitioned section at the end, probably for a kitchen and toilets. There were two design desks with white plastic easels, Anglepoise lights and two computer work stations. The floor was an archipelago of islands of magazines, directories, books of cloth samples and open boxes of fabrics. There were also shoes of all shapes and colours, some in pairs, most in piles, some still in plastic bags.

'It looks like last orders in a Japanese whisky bar,' I said.

'Free samples,' said Amy. 'All imports. Some of them are genuine designs, but most are copies.'

I was about to ask if she could do anything in a size nine Doc Marten, when Lyn appeared from the kitchen area carrying a mug of coffee.

'My, my,' Lyn drawled, 'same clothes two mornings running. What a giveaway.'

She headed straight for one of the computer terminals and hit a button before making a show of noticing me.

'It's always the same with men, isn't it? Easy to pick up but a bugger to shake.'

Perhaps it wasn't coffee in the mug; neat lemon juice had fewer calories, after all.

'I'm not trying to shake Angel, sweetie, I'm hiring him.'

'How sad,' Lyn tut-tutted. 'So young and yet having to pay for it.'

Maybe it was acid. Nah, not in a Snoopy mug.

'As a driver, sweetie, as a driver. Angel has a cab and it could come in very useful. Tonight for instance.'

'What's happening tonight?' I asked, just to remind myself I was still there.

'Tonight's a double-header,' said Amy.

'Don't get his hopes up,' snapped Lyn. 'It means we have two gigs on in the West End.'

'Which is which?' Amy picked up a desk diary and began to flip idly through it.

'It's The Aristocrats first, off Baker Street, and a bunch of girlies from the local oil companies. I processed their questionnaires last week. We hit them with the usual Working Girls range and the TALtop. If we're lucky we might get a couple of M & S staff in there after work.'

'Cheeky,' I conceded, knowing the pub in question and the nearby head office of Marks & Spencer.

Lyn was not impressed and ignored me.

'The other one is round at The Mad Dog and we have to be there by six-thirty. That's a party frock do; two deliveries and up to five potentials.'

'"Potentials" are any friends a customer brings along,' said Amy, without looking up from the diary. 'They get a five percent discount for every three.'

'Clever,' I said.

'We've got to watch it there, though,' Lyn went on, 'after the last time. The Manager put us on a warning for monopolising the ladies loo.'

'No problem. Now we have Angel driving us, we can change in the back of his cab.'

Lyn paused with her mug halfway to her lips, then she glared at Amy, then she glared at me.

'Take that inane grin off your face,' she said.

*

I had an appointment that afternoon to have the tyres on Armstrong II bullet-proofed, I couldn't resist telling Duncan the Drunken about my new job. He wasn't impressed: said it would end in tears before bedtime.

Duncan the Drunken – probably the best car mechanic in the world – had acquired a supply of a large polymer chemical liquid which, once injected into a car' s tyres, slopped around automatically sealing up punctures. Duncan swore blind it was similar to the stuff the Americans used in Vietnam to seal up Jeep tyres when Charlie shot them up and he was pretty sure it contained Kevlar, the stuff bullet-proof jackets are made from.

It wasn't *absolutely* guaranteed to work, he said, if the police rolled out a stinger mat of nails, as they often do to stop joy-riders, but then who would go joy-riding in a black cab? And he wasn't terribly clear as to whether he had acquired the stuff legally, but he swore it was good for fuel economy and made tyres run cooler. So why not give it a try?

'Fashion, you say? Bugger, but that's a shaky business, that is.'

Duncan is the only person I know whose Yorkshire accent gets thicker the longer he lives in London – Barking to be precise. And I'm not convinced he's actually even from Yorkshire.

'And you'd know, would you?' I said, standing aside as he advanced on Armstrong II's rear nearside tyre with a metal syringe that could have given an elephant an enema.

'Nay, lad, I know to stick to me trade. Cars is what I know. Keep up with the technology and ahead of the market trends and you'll not go wrong. If you know what you're doing, that is.'

Duncan wheezed slightly as he pushed down on the syringe.

'When did you ever keep up with the market trend?' I laughed, parking a buttock on the edge of a paper-strewn desk.

'I have to, Roy, I have to. Security, that's the name of the car game these days. Just read what you're sitting on.'

In Ireland they would have said, 'Is anyone reading that paper you're sitting on?' but Duncan didn't make jokes. I shuffled the leaflets and manuals on the table. They all seemed to advertise alarm systems and immobilisers for car ignitions.

'That's cashing in on paranoia, Dunc. Everyone who owns a car in London – except me – is convinced it's going to be stolen, and they're probably right. But that's just common sense, not following market trends.'

'Ah, but it is,' Duncan crowed, moving on to the front wheel. 'You've got to know what sort of security goes with what car at what budget and what the demand is likely to be. F'r-instance, what do you reckon are the top motors nicked? I mean pinched to order, you know, for export like, not for joy-riding.'

I thought about this for a minute.

'The main German ones: the Audi, any BMW and certainly Volkswagen Golfs. Maybe a Saab, especially the convertibles.'

'Not bad, lad,' said Duncan, walking round Armstrong's bonnet. 'You missed out the Renault Espace – very popular – but apart from that you've got the list most insurance companies would agree on. But all those are posh cars owned by people with money. They don't come out here to Barking for an alarm system, they get it fitted when they buy the motor. That's not my market.'

'So what is?'

'Students, secretaries, young married couples, people like that who own second-hand Ford Escorts, Renault Fives or Ladas. People who don't have much cash but who have cars at risk.'

'You mean they're nicked for spare parts?' I knew that around forty percent of the half-million cars pinched each year were never recovered, presumably stripped for parts.

'Nah, for export,' Duncan shouted from inside Armstrong's wheel arch. 'Eastern Europe, lad, fall of the wall, all that shit. There's a big market there and still not enough wheels to go around. They don't have much hard currency, though, so your thief downsizes his operation to meet the demand and suddenly your average family run-about ain't safe on the streets any more. Serious, there's a big demand for Ladas. It's cheaper to nick one here than buy one in Russia.'

'So you're specialising in alarms for second-hand cars?'

Duncan stood up, poked his head around Armstrong and grinned at me. 'Sometimes the alarms are second-hand.'

'Do they work?'

'Sometimes,' he said thoughtfully.

'And this is some sort of social service?'

'No way. It's me identifying a market and cashing in on it.'

'I think you mean, "Responding to market forces," don't you?'

'I know what I mean. Point is this: I know motors, it's my trade. Only thing I do know, really. Because I know the biz, I can spot a change when it comes and jump in. What the friggin' Nora do you know about the rag trade?'

'Not a lot, but I don't have to. These girls have it all worked out, just like you have. They target a specific segment of the market, research it and then deliver the goods with instructions on how to wear them to look your best. The more I think about it, the more it's just like selling a car. When a punter walks in off the street, you size him up and fit what you've got in stock to match. Don't tell me you've never soft-soaped a punter. "These wheels suit you, sir, suit you." "Just what a man in your position needs." "This'll complement your image, sir." So forth, so fifth. Stuff like that.'

Duncan dropped the syringe on a work bench and began to wipe his hands on an oily rag that appeared to have been, in happier times, a Leeds United shirt.

'I see what you're getting at, but it's still different. Cars are solid, women are fickle. Mind you, I did once flog a Volvo estate to a silly tart lived in Stoke Newington. Told her it was the only car guaranteed not to ladder her stockings as she got in and out. She had to sell it back to me a week later; couldn't find anywhere to park something that big. Truth told, she'd have been better off with a bus pass.'

'There you are,' I said, determined to make a point even though I wasn't sure what it was. 'When it comes to clothes, if you're female and you need a bus pass not a Volvo, my ladies will design a bus pass for you. But you'll go away thinking you're wearing a Volvo.'

'Oh, I get you now,' said Duncan worryingly.

He balled up the filthy rag shirt and bowled it, like a cricketer, into a metal bin in the corner. Unlike a Yorkshire cricketer, he hit the target.

'I still think you're out of your depth, Roy, but that's not the real point, is it?'

'What is?'

'Do you get to see them getting their kit off?'

*

The idea wasn't exactly new. What idea was? But TAL had put their own spin on it and it was working.

That much they agreed on, though it was just about the only thing they did agree on during the rush-hour crawl round to Baker Street, as they bounced about in the back of Armstrong, adjusting their make-up, spitting on Kleenex to shine their shoes and wriggling their underwear comfortable while remaining seated, as only women can do.

Part of the concept had come from the craze, a year or so ago, for designer clubwear aimed at the young, trendy and usually zonked. Young clubbers, especially females, would be encouraged to attend makeover nights and strip to the waist, exchanging their boring old tank tops for designer T-shirts or vests. Oddly enough, this had appealed to young males intent on behaving badly rather than clothes-conscious females.

Still, it had shown there was an interest in clothes outside of the normal retail environment (by which I presumed Lyn meant *shops*.) Women certainly bought things in groups or house parties, something Tupperware had pioneered and others had followed, ranging from the National Childbirth Trust to the lingerie evenings of Ann Summers. (Lyn had done a study of their methods.) So it seemed only logical that there should be a scenario where young women could meet socially in a relaxed atmosphere to share a fashion experience with – and be influenced by – their peer groups. And that, to me, translated as down the pub after work with your mates.

The added TAL angle was their market research. Once a group had been identified (similar age profiles, right economic power, convenient wine bar) then they were hit with TAL questionnaires asking what *they* wanted out of practical fashion. As with most market research, the results were analysed on the usual principle: ask them what you want to hear; tell them what you were going to tell them anyway; remind them that this was what *they* had said.

And that way they got involvement in the very design process. The customers had a say, that was the clincher. Lyn persuaded them they had contributed to Amy's designs and Thalia showed them how to wear it.

So it was a genuine two-way process, was it? I asked this while swerving to avoid ramming a real taxi, due to my staring into the carefully-angled rearview mirror when a leg had traversed it from top to bottom. It took me a few seconds to work out that it must have been Thalia cranking up the tension in her black, shiny tights and consequently I missed most of the answer. But it seemed a fair bet that the bulk of their 'presentations', as they called them, were done deals before they started.

Amy had a portfolio of designs, but it was a limited one. The trick was to make it appear different. Take a common denominator of fabrics and one of the colours, then ring the minor changes as often as you could get away with. And keep moving. Don't go back to the same office or firm too often, unless you knew they had a high turn-over of staff.

Was it worth it? I had asked, meaning the door-to-door selling technique and not the sight of Amy changing into a Wonderbra in the mirror. Why not hold a fashion show if the product was good enough?

There was communal laughter from the back.

Did I know that the start-up costs of even a half-hour catwalk show were at least £25,000 these days? And who would come if you didn't have a top-name model strutting the boards? Milan Fashion Week was one thing; Monday night in a church hall in Brentford was another entirely.

And who goes to catwalk shows anyway? Hack photographers, professional hangers-on, resting actors, people wanting to be seen wearing better clothes than those on show, mothers hoping their eight-year-old daughters will be the next supermodel. What about buyers from the chain stores? Buyers? I must be joking.

And as very few customers actually went to shows, why not take the show to the customers? 'Let's do the show *here*,' I offered, but they didn't get it. They just hadn't seen enough afternoon television.

By the time I was turning into George Street, they were just about ready. Lyn had produced a roll of Sellotape and bitten a length off to wrap around her hand, sticky-side out. She used it as a cat uses a licked paw to smooth out her skirt and then brush off her jacket. Then she did a communal preen on Amy and Thalia.

At the kerb outside The Aristocrats, I put my arm out of my window and reached around to open their door just like a real cab driver would – or at least they always seem to do it when they have three attractive females in the back.

Amy asked me if I had their stock and for the fifth time I said I had; two piles of black garments in cellophane bags on the floor in the luggage space next to my driver's seat.

'OK, then,' she said to the other two. 'Let's go to market.'

As it happened, I managed to get a parking space on George Street itself, not far down the road, on a recently-vacated parking meter. I didn't put any money in it, of course. That would have looked suspicious.

So, too, would wandering down into the pub's basement bar and pulling up a chair to join the TAL hen party. Not so much suspicious, perhaps, as suicidal. There were about a dozen young females surrounding Amy, Thalia and Lyn, most of them touching or at least pointing to their clothes and all of them talking.

All three were wearing what Amy had told me was called the TALtop, all three of them in a different way. And they all had plain black skirts; tight and four inches above the knee for Thalia and Amy, knee-length with a pleat at the back for Lyn.

I nodded to Amy as I walked by and ordered an orange juice at the bar. Two businessmen from out of town, with raincoats and overnight 'suiter' bags, watched the proceedings open-mouthed from their table in a corner. The barman served me quickly and without a word, so he could get back to the other end of the bar to be nearer to the women, just in case they needed an ashtray emptying or an olive stuffing.

I caught some of their chatter but even when I did, it didn't make much sense. I certainly noticed that the TAL girls didn't have to buy a drink and there were squeals of delight whenever Lyn consulted her clipboard and then pointed to one of her audience. I watched, trying not to rubber-neck too much, as Amy produced a ring-binder file of design sketches and began to show the assembled girls. Lyn made copious notes on her clipboard; Thalia sat and smoked at the end of the long table they had commandeered. She seemed to be the only one with nothing to do or say.

Then came the trigger they had been waiting for.

A plain, heavy, short-haired brunette, size 14 in a good light, said, 'Oh, but I could never get away with that,' as she pointed to one of the pages in Amy's file.

I saw the glance that flashed from Thalia to Amy and then Amy to Lyn, but I couldn't tell if their new friends did. Thalia stubbed out her cigarette, shook her hair off her face and stood up, holding out a hand to indicate that the brunette should follow. The brunette didn't take any persuading and the two of them marched up the curving half-flight of stairs to the Ladies toilet.

By this time, there were about twenty men in the bar, as the pub's evening trade picked up. The vast majority of them followed Thalia's legs up the stairs with their eyes, and then went back to their drinks or to their mates or their partners. I looked at my Seastar and positioned myself at the bar so I could watch the stairs in the mirror. I was spending my life looking at women in mirrors.

Four and a half minutes later – I was impressed – the door of the Ladies opened and the dumpy brunette stepped out nervously, trying to catch the eye of her friends on the table below her. She was wearing Thalia's black top, V-neck style, just as Thalia had been and the effect was such that her friends really didn't take it in for a few seconds. In fact, she was halfway down the stairs before one of them yelled 'Hey!' and waved and then they were all noticing and chattering.

I was still looking in the mirror and noticing Thalia waiting to emerge, not wanting to steal the brunette's thunder, which she could have done, as she wasn't wearing any sort of top, though she had fastened her jacket with its single, slightly strained, button. She showed a generous V of flesh from the neck and as she skipped down the stairs I spotted an inverted V flash from below the button of her jacket to the waistband of her skirt.

But then I was thinking like a man. The women were all over the brunette, feeling the material of the TALtop, asking her (it seemed she was called Dee Dee) to turn around, reaching for their cheque books.

Amy raised a hand and signalled me to join them. I could feel the barman's eyes like knives in my back.

'… and get rid of the white tights,' she was saying to one of the girls. 'You've got to have absolutely brilliant legs to get away with white. Remember, black takes off ounces; white puts on pounds. Ah, Roy. Is the limo far away?'

Limo?

'Just across the street, boss,' I said straightfaced.

'Good. Can you get me… '

She looked at Lyn, who held up four fingers.

'Four TALtops from the stock box please. Size tens.'

'Sure thing, boss.'

I put down my glass and hopped up the stairs, showing willing. I heard one of the girls say to Amy, 'He works for you?' in a tone which made me make a mental note to return to this pub in the future.

When I got to Armstrong I rummaged through the cellophane packs stacked in the front and discovered they were either TALtops or short black skirts. They all seemed to be Size 10. In fact, the small white label sown in along a seam, which had just '10' printed on it, was the only identifying mark anywhere.

Back in the pub, I noticed that groups of young males had moved from the upper bar to near the top of the staircase, drawn by the sounds of girlish laughter, if not the sight of Thalia below.

I handed the TALtops to Amy and she and Lyn began to dish

them out, Lyn snaffling cheques from four girls plus the made-over brunette who didn't seem to want to give Thalia her top back. Thalia smiled and shrugged that it was OK and the brunette whipped out her cheque book, not even asking for a discount for secondhand. Maybe she was flattered or something.

'Get the cab,' Amy hissed in my ear. 'We have to be round the Mad Dog in ten minutes.'

'No problem,' I hissed back.

As I left I overhead lots of 'Do you have to?' and 'Do you do anything in—?' and similar, with Amy and Lyn making promises to be back the next week, if there were any other fashion victims in the girls' office.

Outside, I had just time to turn Armstrong on his axis and pull up at the pub's front door when they emerged and piled in the back. Two youngish suits drinking from bottles of Beck's lager held the door open for Thalia and both attempted a chat-up line. Both were stopped dead in their tracks by Thalia shouting, 'Sorry, got to rush!' as she peeled off her jacket, revealing a black cut-away bra, as she strode across the two yards of pavement and ducked into the back of the cab. She had the door shut and I had first gear and was moving before their brains unfroze.

'Sling me another top, would you, Roy?' she asked, pushing open the panel between driver and passengers, her breasts filling my carefully positioned rearview mirror.

I fumbled one of the cellophane packs through the gap to her.

'These all seem to be size ten,' I said, my voice strangely hoarse.

'They are,' said Amy. 'Well, that's what it says. Actually, we only do a size twelve, but calling them tens seems to be more consumer friendly.'

They all laughed at that.

'Did you get a result there?' I shouted into the back.

'Not bad,' said Amy. 'Lyn reckons five of them are on over £16,000 a year and they're all unmarried.'

I knew enough about secretarial wages to see why they were pleased with that. West One may be a convenient and safe place to work but the pay wasn't that good as a rule. The better secretarial pay packets were usually in the rougher parts of town.

'So they're on the database, are they?'

'You bet,' Amy laughed.

'And three of them are Capricorns,' said Thalia.

I had to ask.

'Capricorns?'

'Yeah. Capricorns spend like shit,' she explained and nobody laughed.

'You live and learn,' I said.

10.

Later

'Photographs? What photographs? I don't know anything about any photographs.'

11.

Then

'So you want me to snap some tottie for you?' said The Sarge.
'Yeah, that just about sums it up,' I sighed. 'You seem to have
cut to the nub of the matter with your usual precision and
razor-sharp intellect.'

'Kit on or off?'

The Sarge peered at me over the rim of a wheat beer that had been
served in a glass which could have doubled as a plant pot.

'*Per–lease*. I said fashion photography. The clothes are the thing,
not the tottie. Surely, in your vast portfolio you must have a couple of
ten-by-eights that don't contravene the Obscene Publications Act?'

'Suppose so,' he shrugged. 'You gonna eat those?'

I pushed the remainder of my bowl of mussels across the table
towards him. I had been going to eat them, but The Sarge's internal
metabolism was such that he needed them more than I did. Anything
hot, spicy, actively fermenting or, occasionally, still alive, put him in
a good mood.

'So, what's the deal? I don't do weddings or passport pics, you
know.'

'I know, I know. You're a professional, that's why I called you. It's
these girls I'm working with, they've really got their act together I
reckon. They find out what the average working girl wants to wear,
make it for them and then sell it direct. No designer labels, no expensive boutique shops, no catwalks.'

'So, where's the story then?' he muttered through a mouthful of
garlic bread.

'*That was it*. Cut the crap, give fashion back to the women who
wear it.'

'Can't see it myself,' he muttered, waving over a waitress.

We were in a new place called Cafe Racers up in Islington. The
Sarge had suggested it; I was paying. The chairs were plastic and the
tables formica-topped with paper tablecloths. The food was second
division French bistro; the beers imported. The gimmick was that the
waitresses all dressed in athlete's vests and shorts and wore
rollerblades. I'll give it six months.

A waitress wearing a loose white vest and no bra rollered over to us. As she approached our table, The Sarge made a big play of stacking our empty bowls and made sure that a spoon dropped on to the floor. The waitress braked on her blades and, with a resigned expression, bent over to pick it up, fully aware that The Sarge was gazing down her cleavage. The Sarge beamed like the schoolboy who has found the hole in the changing room wall and fumbled nervously with his tie, but made no attempt to avert his eyes.

'Did you get a load of those hooters?' he asked when she had taken the dishes away.

'No, but you did,' I said, trying to give the impression that if you'd seen two, you'd seen them all, but sarcasm was lost on The Sarge.

'Now, I could sell the idea of a spread on this lot,' he nodded to himself, his eyes following another waitress as she glided unsteadily by. 'Tits on wheels, man,' he breathed, 'tits on wheels.'

'Don't grope the staff, Sarge, they can move faster than you can.'

'I don't grope,' he snapped back, but he lowered his voice, making me think I had struck a chord somewhere.

'Well, stick to the business in hand, then.'

'What business? Where's the sexy story? What's the angle?'

'The angle is that this is fashion without the hype. The girls who buy it and wear it help design it. Power to the people and all that. Putting fashion back on to the streets.' I was waffling and I knew it, but hopefully The Sarge didn't.

'Bor-ing!' The Sarge said loudly. 'The cutting edge of fashion is anything totally unwearable and so expensive nobody can afford it.'

'So why does your paper give so much space to it?'

'Same reason we have wine writers when most people drink beer and the same reason we feature snowboarding holidays in the Rockies when most people want a week on a topless beach in Spain with loads of cheap booze.'

'And what reason is that?'

'Buggered if I know.'

A waitress zipped by, almost too far, but just managed to deposit two plates containing a thin slice of steak and a cherry tomato, almost in front of us. She smiled an apology at me and set off shakily back to the kitchen.

'Look, Sarge, this isn't just about the clothes. These girls probably don't do anything you couldn't pick up in a High Street chain store. It's the way they do it that's the story. They involve their customers. It's like democracy… power to the people… in polyester.'

I tailed off there, my train of thought totally derailed by the waitress, unable to stop, zipping by our table, clutching a bowl of *frites* to her chest. She stopped herself by grabbing the corner of an empty table and turned around. As she set off back towards us, I stood up and took the fries as she passed.

'Thanks,' she said breathlessly. 'Can I get you anything else?'

'Two more beers please, darling,' said The Sarge with an evil grin.

'You bastard,' I said, sitting down.

'What's up with you? Worried about the bill?'

I restrained myself from pointing out that he had ordered the most expensive items on the menu, and that his wheat beers cost the equivalent of £7 a pint.

'Skip it. Look, I'm telling you there's a great story here. Course, I've got to clear it with them first, but I can't see them turning down some national exposure.'

'Still don't get it,' he said, piling more *frites* on to his plate. 'This power to the consumer thing, you mean it's a revolt like Punk was?'

'No, not like that. It's more like the Sixties when everybody did a pick 'n' mix from three or four boutiques plus the Oxfam shop and whatever they ended up with was the look of the day. That sort of people power, except we're talking practical office wear here. Stuff you'd go for a job interview in.'

The Sarge wrinkled his nose as if his steak was off. It meant he was thinking.

'Sixties is good. I mean it's a good angle. Sixties-retro is definitely in at the moment.'

'You can say it's post-modern as well,' I said quickly.

'What the fuck does that mean?'

'I don't know, but it might help.'

'Let me have a word at the office. Can't say more than that.'

'Fair enough.'

'Think they've got any mustard? Or chilli sauce?'

We never found out.

Our poor waitress chose that moment to try and deliver our beers. Mine, a bottled St Pauli Girl, wasn't a problem, but The Sarge's wheat beer in its plant pot glass simply wasn't designed for delivery by rollerblade.

As she slid behind him, heading due south instead of roughly east, the contents went over the shoulder of his Hugo Boss suit jacket and soaked his Paul Smith shirt and red silk tie.

He clutched at his tie and flapped at it with his napkin, shouting, 'Shit, shit, shit!' quite expressively.

By the time I had stopped laughing, the waitress had a flush on her the colour of The Sarge's tie and there was a small, balding guy wearing a worried frown standing by our table.

'Please, sir, do forgive us. Please let us get the tie cleaned for you at least—'

He held out the hand of friendship and The Sarge reacted as if he'd been date-raped.

'Leave it!' he snapped. Then he sulked. 'Doesn't matter.'

The management man frowned some more.

'If sir is sure—?'

'Sir is. Leave us alone.'

'Very well, sir, but allow us to do something. There'll be no bill. Please enjoy your meal on us.'

'Most generous,' I said magnanimously before The Sarge could blow it. 'That's very kind of you.'

Another waitress was assigned to our flight path and she delivered more wheat beer and dessert.

'The one and only time you offer to buy me lunch and this happens,' moaned The Sarge. 'You're a lucky sod.'

'My Rule of Life Number One, mate,' I said smugly. 'It's better to be lucky than good.'

12.

Later

'Eugene Sargeant's flat was full of photographs, Mr Angel. He was a photographer, you see.' Stokoe smiled as if butter was refusing to melt in his mouth. 'We worked that out all by ourselves.'

'Weren't you, in fact, trying to get Sargeant to take pictures, him being a photographer?' Sell chipped in innocently. 'Was that because you knew he was a photographer or was it just a happy coincidence? Like, you mentioned you needed some pics and he said I'm yer man, I just happen to have my grandad's Box Brownie about my person?'

'Yes, I've told you—'

'You've told us very little.'

'Less than bugger all, I'd say.'

'I've told you it was my idea to try and get some publicity for the TAL girls. I knew The Sarge, vaguely, and he did work for the nationals, so I set up a meet.'

Stokoe fumbled inside his jacket for a pen.

'That was the meeting down at Canary Wharf you told us about?' he asked, distracted.

'That's the one.'

'Well, this could be important,' he said, looking at Sell.

He produced a click-top ballpoint.

'You got anything to write this down on, Steve?'

Sell frowned, then dug into his jacket pocket and produced a packet of Player's untipped cigarettes which Stokoe took and held like a shorthand notebook, his pen poised.

'Go on, then, Mr Angel. You were saying you set up the meeting with Eugene Sargeant… ?'

They looked at me.

I looked at them.

'Oh, I get it.' I risked a smile. 'You've done this before, haven't you? You sweat somebody in here and when they complain later about harassment, the Crown Prosecution boys and girls ask if any of the officers were taking notes and they say you were writing it all down on the back of a fag packet. Instant discredit of one witness.'

Stokoe handed the cigarettes back to Sell.

'It gets a laugh in court now and then,' he said ruefully. 'We can't put anything over on Mr Angel here, can we, Steve?'

'Doesn't look like it, boss. He's a sharp one, he is. Ought to be in the knife drawer.'

'Speaking of knives—'

'We were talking of photographs,' I blurted out. 'I'm happy to talk about photographs.'

'That's nice.' Stokoe's smile returned. 'Go on, then.'

There was no answer to that, except maybe to tell them the truth. Or at least some of it.

'There's nothing much to tell. I could see after a while that the girls really had something going for them. It was a good idea and I reckoned it was a natural for the newspapers. I knew The Sarge was a freelancer and had contacts in Fleet Street, or what used to be Fleet Street, so I got in touch. He fixed up a session with the Fashion Editor of one of the tabloids.'

'But he never got around to taking any pictures?' asked Sell and Stokoe flashed him a half-glance, as if he was jumping the gun.

'No he didn't and now it doesn't sound as if he will,' I said.

'You can put money on that,' said Stokoe. 'But fill in a gap for me.'

'What gap?'

'The gap between you starting to work for these women as a driver and general gopher and you suddenly becoming their public relations man. How did they take to that?'

'Well, I just suggested it,' I said with a shrug. 'I'd got to see most of their operation and started to chip in a few ideas.'

'Hmmm,' Stokoe muttered, scratching his chin. 'That sounds interesting.'

'What does?' I was instantly suspicious.

'Their operation, the TAL set-up.'

'You're right, boss, that does sound interesting,' Sell chirped.

Stokoe leaned back on two legs of his chair.

'Tell us about that. Tell us about the TAL operation.'

13.

Before

'We've had a meeting,' Amy told me the next day, 'and we've decided to offer you a job.'

'That was quick,' I said unloading plastic cups of coffee from half a shoe box. 'You girls don't hang about.'

'If you're in a meeting, you ain't with a customer,' said Amy.

'Don't call us girls,' said Lyn.

'You'll be the decaff,' I said sweetly. 'So what do I call you?'

'Boss,' said Lyn, not smiling.

'Mistress,' said Thalia, swinging her legs up on to her desk and crossing them at the ankle, her skirt sliding up her thigh. She held out a hand. 'Mine's the *cappuccino*.'

I had to walk the entire length of her legs to give it to her.

'Of course we can't pay you,' Amy was saying, as if I was thinking about money. 'Well, not officially, not like you were an employee. I mean tax and National Insurance and all that stuff.'

'No. I mean yes. Sure. Understood,' I rambled, as if I was thinking about income tax.

'We'll pay you out of petty cash,' Lyn sneered.

'How petty?' I managed to break out of Thalia's laser-guided eye contact. Houdini would have been proud of me.

'Black cab rates for any driving job and waiting time if you have to hang about. Most runs will be around the West End or down to our suppliers in E1 and we should know when we'll need you at least a day in advance. Won't be every day and it'll be some nights.'

'So you don't have to hang around here all day,' said Lyn turning away to consult the screen of her computer.

'Pity,' said Thalia softly, dipping the end of a finger into the froth of her *cappuccino*.

Before she could do what I knew she was going to do, I gulped at my own piping hot double espresso. The caffeine rush and the scalding sensation on the roof of my mouth seemed to do the trick. Pain, the great restorer.

'So what happens? Do I ring in every morning to get my orders for the day?' I croaked.

Amy walked over to her designer's desk and pulled a box out from underneath it, using her foot. She crouched down, holding her coffee out to one side and rummaged in the box, until she produced a black, rectangular object. As she straightened up, she turned and threw it at me, like a gunslinger.

The weight of it surprised me but I managed to catch it one-handed whilst not pouring coffee into my crutch. The warning wasn't lost on me though. I moved away from Thalia's desk and studied the Motorola flip-out phone.

'What's this?' I said stupidly.

'Told you he was thick,' snarled Lyn. 'Bet you he says 'Beam me up, Scottie' into it.'

I certainly wasn't going to now.

'It's a mobile phone and it's on our account. There's a charger for it somewhere but the battery should last eight hours. We'll keep in touch.' Amy, all business.

'Next best thing to electronic tagging,' I said, weighing the phone in my hand. 'And I can call out?'

'Yeah, but don't go mad, we get itemised bills.'

I doubted that. I suspected it was a cloned number, so someone would get an itemised bill but it wouldn't be TAL.

'And it doesn't work on overseas calls or the 0898 porn lines,' Lyn added, unnecessarily I thought.

'And you can't call International Directory Enquiries from a mobile phone,' I said. It was the one thing I knew about mobiles. They didn't seem impressed.

'I'm not going to get rich on this, am I?' I tried to appeal to their commercial ethics. I guessed there was little point in appealing for sympathy over what might happen if a real cabbie, or even a mini-cab company, caught me moonlighting their business.

'We pay you for three trips for every two you do,' said Amy. 'And you can start this morning. Right now, if you want.'

'But we'll need receipts.' This from Lyn, not looking up.

'Receipts? No problem. How many do you want?'

Amy gave me an address in the East End and a dozen TALtops in clear plastic bags. She stuck a sheet of paper to the top one and wrote: 10 x Design B. It meant alterations, she said, and I was to hand them to a man called Mujib Ur Rehman and nobody else, unless I had a problem with that.

I had said no problem, I could find it easily enough and she said that was OK, there was no rush, sometime today would do. I made finger-puppet signs to suggest we might get together later and she said she would ring me.

As I made to leave, my arms full of TALtops, I asked what the number of the mobile was and Lyn told me I didn't need to know. I muttered something about not being able to put it on my business card and Thalia smirked as she held the door open for me.

That must have triggered a thought somewhere in the back of my mind and connected it to Lyn's insistence that I produce receipts, so I took a detour south of the river before making my delivery.

Printer Pete's Place is buried away in Southwark, a chain clink away from the old Marshalsea Prison. Not that Peter, who ran it, had ever been in a prison as far as I knew, though he had come close once after assaulting the typesetter who left the 'r' off his name on the first lot of business cards he had had printed.

He was very sensitive about being Peter, not Pete, but at the time could not afford to have them changed so he used them and the name stuck. People even said they thought it was catchy, so he made a fundamental business decision on the experience. Anyone who called him Peter got a discount, those who referred to Pete got a surcharge. It doesn't have to make sense; business decisions have been made for dafter reasons than that.

Stuck in traffic down by the Aldwych, I phoned Peter to see if he was in. It wasn't really necessary, it was just that I was itching to use my mobile phone on the basis that, like most things in life, use it or lose it.

There was also the added *frisson* that a taxi is the one vehicle the cops don't pull over if they see a driver using a hand-held phone. The hands-off microphone system is, of course, much safer, but a real bummer if you want to show off, as other motorists don't realise you are important enough to be receiving calls.

Peter was in and I told him I was on my way to see him to do a bit of business.

'Just got a mobile phone, have you?' he said.

'What makes you say that?' I mumbled, the phone pressed deep into my shoulder, as I was forced to change gear thanks to a cyclist with absolutely no consideration for other, bigger, road users.

'Always happens with new toys. Hello, they'll say, I'm phoning from a traffic jam down the Aldwych. Or, hello, I'm phoning from the beach or the train; or, hello, I'm sitting on the lavvy parking the breakfast... As if you were fucking interested in where—'

'Sorry, Pete, you're cracking up,' I said and snapped the phone shut.

To hell with the discount.

'Taxi receipts?' Peter said through a gob full of bubble gum.

'Yeah, those little books of receipts which say "Licensed London Taxi" or similar.'

Peter blew a pink bubble of gum until it burst with a plastic crack. I hadn't seen anyone do that in years.

'How many?'

'Dunno. Three or four books, different designs if possible.'

'OK. Oi – Star Trek!'

A teenage black kid in an ink-stained brown work coat wandered over from the laser copier he was minding and joined us in Peter's office. It wasn't actually an office, just one end of the main (and only) print room, kitted out with a desk, two chairs and a battered green metal filing cabinet.

'Yes, Captain?'

'Nip into the security room and bring me one each of the little books of taxi receipts. They're on the second shelf, next to the holiday brochures, about this big.' He held up the forefinger and thumb of each hand to form a square. 'And don't touch anything else in there. Got it?'

Star Trek gave a short, formal bow.

'Beaming over immediately, Captain.'

He turned on the heels of his trainers, making a squeaking noise as he did so, and was off at the trot.

'Security Room?' I settled in the spare chair without waiting to be asked.

'We do security printing from time to time. Good business.'

'What, company reports and stuff?'

If that was the case, Printer Pete's Place had come on since I first knew him from the days when I had lived in Southwark.

'Mostly holiday brochures,' said Peter thoughtfully, chewing on.

'Where's the security angle on holiday brochures?'

'They're for the year *after* next, and they've got the prices in them.'

'I see. Business booming, then?'

'Doin' fair by staying small. It's the only way. I've seen the book trade move out of London and the colour work go to Italy or Singapore. Now, everybody's got desktop publishing and colour copiers, God knows where it'll end.'

And I thought it was farmers who were supposed to be manic depressives if you ever asked them how they were doing.

'You don't look too busy,' I said to annoy him.

It was true. There were half a dozen print machines of various sizes in the place and only one, apart from the copier Star Trek had left churning away by itself, was running, another young black kid watching it half-heartedly while swaying to the beat echoing in his personal CD player earphones.

'You've caught us at shift change,' said Peter. 'Here comes the afternoon shift now.'

As he spoke, three young girls, all mixed race and not one of them over eighteen, entered the print room at the far end and began to swap their street clothes for the brown work coats hanging on pegs by the door. If Peter was changing shifts at noon and this was his workforce, then he was using part-timers or Work Experience kids. In other words, cheap labour. In an odd sort of way it was almost reassuring to know that I was dealing with the same old Pete.

Star Trek appeared again, nodding to the newly arrived girls, even saluting one of them.

He held out four small square notepads to Peter.

'I have made it so, Captain.'

'Thanks, Star Trek,' said Peter, shaking his head slowly. 'Get back to work now.'

Star Trek clicked his heels and bowed again.

'Engaged,' he said before trotting back to his machine.

I wasn't going to ask.

Peter weighed up the notepads, all of different design, two with little black silhouettes of the traditional Austin FX taxi on them.

'You going legit with these?' he asked, having parked his gum over a cavity. 'I didn't know you'd done the Knowledge.'

The Knowledge was the awesome driving test all officially licensed London cabbies have to take. It involves swallowing the *A-Z* map of London and riding around on a moped for a couple of years, finding out where this or that Mews is and which streets the cabs can use but the civilians can't. Mini-cab drivers, however, don't have to do the Knowledge and quite often like their passengers to hold the map for them as they drive.

'Thinking of a bit of mini-cabbing on the side, Peter, that's all.'

'You still driving that black cab?' He narrowed his eyes.

'One like it,' I said guardedly.

'You're going on the tout, aren't you?'

The Tout was a particularly naughty practice which happened whenever there was a strike on the Underground or on the buses or, say, when it was Wimbledon fortnight. Black cabs would actively tout for business at bus stops and tube stations, picking up four or five people going in roughly the same direction, each one paying slightly less than the normal fare but getting a receipt for the usual amount. The cab's meter shows one journey but the cabbie takes four or five fares.

'It's nothing like that, Peter,' I said innocently. 'Just a bit of fetching and carrying. Delivery stuff. I'll take all four of those. How much?'

'Half a long one,' he said without thinking about it.

'Hey, reality check, Peter,' I came back. A long one was £100; a half, £50. The retail price of the booklets was about £2. 'Give you twenty.'

'Forty.'

'Twenty-five, if you give me a VAT receipt.'

'Twenty, then, but there'd better be a drink in it somewhere.' He tossed the receipt pads and I caught three but dropped one.

As I bent to pick it up, I noticed one of the girls from the new shift walking across to her machine. She was pulling on her brown work-coat over what looked suspiciously like one of the TALtops I had in the front of Armstrong II outside.

'What's her name, Peter?' I asked, pointing to the girl. Peter choked back a bubble of gum. 'Dunno. Why?'

'Just wanted a word with her, that's all. About something she's wearing.'

Peter looked at the girl then at me.

'I always thought you were weird, Angel. Oi! Star Trek, come 'ere.'

Star Trek left his machine again and jogged over but Peter cut him off before he could entreat us to live long and prosper. 'What's her name?' Peter pointed. 'The Asian babe on the four-colour job?'

'Crusher, sir,' said Star Trek.

Peter looked confused.

'There's nobody called—'

'Just ask Beverley to come over here for a word, would you?' I intervened.

'Engage,' said Star Trek.

'What was that all about?' Peter asked, genuinely confused.

'Leave it, Peter. Life's too short.'

Beverley got the message from Star Trek and looked over to us nervously. Peter waved her on and she stuffed her hands deep into the pockets of the brown coat as she walked. She was suspicious, not nervous.

'Roy here's a friend of mine,' Peter said, 'and wants to chat you up.'

'Chat *to* you, Beverley,' I said quickly. 'It might sound strange but I wanted to ask you where you got the top you're wearing. I noticed it when you came in and I want to get my girlfriend something like it for her birthday.'

'What? This?' Beverley pulled open her coat.

She was wearing the TALtop as Thalia would, in plunging V-neck mode. It could have been one from the delivery I was supposed to be making, but I couldn't be sure. I hadn't looked at them closely.

'They're great, til' you wash them.'

She pulled the sides of the top to show how it stretched.

'Bit cheap, I reckon. Shoddy goods me mum said.'

'Thank you, Beverley,' Peter interjected. 'Best get on with your work now, love.'

'Can I ask where you bought it, Beverley?' I said, shooting Peter a killer look.

'Oh, I didn't buy it, I *earned* it, didn't I? This was my overtime bonus for weekend working 'bout three months ago, wasn't it, Mister Pete?'

'*Thank you*, Beverley—'

'First and last time I get conned into—'

'Thank you, Beverley. There are two million unemployed, you know. Don't let's make it two million and one.'

Beverley wrinkled her nose at him and marched off.

'You might have said,' I accused Peter.

'How the buggeration was I supposed to know you were going to ask the little tart about her blouse?'

'It's not a blouse—' I started, then realised what a dumb argument this was likely to turn into.

'Look, Peter, I'm delivering some samples identical to what she's wearing and I thought she might have hoisted it from the back of my cab.'

'You should've said straight up. Nah, my kids wouldn't hoist from the back of a cab, they'd take the cab. You remember Lally French? Now *there* was a hoister.'

Lally French had been a legend in the East End and the scourge of West End store detectives, especially on late-night shopping days. She had shoplifted all her clothes and complete wardrobes for her three daughters during her career and it was rumoured that when she died, three year's back, she had been laid out in a Vivienne Westwood original.

'She was the best, so I'm told. Anyways, where did you get your little bonuses from?'

Peter attempted another bubble, relaxed again now, but the gum must have lost its tensile strength or something because he gave up, plucked it out of his mouth and flung it into a plastic dumpster which had RECYCLABLE stencilled on it.

'They were a freebie from a client,' he said, wiping his fingers down his shirt front. 'Picked up half a dozen of 'em. Gave one to the wife, matter of fact. They were just lying around and I said I could use one of them, good bit of schmutter, blag, blag, and the client said help yourself. So I did.'

'Was this client up west?'

'Might have been.'

'Anywhere near Seven Dials.'

'Perhaps.'

'Was it a company called TAL? It's a fashion business.'

'Nah, never heard of it.'

I knew Peter well enough to know he wasn't lying on that one, but he was being cagey about something.

'You're sure about this, Peter?'

'Sure about what?'

He stared me out as he unwrapped a plug of gum which I could smell – that peroxide smell you get in hairdresser's – from where I was sitting. I wished he'd take up smoking. I was sure there were risks from passive chewing.

'Sure it wasn't a company called TAL, T-A-L, run by three stunning bits of skirt, any one of whom could give you a right trousering?'

'Now you're talking my language, Roy,' he grinned. I knew it. 'You think I'd've forgotten something like that? Nah, it was a computer company. Maybe they did some work for these tarts of yours and got paid in free samples. It was Seven Dials, though, that I do recall.'

'Fair enough, Peter. Sorry I suspected your young Beverley of a naughty.'

I held out a twenty-pound note and he snaffled it into an ink-stained hand.

'No worries there, Roy. This fashion company… these birds… do they… ?'

'Do they what?'

'Give free samples… if you know what I mean?'

'You've been proof-reading your own pornography again, Peter,' I sighed. 'I do know what you mean and they don't.'

'Pity.'

I stood up and stuffed the taxi receipt books into various pockets, then zipped my jacket.

'By the by, Peter, why is Star Trek called Star Trek?'

'D'you know, Roy, that's always puzzled me.'

'I guessed it had,' I said.

*

The address Amy had given me to deliver the TALtops (to Mujib Ur Rehman and nobody else) was on one of the cut-through firetrap alleys between Commercial Street and Brick Lane. It was an area of London that had seen just about everything in its time: waves of immigrants from all points east, prostitution, Jack the Ripper, fascist marches, communist counter-marches, pubs which opened at 5 a.m., the oldest brewery in the country, legendary gangster families, the best Italian leather jackets outside Italy, and the best balti cooking this side of the pass beyond Kashmir – or at least this side of Wolverhampton.

It did not surprise me that TAL were buying in from the area, because clothing, along with fake Nike and Reebok trainers, was a key sector of the local economy. It probably got a government grant. There is even a Fashion Street, though that had been there since the 1880s when the area was fashionable for cheap, brain-numbing gin and very unsafe sex.

What surprised me was that my destination turned out to be a camera shop.

I checked the address again, even consulted the battered A-Z street map I keep behind the sun visor. This was it, a single unit shop front with one window protected by an iron grill above which a sign said SECONDHAND PHOTOGRAPHIC in faded lettering. Sure enough, the window contained a display of cameras, lenses, flashguns and even a tripod. Nothing very old or valuable as far as I could see, but worth having the grill up to deter the passing smash-and-grabber.

I parked Armstrong down the road and went back on foot for a closer look. It was a camera shop and seemed to be open for business and I thought I could see someone moving about inside through the smaller-mesh grill which protected the glass door.

Maybe this was Mujib Ur Rehman's day job and he only did tailoring alterations at night. What did I know? There was only one way to find out, so I went in.

The shape I had seen moving around was a Bangladeshi woman in a dark green sari. She smiled at me as I entered and she smiled when I asked for Mujib Ur Rehman.

'I have a delivery for Mujib Ur Rehman,' I said and she smiled again. 'It's outside, in my taxi,' I said lamely, pretty sure she had seen me drive by.

She smiled and shrugged her shoulders slightly.

'I'll go and get it,' I said to myself.

It only took me a minute to get the sample TALtops out of Armstrong II, but I must have asked myself half-a-dozen times whether she couldn't, or wouldn't, speak English. If she didn't recognise the name Mujib Ur Rehman, she might recognise the garments.

She didn't have to. When I got back to the shop there was a young Bangladeshi male standing by her side behind the camera counter. He must have come in from the back, because he hadn't passed me on the street. He was tall and wiry and no more than about seventeen, judging by his moustache that looked as if it had been applied with the stub of a pencil.

'Yes, please?' he asked before the door had closed behind me.

'I've brought these for Mujib Ur Rehman, I said, holding up the samples of TALtops.

'This is a camera shop,' he said, straightfaced. Then he added, 'Secondhand mostly.'

'I can see that. It puzzled me too, but this was the address I was given.'

'This is a camera shop. Do you want to buy a camera?' he said.

'No, I just need to—'

I didn't get any further because I was interrupted by a strange warbling sound and for a moment I wondered how the woman was making such a noise whilst still smiling vaguely at me.

The warbling trilled out again and the young Bangladeshi pointed a finger at me and nodded enthusiastically.

'Oh. Er… excuse me a minute.'

I transferred the TALtops to my left hand and took the mobile phone out of my pocket, fumbling it open and jamming it to my ear.

'Hello?'

'Are you there yet?'

It was Amy.

'Sort of. Can I just check the address you gave me? It's a—'

'Camera shop, I know. I just remembered that I forgot to tell you. Is Mujib there?'

'I don't think so. I'm not getting very far, I'm afraid.'

'Tell them you work for Miss Amy,' she said.

'Miss Amy,' I repeated out loud. 'OK, hang on.'

But there was no need. As soon as I had said 'Miss Amy', the Bangladeshi woman nudged the young lad with her elbow and said, in perfect English, 'It's all right, Miss Amy sent him. I told you we should have belled her.'

The kid muttered something in Bengali and reached behind a poster advertising Fuji film to open a door into the back of the shop. He waved at me to follow him.

'I've just got a green light here,' I said into the phone. 'Your name seems to be a positive Open Sesame in these parts.'

'Glad to be of service. You behave yourself. I'll see you later.'

'Tonight?'

'No, not tonight, I've got a meeting.'

'I thought you said if you were in a meeting, you weren't with a customer.'

'Don't flatter yourself. You're not a customer.'

She hung up and I snapped the phone off like I had been using it all my life and slipped it into my pocket.

'Are you Mujib Ur Rehman?' I asked the lad.

'No, just one of his idiot nephews,' said the woman, who wasn't smiling any more. 'But we have to be careful. Moklis will take you through.'

Moklis was already on his way. I followed through the door

behind the Fuji film poster and into an uncarpeted corridor that ended in another door. This one had definitely not come with the original building plan. In fact, it looked as if it had been pinched from a recording studio. It was thick and padded with foam, with a two-inch wide rubber seal around the edge.

The need for soundproofing became apparent once Moklis opened it. From somewhere behind and, I thought, up above, came a regular hum from one sort of machinery and an irregular clunk from another, heavier, machine. There was a weird smell too, a mixture of dust and detergent, as if somebody had spilled a box of washing powder.

Somebody had, and I found myself leaving footprints as Moklis led me into a stone-floored room which housed three launderette sized washing machines, a huge tumble dryer and what I guessed, from its own chemical smell, was a dry-cleaning machine.

Moklis turned left through a doorway without a door and into a larger room. Even my sense of direction realised that we were now in the property next door to the camera shop, although from the street it appeared boarded up and empty.

There was no natural light, but it was bright with the light of a dozen or more naked hundred-watt bulbs suspended at random by cables from the ceiling. It was noisy with the chattering hum of eight sewing machines, double banked on dangerously swaying trestle tables and there was a radio or tape-deck somewhere playing Hindi rap.

And it was hot. There were eight Bangladeshi women working the machines, two more operating steam-presses and another in the far corner stirring a cooking pot mounted on a bottle gas-fired double burner.

There was no obvious ventilation and a lot of busy people in a relatively confined space. Of course it smelled of sweat.

I was in a sweatshop.

14.

Later

'So, you see, I don't really know anything at all about the TAL operation, as you call it,' I said. 'I was just the driver.'

They exchanged knowing glances and slight nods as if that was the answer they expected. As if that was a fair answer. As if they believed me.

'Lying through his…' said Stokoe.

'…fucking teeth,' completed Sell, then added, 'Sarge.'

God, they were good.

'My thoughts exactly,' Stokoe said to Sell as if I wasn't there any more. 'I think we'll have to adopt another tack with our Mr Angel.'

'With you on that one, boss, all the way. But which of our many stratagems, ruses, tricks, ploys or schemes should we employ?'

'Tricky decision, that, DC Sell,' said Stokoe, faking concern like a bad stage direction. If a cartoon lightbulb had appeared above his head and lit up, I wouldn't have been at all surprised.

'Got it!' he said, slapping a hand on the table. 'We'll use the one where you leave the room to make some tea and I talk about you behind your back.'

'Think it'll work, boss?' Sell asked, hamming it up.

'It's the only plan we've got, Steve.'

Stokoe was a bass note away from a full John Wayne. I bet myself it was his party piece when they got the karaoke machine out at the Policeman's Ball.

'Then let's go for it,' said Sell. He switched from stage whisper to Public Address mode. 'I'll see if I can rustle up some tea, shall I, Sarge?'

'Good idea, Steve. Initiative, that's what that is. I could murder a cup. Oops, sorry about that, no pun intended.'

'None made,' I said under my breath.

'And I'm sure Mr Angel would appreciate the cup that cheers but does not inebriate.'

No, he wouldn't. A bottle of scotch with the top off would have been more to my liking, but I nodded wearily.

After Sell had gone, Stokoe began to speak, holding up his right index finger to indicate that he didn't expect either interruptions or answers.

'I think I mentioned that DC Sell and I are attached to what is known as AMIP – that's an Area Major Incident Pool. Let me explain. A Major Incident is something like a murder, in this case that of the late Mr Eugene Sargeant, and he was found in a particular area, so that explains the Area bit of AMIP. So far, so clear, right?

'Now, the really interesting bit is Pool, because that means we on this side of the great law and order debate, get to pool our rich and varied resources. Normally, we all work in our little ruts, everyone chasing their own speciality, bidding for staff, justifying budgets. Give us a Major Incident and we get together and we find out what each other's doing. It's really great. We love a good murder, because the left hand gets to find out what the right hand is doing.

'My colleague, DC Sell, for example, has a speciality and he's brought all his special knowledge and experience into this investigation, a bit like bringing a bottle to a party. And I'm telling you this because DC Sell is very keen to use his special knowledge on this investigation. He thinks he can crack this one because of his special experience, and he is an ambitious young copper. I wouldn't like to be the one holding things back from him.'

'And I am holding something back?'

'He thinks you are, I can tell,' said Stokoe.

'About what, for Christ's sake?' I snapped, knowing I was playing Stokoe's game. 'What is his special fucking speciality, anyway?'

Stokoe had been waiting for that.

'He's done three years in what you might call Community Relations. Well, if you were an Assistant Chief Constable, that's what you'd call it. Me, I prefer to cut to the chase, get to the nub of things, call it like it is.'

'Any day now,' I said under my breath.

'DC Sell,' he went on, 'has spent the last three years trying to prevent the coming civil war. He's very dedicated to that.'

'I'm sorry?' I shook my head. 'Did you say civil war?'

'You heard.'

'Between whom?'

'Between the Turks in Islington and the Bangladeshis in Shoreditch, of course.'

He drummed his fingers on the table and looked at me, head on one side, almost friendly.

'You're going to tell me you have no idea what I'm talking about, aren't you?'

'I have no idea what you're talking about,' I said obediently.

15.

Before

'It's because of the Turks,' Mujib Ur Rehman told me when I knew him better. 'And the Nazis, and the skinheads, and the social workers, and the taxmen, and the National Insurance inspectors, and the council, and the immigration authorities. But mostly the Turks.'

It had taken me three or four visits before it had clicked. Something had bugged me from the start about the set-up, something farcical. Then, one morning, while collecting an experimental sample of a TALtop done in chocolate brown ('It'll never replace black, but it's the flavour of the month.'), it hit me.

It was to do with the camera shop which fronted the business. You went through a shop cluttered with optical technology and then, a bit like Alice, entered another world, a world of steam irons and clothes presses and sewing machines. Why should this seem oddly familiar? Weird was fair enough, but *familiar*? Then I remembered all those episodes of *The Man From UNCLE* (I'd seen reruns on cable twenty years on) where the dapper agents would enter UNCLE's high tech headquarters (computers as big as a wall, but it was the Sixties), through a dry-cleaner's somewhere in downtown New York. They used a laundry as the front for covert operations invariably involving lots of electronic gadgets. Mujib Ur Rehman used a shop full of electronic gadgets to front a sweatshop and laundry. There was some sort of synergy there, but it was lost on Mujib Ur Rehman. As far as he was concerned, a Man From UNCLE was a distant relative out to collect a debt.

But that first time, when Moklis Ali had shown me through the back and into the business end of things, there had been no opportunity for small talk.

Young Moklis had introduced me to a small, middle-aged man with a straggly white beard that had gaps where he tugged at it when agitated.

'You say Miss Amy sent you?' he said, tugging at his beard.

'Yeah, I'm bringing these in for alteration. She said you'd know what to do.' I indicated the pile of TALtops I was holding.

He tugged a single white hair from his chin. 'She give you a phone?'

'As a matter of fact she did. She just rang a minute ago, down in the shop.'

He shot a glance at young Moklis and said something I wouldn't have caught even if I had spoken the language. Moklis answered him with a shrug of his shoulders.

'What's the number?'

'What?'

'What's the number of this phone?'

'I don't know. I forgot to ask.'

He held out a hand and said, 'Let me look.'

I pulled the phone from my pocket and slapped it into his hand. He pressed a couple of buttons and the liquid crystal display lit up. Then he reached behind him to the waistband of his jeans and pulled an identical phone out of a leather holster, pressing buttons with his thumb. He looked at both and seemed satisfied.

'Same series,' he said, handing mine back. 'Miss Amy gives them out so she can stay in touch.'

But the junior staff don't get the leather holsters, I noted.

'You got to wait for these alterations?'

'She didn't say I had to.'

He took the TALtops from me.

'Be seeing you, then.'

'Could be,' I said, stuffing the phone into one of the flap pockets of my leather jacket.

'Nice jacket,' said Mujib Ur Rehman. 'Is it a Max Mara?'

'Hardly,' I laughed and opened it to show him the chain store label over the wallet pocket.

'Do you want one?' he asked, steely-eyed.

'How much?' I countered.

'On the house.'

Some house. There had to be a catch. It was a trap or a test of some kind. Best to walk away.

'Love one.'

'OK,' said Mujib Ur Rehman, dead cool. 'Slip it off and one of the girls will sew in a label for you. Five minutes, tops.'

*

'You could have had Versace, Ungaro or Paul Smith and they do Nikes and Reeboks as well,' Amy had said later. 'If it's leather, you can get it in Brick Lane.'

She had rung me that evening, just as I was about to leave Stuart Street for a meet and a drink or three with an old musician mate called Bunny, in search of work. Having blown it with Danny Boot's mate Topher, I was going to pull in a few favours with Bunny, probably the most versatile and permanently in-work pub musician I knew. Even with every other pub in town being converted to an Irish bar (and I don't play fiddle or penny whistle), Bunny would know where there would be an opening for a hack horn player. If he didn't, no one did. But once again, TAL intervened to divert me from my quest for honest employment.

I had opened the front door only to be confronted by Fenella trying to juggle three bags of shopping while trying to get her house key out. Being a gentleman, I held the door open for her.

'This cat food weighs a ton, Angel,' she wimped. 'I thought you were going out with your friend Rabbit?'

'I was. I am. I'm just...'

'What's that?'

'What's what?'

'You're *trilling*,' she said, wide-eyed. 'That noise. It's in your pocket.'

I slapped myself gently on the forehead.

'Sorry. Phone.'

'You've got a mobile phone?'

'Yes, and I'd better answer it.'

'How long have you—?'

I ignored her.

'Hello?'

'It's me.'

'Amy?'

'Who else were you expecting?'

'Nobody, I just—'

'Hey, Lisabeth, Angel's got a mobile phone.'

'Who's that shouting?'

'My neighbour. Never mind. What's up?'

'Nothing special. Yet.'

'Binky, don't shout on the stairs. You know I hate it.'

'Who was *that*?'

'My neighbour's... er... neighbour,' I said carefully, as Lisabeth was now on the stairs and within range. 'So what can I do you for?'

'I've finished my meeting earlier than I thought and I'm at a loose end,' Amy said in my ear.

'Where?'

'Binky, have you been doing Angel's shopping for him again?'

'He's been busy. He's on the phone.'

'And not hearing a bloody thing! Keep it down to a dull roar, will you?'

'Are you at Paddington Station or something?' yelled Amy.

'Nowhere so restful. Where are you?'

'I'll be in the All Bar One in Hanover Street in about ten minutes. Can you make it for a quick one?'

Lisabeth cut off my obvious (but favourite) reply.

'Has he paid for all this cat food?'

'I'll give it to you in the morning,' I shouted up the stairs, then stepped out and slammed the door behind me.

'That's nice,' said Amy down the phone, 'but shall we have a drink first?'

'Nikes, eh?' I said. We were in bed back at Stuart Street after a couple of drinks and a pizza supper. Stuart Street because her place was 'a mess' again. 'Well, that's my Christmas present list sorted.'

'They're not real, of course,' Amy murmured sleepily. 'The shoes, I mean. The labels are.'

'Oh well, that's all right then. None of my friends will notice.'

The trouble was all the people on my Christmas list probably would.

'It sounds as if you've been accepted. That's good. Mujib and his crew don't normally take to strangers.'

'It goes with the territory,' I said softly, nibbling her ear. 'Brick Lane has always been a transit camp for the dispossessed and if they manage to make a living, people get jealous and hold it against them.'

She rolled over to face me and opened her eyes wide to meet mine.

'You're not just a pretty face, are you? You think things through.'

'I wouldn't go that far,' I said. 'Breakfast is about as far ahead as I plan.'

'That's not what I meant,' she whispered, her hands moving down under the duvet. 'Would you be willing to do more runs down Brick Lane for us?'

'Sure, if you're paying for the diesel.'

'Good. See, I knew you'd thought things through.'

I didn't follow the logic of that at all.

'Are you sure *you* have?' I asked, but she seemed to deliberately misunderstand.

'Oh yes. I had a really good meeting today and we have some gangbuster business lined up because of it. So I thought I'd give myself a treat.'

Her hands began to move again.

'And what are you treating yourself to?' I asked, knowing the answer.

'You.'

*

Amy's idea of me doing a few more 'runs down Brick Lane' turned into an almost full-time job over the following weeks, so much so that I abandoned my attempts to find a gig to play at. Some might say that the fashion world's gain was also the music world's gain.

I found parking spaces, delicatessens, pubs and unfashionable balti restaurants (unfashionable because they worked at remaining undiscovered by the West End restaurant critics) I had forgotten, or never knew, existed. Armstrong II became recognised and accepted in the area, so much so that after a week, young Moklis confided that I could park on Brick Lane itself after dark and still expect to find all four wheels in place. Some worthies get the Freedom of the City and are allowed to drive a flock of sheep over Westminster Bridge. I get to park in Brick Lane; and I reckon I get the better deal.

Moklis Ali showed me most of the ropes and told me that his uncle Mujib got quite a kick out of having a black London cab doing his deliveries for him. It didn't surprise me, therefore, that after half a dozen runs for TAL, Mujib asked if I would do a run for him – a couple of sealed boxes out to a warehouse in Southall, out towards Heathrow. Naturally, it was a cash-in-hand job and a generous one, because it had to be done immediately. Time was of the essence. Very urgent.

So urgent that he would time me and when I eventually found the delivery address – one anonymous unit on an anonymous industrial estate – there was my contact, another Bengali called Tozammul Hussain, timing me as well.

I hadn't been told whether Tozammul was a relation, but he was closely in touch with Mujib Ur Rehman, quite literally – on the end of a mobile phone. As I pulled up in front of him, he made a point of letting me see him consult his watch, then he spoke into the phone, before switching it off and stuffing it into the pocket of his padded anorak.

'You are half-an-hour late,' he said, helping himself to the pair of boxes in the back of Armstrong II.

'The traffic was terrible,' I told him. 'Plus, I've been tooling around this estate for twenty minutes trying to find you.'

Tozammul snarled at me, grabbed his boxes and scurried off towards the warehouse. It didn't look as if I was going to get a tip or a cup of tea or a thank you, so I started Armstrong up again and turned around, heading for the M4 and all points east.

The traffic had been bad, that much was true, and I had guessed that they would allow me twenty minutes or so leeway. That had been just long enough to pull into a pub car park in Chiswick and carefully open Mujib Ur Rehman's boxes just to make sure I wasn't being set up to boost the Drugs Squad's arrest statistics. Unless the Drugs Squad was suddenly interested in two dozen pairs of size 10 Reeboks though, I felt I was safe.

Because I had resealed the boxes, stolen nothing and asked no questions, I passed the audition and more little delivery jobs from Mujib followed. Sometimes I tacked them on to the back of a TAL job, sometimes Mujib rang me direct on the mobile. I trucked boxes out to Southall, down to Brixton and even, after dark, to the back service entrances of a couple of well-known department stores in the West End.

Mujib remained businesslike and somewhat aloof but young Moklis seemed to warm to me, as did the woman I had seen him with the first time I visited the camera shop. Her name was Roshan Ara and Moklis told me she was no more than seventeen, some distant cousin of his and, in family circles, a bit of a problem. That probably meant she would end up running the business. She certainly had no inhibitions about coming on to me, though I didn't encourage her. For some reason I was worried about Amy hearing untoward things on the grapevine or, more likely, the mobile phone.

Still, the chance to flirt with Roshan Ara was an added bonus to my trips to Brick Lane, and it was instructive too. She told me that Bangladeshi names were flexible, to say the least. She was Roshan Ara and it was always said in full, whereas Moklis Ali could be just Moklis, but that a distant relative, Mohammed Ali, was always Mohammed Ali, and I said I'd heard of that one.

One morning, I impressed her, briefly, by greeting her with *Namaskar* in Bengali (or *Bangla* as she called it) and then she pointed out that as 85 per cent of Bangladeshis were Muslim, *Salaam mellekum* would be more appropriate. She treated me to a lunch of *malchi*, dried fish boiled up with white rice, and taught me how to roll it into balls and eat with my fingers, whilst never missing a beat from whatever was playing on Sunshine Radio at the time.

Any mention of food got her on to her favourite subject of how the vast majority of Indian restaurants in Britain were in fact owned and run by Bangladeshis and how their names were set to change to reflect this. After twenty-five years educating the British palate under mock colonial names such as Star Of India, Taj Mahal or even Jewel in the Crown, the coming trend was for more authentic Bengali names, such as The Sugonda or The Sundarban or using the crescent and star to indicate the Muslim origins. Rosham Ara had obviously thought about this in depth and saw herself as a mover and shaker in the catering business, rather than in the rag trade. Give her three years at business school and she would be talking franchises and export markets and opening the first chain of tandoori restaurants in Latvia.

But before then, she needed my help.

It was late on a Wednesday afternoon and I was running late, trying to pick up a consignment of TALtops and get back up West for the girls to do an early evening show in a pub in Notting Hill.

I was cutting through a deserted Spitalfields market to get to Brick Lane when Roshan Ara ran into the corner of my eye, coming out of an alley. My instant assumption was that she was heading for The Gun (a fine pub where they haven't changed the juke box since I was a student) on Brushfield Street. Then I saw she was wearing a TALtop and guessed she was hurrying somewhere to get changed before going back to the shop as I knew, from her, that Mujib didn't approve of the staff modelling the merchandise. And then I noticed that her hair was not plaited and was blowing wildly as she ran and that it came down to her hips. And then, finally, I noticed that she was waving at me. And shouting. And then banging her hands on Armstrong's bonnet and running around to the driver's door as I stopped.

'It's Moklis,' she yelled in my face. 'They're killing him. You've got to help. Down there.'

She pointed down the alley she had run from.

I could have pointed out that there were two police stations (City and Metropolitan) within a minute's run. I could have offered her my mobile phone. I could have asked who was doing what to Moklis and why.

'Is that a dead end?' I asked instead.

'No,' she said, 'it goes through to—'

'Get in.'

I had Armstrong moving before she slammed the door and as I swung into the alley, she bounced across the back seat trying to get purchase. Fortunately, I needed no further directions from her.

Halfway down the alley there was a ruck in progress which involved maybe seven or eight bodies, one on the deck on the pavement, the others milling around furiously, pushing, shoving and shouting. It was par for the course for a real live street fight. Unlike in the movies or on television, fights are usually childish, disorganised and, fortunately, quick. At least, that is the case when a brawl takes place in daylight, in public, and involves participants with an average age of sixteen. (These rules do not apply to middle-aged Glaswegians under five-foot-two-inches tall after the pubs have closed.)

I turned on Armstrong's headlights and hit the horn in a continuous blast only giving a half-thought to wondering whether I had asked Duncan the Drunken to check the brakes.

The mob split before I began to slow and were running out of the alley almost on to Commercial Street before Armstrong stopped opposite Moklis, who was leaning against a wall panting heavily. Across the alley, lying in the gutter, was another Bangladeshi huddled in a near foetal position, a stained tweed overcoat pulled up over his head as if for protection, a pair of scuffed trainers sticking out of the other end. He had a thin, straight moustache and his eyes were wide and white and screaming.

Roshan Ara was out of Armstrong and dabbing at Moklis' nose with a tissue before I had the handbrake on. I waited until the last of the scrappers had disappeared out of the alley before I risked getting out. I hadn't seen anything much of them apart from anoraks and jeans and a vague impression of dark, youthful faces and curly hair.

Moklis had a nose bleed and a tear in the knee of his jeans.

'You'll live,' I reassured him. 'What's going down?'

'They were selling drugs to this worthless piece of shit,' he said, flinching as Roshan Ara dabbed his nose.

The young man in the gutter, and I could see now just how young he was, began to rock gently on his back and moan to himself.

'Who were they?'

'Turks,' he said dismissively. 'One of the Islington gangs.'

'Good job the Neighbourhood Watch was around, then, wasn't it?'

The guy on the ground yelled something in Bangla.

'What's he saying?' I asked.

'He doesn't appreciate our help,' said Roshan Ara.

'He was trying to buy,' said Moklis.

The man in the coat staggered to his feet and turned his eyes on us, then took a couple of swaying steps towards us. I could see ancient vomit stains down the front of the coat and I could smell him now and knew he had lost control of his bowels. As he stood in front of us, his shoulder muscles began to twitch. I guessed heroin and that he was a relatively new user, about twenty-four hours from his last hit.

He drew himself up and spat professionally over Armstrong's nearside headlight. Then he let go a stream of invective in Bangla before limping off down the alley.

I didn't bother asking for a translation.

*

I never mentioned the incident to Amy or Lyn or Thalia, but a couple of days afterwards, Amy told me, right out of the blue, that Mujib Ur Rehman had a very high opinion of me.

She didn't volunteer any details and I didn't push it.

'That's cool,' I said. 'They seem to have a good set up down there.'

'Yeah, bless 'em,' said Amy. 'They're fast and reliable and cheap without being shoddy.'

'Are they legal?' I ventured.

'As much as anyone cares these days. Sure, the building's a fire trap and the wages are crap and they probably don't have an annual works outing to Brighton or a union, but nobody works there against their will. It's a family business and they keep it tight.'

I bit my tongue, not wanting to get into that argument.

'How on earth did you find them?'

Amy was non-plussed.

'From a directory.'

'What, like Yellow Pages?'

I made a mental note to look up 'Sweatshops' the next time I was in a phone booth.

'No, one of Lyn's directories,' said Amy. 'On the Internet.'

16.

Later

'It's coming here via Germany,' said Stokoe, 'but the port of origin is Karachi. Daft, isn't it? When you think about it. All that high grade elephant – OK, so some of it is cut nine-tenths with talcum powder – coming all the way from West Pakistan to end up being retailed in Brick Lane to East Pakistanis.'

I said nothing. It wouldn't have got me anywhere to have pointed out that East Pakistan had been Bangladesh for over twenty-five years and that no one had used *elephant* as slang for heroin for about ten of them. He already knew that, he was just wondering if I did.

'Now, we've always kept an eye on our brethren from the subcontinent… Don't look at me like that, I'm stating a fact, not an opinion. We've always looked at anyone and anything coming in from an opium growing area, that's our job. But this particular trade is interesting. I'm not boring you, am I?'

'No, no,' I blurted. 'I'm riveted. Well-focused. Tuned-in. Carry on.'

He narrowed his eyes at that, but went on.

'OK, then. This scenario is interesting because it's being imported by certain elements of the Turkish community – is that politically correct enough for you?'

'I get your drift.'

'Good. Well, certain Turkish toe-rag bastards are dealing the stuff to the Bangladeshis. Not your average work-all-hours-keep-your-nose-clean immigrant family that wants to get ahead, though. We're talking young, male, second generation immigrants getting a taste for it. Do you know what they say about heroin?'

'You're going to tell me.'

'Cocaine is the drug of choice of the rock star or the stockbroker. Ecstasy is the drug of choice of the young rave-goer and the fashion victim. Valium is the drug of choice of the housewife. Heroin is the drug of no choice at all.'

'And nutmeg is the drug of choice of the idiot vegetarian,' I said before I could stop myself.

'What?'

There was a flash of anger there from Stokoe, the first one.

'Sorry, didn't mean to spoil the lecture. It's just that I have actually met some people who smoked ground-up nutmeg. Usually just before they chained themselves to a tree.'

'Is that supposed to be funny?'

'Not especially. I'm just saying there's drugs everywhere.'

'You approve of that?'

'I'm not surprised.'

'What? Not surprised at the Bangladeshis, or just not surprised?

I had no idea where this was going but I had that shoulder blade tingle telling me to be careful.

'Look, drugs are a cash crop. Poor countries grow the crop and need the cash. Rich countries have the cash. London is a big place, easy to get to and multi-cultural. There are drugs in London. Stands to reason. I didn't know about the Bangladeshis, but why should they be immune to temptation?'

'And it doesn't worry you?'

'The politicians and the newspapers do the worrying.'

'And that's enough?'

'Oh, and the police. They worry about drugs as well.'

He shook his head slowly.

'My colleague DC Sell certainly does. He takes these things very seriously indeed. Personal, almost. He doesn't like drugs on his patch and he won't like it if you don't take things as seriously as he does. Could turn ugly.'

I would have nutted my forehead on to the table if I thought it would have made an impression on anything other than the Formica. Stokoe would only have laughed. Probably the biggest chuckle he would have had since he'd read the Police and Criminal Evidence Act. If he ever had.

'Look, what's going on? Just what are you getting at? This stuff about Turks and Bangladeshis and heroin, what's it got to do with me?'

'You live in Hackney,' he said, but he knew it sounded thin.

'Well, that narrows it down then, doesn't it? Yes, I know some Bangladeshis and some Turks too. What next? Saliva tests to see who's drunk Turkish coffee or DNA sampling to check who likes curry?'

'You're streetwise, you go down Brick Lane.'

'So I drive around. I'm a driver. That's what I do – mostly.'

'Do you ever use that cab of yours as a real one?'

'I might be stupid but I'm not suicidal.'

He snorted approval at that. We both knew what a mob of angry London cabbies could do.

'Oh, I don't think you're stupid, Mr Angel. We're good with stupid, we know how to handle them. Most of them are very helpful.'

'And I'm not?'

'About as helpful as a vibrator with a flat battery. You can't—'

'But I might come in useful,' I said, spoiling his punchline.

'Something like that.'

'You're not helping,' I said as condescendingly as I dared.

'Oh, aren't I? Oh, well, naughty little me.' Stokoe feigned shocked surprise. He was good at surprise. 'I just knew it would all be my fault. Where have I gone wrong? What can I do to make it up?'

I ticked off the options on my fingers in front of his face, just to see how far I could go. Most coppers are careful when they are on their own, even in a police station. Probably, especially when they are in a police station. My word against his. I'd been there long enough without being charged and being questioned only informally, for it to be odd. Odd enough for me to claim he had thumped me? It was always a risk they ran, that's why they always go around in pairs and never question suspects alone, unlike most of the cops on television.

'One, you can let me go. Two, you can charge me with something – anything – and let me get a solicitor. Or three—'

'Am I going to like three?'

'Doubt it. Three, you can tell me exactly what the fuck is going on. Are you investigating a murder or a drug war, and what have I got to do with either?'

Stokoe shot out a hand, very fast, and grabbed mine firmly but he didn't apply any real pressure. We were locked for a second like a couple of arm-wrestlers. His thumb carefully bent down my index finger.

'One, you can go any time you like, but I'd take it as a favour if you'd wait for DC Sell to return. He'd be so upset if he didn't get a chance to say goodbye. Two…'

He bent down my middle finger ever so gently. I relaxed and went with the flow. He wasn't hurting me yet.

'We won't be charging you with anything today, so you won't need a brief. That's not to say we won't haul the arse out of your trousers tomorrow or the next day, if only for withholding vital information.'

I wasn't sure there was such a charge but I didn't want to argue. He was the policeman after all.

'Three. This little piggy…'

He closed down my third finger. It was like a magician's trick. My hand was inside his and any second now he would blow on it and my hand would disappear.

'Yes, we are investigating a murder, which may or may not be connected to other crimes or on-going investigations.'

'This drug war?' I looked pointedly at my hand and he released his grip slowly.

'I never said it was a drug *war*; that's when two firms go head-to-head over territory. This is one-sided, a new conduit. Someone is deliberately targeting the Bangladeshis.'

'A Turkish firm?'

'Maybe.'

'But you said—'

The door to the interview room opened, as if on cue. It was DC Sell, pushing the door with his foot whilst balancing two styrofoam cups on a large stiff envelope, the sort that has DO NOT BEND in big red letters on the front. He put one cup down in front of Stokoe and the other in front of his chair. The envelope he flopped on to the table in front of me.

'Sorry about the wait, guv,' said Sell. 'It would have been quicker to take them round to Mr Patel's One-Hour service.'

'Don't worry about it, Steve,' said Stokoe, all genial again. 'It keeps the lab boys in a job and I've been keeping Mr Angel entertained.'

'He hasn't confessed yet, then?'

'Not to anything we could stitch him up for.'

They both sipped their tea and stared at me as if daring me to ask where mine was. When I refused to rise to the bait, Stokoe looked at his watch then said: 'You'd better look at them or we'll be here all day.'

'What are they?' I asked warily, not offering to touch the envelope.

'They're photographs. We told you there were photographs.' This from Sell.

'Of what?'

I had a nightmare freeze-frame vision of technicolour head wounds, a blood-smeared carpet, the handle of a breadknife protruding from bone and scalp.

'Well, they're not holiday snaps, that's for sure,' Sell said to Stokoe. 'I suppose he would have called them "work in progress" or something poncey like that.'

'The Sarge took them?'

Sell nodded and I allowed myself to breathe again. If The Sarge took them, he couldn't be on them, or at least not dead on them. Unless, of course, he was a much better photographer than I had ever given him credit for.

'Go on then,' Stokoe chivvied me, not quite sure why I was hesitating. 'They won't bite.'

How many times had I heard that about cats? Or women?

I picked up the envelope gingerly and tipped the contents out on to the table. There were seven black-and-white prints and from the way they were all grainy and washed-out, I guessed they had been blown up and/or copied from smaller prints. I used a fingernail to move them around so that I could see them all, having read somewhere that photographs were really good for picking up fingerprints from the unwary.

Three were so grainy it was impossible to make out what they were. Either they were totally out of focus or the subject had been moving at lightning speed and photographed through the wind-screen of a moving car by an alcoholic with a bad case of the shakes. They could have been used in a trailer for the *X-Files* and I was about to say so when I flicked one away to find myself looking at me.

It was as grainy a shot as the others but it was clearly a face. My face, and taken close up, almost *in* my face. And for the life of me I could not remember The Sarge ever having taken such a shot. He would have had to have been so close, to get me full-frame in that way, that I would have been able to identify his toothpaste.

Stokoe and Sell said nothing and I tried to concentrate on not giving them any cause to do so.

I scratched at my portrait (almost a full profile, with a bit of a smile but not showing my teeth off to the best advantage) until I moved it enough to see the print underneath.

To the untrained eye that one was easily explained. It was the rim of a flying saucer as it hovered over a series of dust dunes on the moon. Only a skilled observer like me realised it was the cleavage of a waitress on rollerblades delivering a bottle of Belgian wheat beer. And that explained where the photograph of me had been taken; but not how.

But the last two photographs were the most interesting. The penultimate one was another cleavage, a literal full-frontal, with no head showing and no background clues. It was Thalia and I knew it had been taken during our drunken afternoon in the pub down at Canary Wharf.

Finally, there was a head and shoulders of a young white male in three-quarter profile. It was the sharpest of the seven prints and clearly showed, maybe because of the black-and-white film, that its subject had white or blonde hair cut short almost in what used to be called *en brosse*.

I knew him too, as well as knowing the previous bosoms.

Stokoe was talking.

'Mr Sargeant had a lot of photographs in his flat. Well, he would, wouldn't he, being a photographer? But these were a bit odd, not like all the others, so to speak. And that's the only one we found of you, Mr Angel, which makes it doubly odd.' He paused. 'But at least we can make you out on that one, not like the others you've got there. Difficult to tell who they are or what they are. You couldn't help us out there, could you?'

'I don't remember any of these being taken,' I said carefully and it was sort of true.

Stokoe looked at Sell.

'That's not being helpful is it?'

'No, guv.' Sell shook his head. 'Getting a bit boring, isn't he.'

Stokoe nodded as if agreeing, then turned back to me.

'Let's change the subject, Mr Angel. I am very disappointed in you.'

He wasn't alone there, but I thought it best not to volunteer the information.

'You see, I told you that DC Sell here brought his own special expertise to our little AMIP investigation. His experience in some of our ethnic communities is throwing new light on this case. Well, so am I in my own small way. But you never asked what my speciality was, did you?'

I eyeballed him but didn't push it. He wasn't kidding suddenly.

'You're going to tell me, aren't you?'

Stokoe reached over and tapped the last photograph, the one of the blonde guy, with his index finger.

'My speciality is him,' he said, 'and you know him, don't you?'

I sensed it was time to stop messing about.

'Yes,' I said weakly, clearing my throat. 'His name is Wolf.'

17.

Then

I was in the TAL office making coffee, unjamming the photocopier, offering to sweep the floor, anything to kill time; basically just getting in the way.

'I told you,' Lyn said, without looking up from her computer screen, 'she left a message on the answerphone, said she'd be in around lunchtime.'

She had told me and that made the fifth time.

Thalia was trying on shoes, dozens of them. She would sit on the floor, take a new pair from one of the boxes scattered all over the office, put them on, stretch out her long legs and waggle her feet. Then she would stand up, walk over to me and go into the pose, the right leg bent slightly, the foot at ten-past-the-hour. She was wearing thick black leggings rather than tights, so the effect was muted but still impressive.

The first time she had said, 'What do you think?' I had told her to walk about the office a bit, see what they felt like, were they comfortable? She had looked at me as if I had slithered out of a mescal bottle and said, 'I'd wear trainers if I wanted to walk anywhere.'

After that I restricted myself to simple, monosyllabic answers.

She approached wearing a new pair and I lowered the magazine I was pretending to read.

'Angel?'

'Too low. Too square.'

She pondered this judgement for all of a second.

'You're not wrong,' she said, kicking them off and mooching over to another pile of boxes.

'Do you have to encourage him, Thalia?' Lyn growled, bashing her keyboard. 'He's determined to get in the way.'

'He's harmless,' Thalia drawled, plopping herself down on the floor and ripping open another shoe box. 'He's just missing Amy. It's not his fault she's such a busy girl these days.'

She gave me a sideways look from under her fringe; half smug, half come-on, totally sly. But by then I knew Thalia only flirted with me when she had an audience and as Amy wasn't around, Lyn would have to do.

I buried my face in the magazine and scanned an article on how market researchers had invented new categories of young, affluent consumers.

'Here's one for you,' I read, 'put these into your database. "The eighteen to twenty-four age group can now be image-divided into six groups: Cyber Gens, Mind Blows, Eco Pagans, A-Genders, Glam Bangers and Street Sporters." Hope you've got them all tagged, Lyn.'

'What *are* you talking about?' she said, bored. She was good at bored.

'The latest style definitions. Cyber Gens and Mind Blows seem to be much of a muchness, computer nerds and Internet anoraks. The Eco Pagans, well, I suppose they're the Body Shop vegetarians. A-Genders are those with the androgynous waif-model look, or maybe young blokes who want to sing in bands like Suede. "Glam Bangers," it says here, "adopt a retro-seventies style, but with a post-modern sense of irony." I'm glad about the irony, aren't you? And Street Sporters, it looks like they're the young thugs who rollerblade through the shopping precincts on Saturday afternoons.'

'What about these?' Thalia was standing in front of me again, closer than ever and looming over me in four-inch heels.

'Not spiky enough,' I said.

She looked down at her feet and then shrugged as if she agreed with me.

'You're making this up,' Lyn muttered.

'No, I'm not. It says here that anyone selling anything must appeal to "the cyber-centric, surf-seeking new-ager". It could be you, Lyn. Don't you see yourself as a cyber-centric, surf-seeking new-ager?'

She leaned back from her screen and pretended to think about it.

'Some days I am,' she said slowly, 'and then some days, I just can't be arsed. Now shut the fuck up, will you? I'm working.'

I sat down in Amy's chair and threw the magazine on to her desk, muttering, 'Just trying to help,' and wondering what to do next.

It had been a weird sort of week. I had run three or four delivery errands for TAL and had one job down a seedy club in Camden, playing one set for a self-styled torch-singer, backing her with all of about six different notes on *Walk On By*. When I asked the pianist why she called herself a torch-singer he'd said, 'Dunno. Got any lighter fluid?'

I had asked Amy to come to the club with me, thinking she had never heard me play and might be interested. She'd said she had to see her landlord, something about her tenancy agreement. And I'd suggested a night at the Comedy Store (doing her laundry), a meal in the rudest Chinese restaurant in Soho (staying in to finish off some new designs) and a drink in Callaghan's Irish bar at Marble Arch (meeting with a new client). I was getting the distinct impression that she was avoiding me.

'What's up? Amy avoiding you?'

Thalia was standing a matter of inches away, hands on hips, looking down at me.

'Are you psychic?'

'Of course.' She pushed her hips with her hands and the effect was to emphasise the thrust of her breasts. 'So what do you think?'

'Very nice,' I said without thinking, then realised she meant the shoes. 'Really nice. Honestly, dead smooth.'

'Wrong answer,' she grinned, reaching out and ruffling my hair. 'I win. I wore these three lots ago. You said they were too chunky then.'

I gawped at her like a surprised goldfish as she marched over to Lyn and held out a hand. Without looking at her, Lyn reached into the pocket of the jacket she had hung over her chair and produced a one pound coin for her.

'What was the bet?' I asked sheepishly.

'I said you were mooning for Amy and wouldn't pay attention to my legs. She said you were a man and given half a chance would try and get in my pants by taking an interest.'

I noticed that Lyn blushed faintly but she kept her eyes locked on her screen.

'In most cases, I'd have backed Lyn,' I said.

'Yes, but you're not psychic,' said Thalia doing a little pirouette in her new shoes. 'You're a Libran.'

I wasn't going to ask her how she knew I was a Libran; the answer would have been because she was psychic. So I said, 'What makes Librans bad psychics?'

'They're just no good at it.' She did another twirl. 'If you were you'd know I wanted you to go to Carluccio's deli round on Neal Street and buy me one of his praline chestnuts.'

She flipped the pound coin at me and I managed to catch it without quite falling off Amy's chair.

'Just the one?' I asked.

'That's all you've got the money for.'

I stood up and zippered my jacket.

'I was right about the shoes, though,' I said, walking to the door, my back to her. 'They are chunky. They really fatten your ankles.'

As I reached for the office door handle, I said, 'Made you look.'

Lyn's burst of giggling told me I didn't have to turn around.

Thalia wasn't far wrong though on the price of praline chestnuts in the delicatessen and I got some funny looks when I only bought one after half-an-hour's mooching around the shelves of bread and pasta and olive oil priced at something over £150 a gallon if my maths was accurate.

I tried to look knowledgeable while examining the eight or nine different types of mushrooms – OK, *funghi* – on display which I knew would be on the menu in the restaurant next door. I taxed my powers of mental arithmetic some more trying to estimate when I might be able to afford to eat there again.

The pub on the corner was opening up and I thought, what the hell, put it down as a sign from God and have a drink. It was the sort of pub where you didn't order the ale until you had seen someone else take one out of the pipes, so I asked for a lager and change for the cigarette machine, telling the Australian barman that I knew perfectly well how to switch the machine on. Then I had to go back and ask him for the loan of a match.

I sat on a bar stool near one of the windows looking out on to Seven Dials and with a great effort of willpower managed at least twenty seconds before pulling out my mobile phone. I dialled Amy's mobile, using the Memory, having finally worked out how to program it, only to be told, again, that the Vodaphone I was calling may be switched off and would I please try later?

I snapped the thing shut. I was trying later, though I had lost track of exactly how many times since the weekend. And that had gone well enough, hadn't it? Amy had spent two days and nights at Stuart Street, which is not something you would normally do unless the Appeals procedure failed. She had got on like a house on fire with Lisabeth and Fenella downstairs and Springsteen hadn't laid a paw on her. On the Saturday night we drove out to Romford to catch a new band I'd had a tip on, doing a pub gig. We agreed they were good but only if you'd never heard of The Kinks, left early and stopped on the way back for fish and chips and cans of 7-Up in the back of Armstrong. Having sampled so much of the high life, we decided to stay in bed most of Sunday.

Since then though, it seemed as if I was getting the big elbow treatment and the only contact with Amy had been via the mobile, her to me, with instructions for a run down to Brick Lane or a delivery to somewhere in the West End. She had studiously avoided anything other than strictly business contact. It was not that the vibes she was giving off were cold or hostile, it was just that there were no vibes at all. That irritated me and the fact that it did really bugged me.

And it also bugged me that I couldn't come out and ask the others what was wrong. Thalia just wouldn't take it seriously; Lyn would. And I didn't even know where Amy lived. Every time the subject had come up she had been evasive. Her place was always a mess, though she had seen my gaff in Stuart Street and if hers was a mess in comparison, then it must have been trashed by experts. And she had never exactly specified where it was, just 'Islington way'. She wasn't in the London residential phone book, at least not under Amy May, but then again, that meant nothing. Mobile phones and the fear of sicko callers had removed most single women from any listing which could give their address. Assuming, of course, she was single.

But now was not the time to worry about it unduly. The time to do that was when I didn't have Armstrong parked round the corner and I could afford to get a serious drunk on, so I finished my lager and stubbed out my cigarette. I thought about leaving the rest of the packet on the bar, and then asked myself who I thought I was kidding?

I drifted back towards the TAL office, stopping at a streetside trader offering CDs and tapes, to see if I could spot the pirate versions or, even more difficult, spot the ones I had played a backing track on. It was only because I was tooling about wasting time at the market stall that I was in a position to see the van arrive.

The driver didn't so much park as abandon the van, a small white Ford, half-on the pavement. Such was the angle he was at, when he opened his door the bottom corner scraped and sparked on the tarmac of the street.

The guy running the CD stall winced and shook his head.

'Just look at that, an' not a bleedin' warden for miles. But when we set up in the morning, fuck me if they ain't all over us like flies on…'

But I wasn't listening. The van driver with the cavalier attitude to parking was already scuttling into the TAL building, clutching a parcel under his arm. He was moving at Mach One, or maybe that should be Warp Factor Five, as I clearly recognised him from Printer Pete's place, where he was called Star Trek.

I gave the white van a good once-over as I walked by. The only thing of note was a bunch of small parcels on the front seat, all wrapped in brown paper with one sample of what was inside taped to the wrapping. There were business cards and With Compliments slips, standard printer's stuff. I wondered why Pete had lied to me when he said he had never done business with TAL.

I met Star Trek halfway up the first flight of stairs. He was coming down them in two-footed jumps, two steps at a time, just like a kid.

He froze, wary but not embarrassed, when I said: 'Hi there, how boldly goes it, Star Trek?'

'I know you?' he asked and for a moment I tried to think which character he was assuming, then I realised he was being himself.

'Pete's place. I was down the print works the other week.'

'Oh, yeah, right,' he said, unconvinced.

'You delivering?'

'That's right, man, it's delivery day.'

He eyed up the stairwell behind me as if he thought I might block him. 'Special deliveries.'

'From Pete?'

'Sure. Who else? Special delivery. In, out, don't hang about.'

'Pete told you not to hang about, eh?' We nodded, agreeing with each other. 'What, scared the girls will get you?' He stared at me as if I had switched into Klingon. Actually, he would probably have understood me in Klingon.

'Girls? What girls? There ain't no girls up there.' He must have seen something in my face.

'Straight, man. No girls up there, just the weird guy, Blondie.'

Blondie? Weird *guy*? I now knew for sure that television rotted your brain.

'I've got news for you, Star Trek. The only weird blonde up there is called Thalia and she is definitely female, with all the bits in the right places. I think Pete's been working you too hard.'

'Hey, listen Mister Whoever, if I'd seen a female, I'd know. Nothing wrong with my eyes. You want to buy Blondie up there some flowers, then you do that, but get Interflora to take them up to the third floor, cos I won't. He's got the evil eye on me already.'

'Hold everything. Did you say third floor?'

'Hello there, channels open at last. Put it on screen for you?'

He reached into the pocket of his jacket and produced a slip of paper and unfolded it using the fingers of one black hand, a bit like a card sharp.

'On screen,' he announced, holding it up to my eye level.

It was a POD, a proof-of-delivery slip with an unreadable signature acknowledging that whatever he had delivered had been received in good condition. The address it gave was this building, but the company was WEB 18, third floor.

'Sorry, Star Trek, wrong office.'

'No problem. You had me worried. If there were women up there, my sensors would have picked them up.'

'I'm sure they would have,' I laughed but he wasn't smiling, he was back in character. 'Give my regards to Pete.'

'Acknowledged,' he said, and jumped by me down the stairs. 'Live long and prosper,' he said over his shoulder.

Thalia was putting her coat on as I entered the TAL offices.

'Brilliant timing, Angel,' she said gleefully. 'You just missed her.'

'Amy?'

She put her head on one side and stared at me with no more than half a ton of fake pity.

'Aw, just look at him, would you? He's like a little puppy, isn't he?'

Behind her, still at her console, Lyn snorted.

'She's not coming in today,' Thalia wagged a finger, 'so you'll just have to contain yourself. She just rang in, said she had to go to Leicester to check out some sample fabrics. If you hadn't taken so long buying my chestnut, you might have been here and talked to her yourself, though she didn't ask after you and I quite forgot to tell her you were hanging around here pining for her. You did get my chestnut, didn't you?'

I reached into my pocket and squeezed the praline before I produced it for her.

'It's melted a bit,' I said meekly. 'Sorry.'

Thalia took it and, stretching her neck, she rubbed the chocolate, still in its foil wrapping, over her throat.

'They're easier to apply when they're melted,' she said huskily, then she laughed, flipped the chocolate once, caught it and flounced towards the door.

'I'm off to…' she started, but then the door opened before she got to it and whatever she was going to tell us turned into, 'Well, well, more men. Men everywhere and not a one for me.'

I couldn't see who she was talking to as she was blocking the doorway from the inside and she was determined not to let whoever was there see in. Deliberately, she danced from one foot to the other, holding the sides of her coat out like wings, to block his view, but she reached her boredom threshold mercifully quickly.

'Oh, don't worry, she's here,' she said, standing to one side to allow him in.

He was an inch, perhaps two, above six feet tall and powerfully built. He was wearing a short-sleeved linen shirt and a red silk tie with small black dots, fashionable wide-cut khaki trousers and brown loafers which looked so naff they had to be fashionable and expensive. His arms were muscular and the shirt showed off an impressive tan. His hair was short, spiky and bottle-blond, which had been fashionable with footballers that season. I had no doubt that this was Star Trek's Blondie from Web 18 upstairs.

'Lyn, come.'

That was all he said. Two words only, but enough to suggest a strong German accent.

'Her Master's Voice,' Thalia said nastily, waving Blondie in with an exaggerated bow.

But Blondie did not want to come in, not now he had seen me.

He fixed me with eyes so light blue he must have been wearing coloured contact lens and we stared each other down. I was expecting Thalia to say something but it was Lyn who broke the deadlock.

She stood up and switched off her computer, not logging out or anything, just hitting the power switch. Then she marched out from behind her desk, and I mean marched, almost in a straight line, gazing at Blondie as if hypnotised.

'Mind the phones, Thalia,' she said without breaking stride, 'I won't be long.'

Thalia stepped aside to let her pass and Blondie nodded slightly and followed. Before he closed the door behind him, I saw Lyn clumping up the stairs to the next floor like a zombie.

'What was *that*?' I asked, remembering to breath again.

'*That* was Wolf,' said Thalia, pulling a face and then miming two fingers down the throat in the universal semaphore for vomiting.

'And who is Wolf?'

'Lyn's bit of stuff,' she said, bored already. 'They've been at it like knives for months now. He runs a computer company or something upstairs. When he wants something he just snaps his fingers and little Lyn trots up there like a riding school pony.'

I hadn't known Lyn, or any of them, long, but even so I could not see me ever describing her as anyone's My Little Pony. Thalia saw me thinking it. Maybe she was psychic, or perhaps I was just too obvious and too male.

'Oh, don't tell me,' she said with mock horror. 'You thought she was gay as well?'

'It had crossed my mind.'

'My, my, but I bet that used up a few grey cells. But you're not alone. Most men reckon she's bent, but she doesn't have the imagination for it. You can tell that by the way she's smitten with the stormtrooper up in the attic.'

'How did they meet?' I asked, still shocked at Lyn's abrupt change of behaviour, the like of which I had never seen before without chemical stimulus. 'He popped down to borrow a cup of sugar or something?'

'Wouldn't you know it, they met on the Internet,' Thalia said, buttoning her coat, bored.

'Just how do you do that? I've never understood.'

'Don't ask me, sweetie, I'm an eco-pagan, not a cyber gens. Ask someone who looks good in an anorak.' She looked at her watch. 'Oh bugger, I'm late for my aromatherapist. Listen, Angel, why don't you *be* an angel for once and mind the store? Amy's gone off to wherever it is and she won't be back, so it's not like you've got anything else to do, is it? And anyway, Lyn'll be back shortly. They never go into shag mode this early in the day. Well, hardly ever. Go on, say you will...'

'You trust me to mind the shop?'

'It's not a shop, darling, do try and keep up. We don't actually sell anything from here. The most exciting thing that's going to happen is the phone might ring. You'll manage. Somehow.'

'But what if something does happen? What if something goes missing? I'll get the blame.'

I whined on, not really wanting to argue the toss, just make her late for her aromatherapist.

'Don't worry about the stock, there's nothing here under a size twelve or in your colour. But, yes, you'll get the blame. You're a man, aren't you? I'm out of here.'

And with a flounce, she was.

I mooched around the office for five minutes trying to find a magazine I hadn't read or something to eat. There was one out-of-date carton of raspberry yoghurt in the office fridge, so I read that.

I sat down at Lyn's work station and stared at the screen of her computer, which told me I could explore the joys of Windows '95 if only I knew a password. I typed in 'Bill Gates' but nothing happened.

I tried turning it off and then on again. I clicked the mouse until I had quite a flamenco rhythm going. Nothing. One of these days, I said to myself, I would catch up on twentieth-century technology, while there was some of the twentieth century left.

I turned off the screen and looked at my reflection in the shiny dead plastic. I found I was weighing up the mobile phone, trying to decide whether to call Amy again. I pointed the phone at my reflection and said aloud, 'I know what you're thinking, punk. You're thinking has he made six calls or was it only five? Well, to tell you the truth, punk, in all this excitement I'm not rightly sure myself. But being as this is the most powerful mobile phone in the world – and could just blow your ear off – you've got to ask yourself, Do I feel lucky? Well, punk, do you?'

This was getting ridiculous. I had to do something constructive, like annoy someone and the only targets within range were Lyn and Wolf upstairs. I hoped they were doing something intimate when I used the mobile to dial Lyn's office phone.

When it rang, I picked it up and laid it on her mouse mat, then I cut the mobile and stuffed it in my pocket.

Taking my time, I left the office and quietly climbed the stairs to the next floor. There were two doors there. One had a brass plate bearing the legend: SAGER INTERGALACTIC ADVERTISING and a logo of the earth as seen from space. Beneath it was a sheet of paper out of a word processor, decorated with pictures of balloons. The message, in computer script, read: 'Gone To Lunch. Back in November. These premises are guarded by my mother.'

I liked that. It was cool. To me, that was a company I could do business with; if I had a business and, of course, when they got back from lunch.

The other door, though, just had a plain white postcard thumb-tacked to the frame. On the card, printed in red ink, was simply: WEB 18. They seemed about as keen to attract business as Sager Intergalactic Advertising and this was hardly the image a high-tech computer programmer should be presenting. But then, what did I know? The last time I had seen postcards pinned to door frames was before Soho was redeveloped and the services they offered were anything but high-tech.

But there was something odder than that about the door to WEB 18. It had a keypad lock for a start, a newly-installed expensive one. And it had a viewing hole at head height for checking out callers. That must have been installed specially, unless they had bought the door job lot from a derelict hotel.

Short of a video camera, they seemed to have thought of most things and anyway, a camera would have simply attracted burglars rather than deterred them. (I actually know a burglar who steals nothing but video security cameras.) In an odd sort of way, WEB 18 had gone out of its way not to draw attention to itself, which was probably the most elaborate security it could have.

I pressed the call button on the keypad and heard a deep buzz from inside. Then I dropped to one knee and rapidly undid the lace of my right Nike trainer – a present from Amy at the weekend. That way whoever was peeping through the spyhole wasn't spying very much.

It didn't take as long as I had thought. There were two electronic clicks – a double lock – and the door flew open and I found myself almost at crutch-level with a pair of wide-cut khaki trousers.

As my options for looking up were unappealing, to say the least, I concentrated on tying my shoe lace as I talked.

'Sorry to bother you guys, but there's a call downstairs for Lyn. Wouldn't leave a name but says it's important. He's hanging on.'

Through his legs, when I did glance up, I could see Lyn standing at a trestle table piled high with brown envelopes and piles of paper. She was looking at me and it was a toss-up whether she was more surprised than she was guilty. Maybe it was just the sight of me smiling at her through her boyfriend's legs.

Then I noticed that Wolf was clenching and unclenching a fist not more than six inches from my face.

I stood up slowly and met Wolf's dead-eyed gaze.

'Er… telephone—' I started.

'I'm coming,' Lyn shouted from behind him. 'Where's Thalia?'

Wolf was expanding in front of me, drawing himself up, squaring up to me and not saying a word. It was unnerving and a very effective way of stopping me looking into the office.

'She had to pop out,' I said, taking a step back, almost expecting Wolf to follow, but he stayed where he was, one hand on the door, starting to close it.

'Dopey cow,' Lyn shouted to herself. 'I'll be down in two seconds.'

Then the door closed and the lock clicked.

I decided not to hang around for when Lyn found a dead phone line so I took the stairs two at a time and kept going beyond the TAL office and down to the street and around the corner to where I had parked Armstrong.

It never occurred to me to think why Lyn was moonlighting to help stuff envelopes in the virtually empty office of WEB 18, whatever that was.

18.

Later

It was all about photographs.

They had told me Amy had identified me from a photograph and now they were asking me to identify people from photographs. I was in a photograph I had no recollection of having been taken. The Sarge had been a photographer. I had sold him the idea of photographing the TAL girls for the newspapers and fashion magazines. Had that got him killed?

'So how do you know this Wolf?' Stokoe was saying, snapping me back to reality.

'I don't, really. He works upstairs from the TAL office. I met him through Lyn, one of the girls. They're an item.'

'That would be Lyn Buttress, wouldn't it?'

Suddenly, Stokoe had a black, flip-over policeman's notebook open on the table in front of him and he was drawing a pen from inside his jacket like a gun.

'Is this on the record?'

'You know the score, Mr Angel. It might be, it might not. It depends how we feel when we're writing up our notes. Come on, you know we make it all up afterwards if we have to.'

I shook my head in defeat.

'What do you want to know?'

'I told you,' said Stokoe, tapping the picture of Wolf. 'I am very interested in this man. I want to know what contact you had with him, what he said, what you think of him.'

'I've had no contact with him. I've seen him around the TAL offices, that's all. It's not like we were introduced or anything. I don't even know his last name.'

'Mansfeld,' said Stokoe automatically.

'Whatever. We used to call him the Nazi in the attic.'

'That's funny,' said Stokoe not smiling, 'so do we.'

'When was this taken?' Seil asked before I could react.

'I don't know,' I answered truthfully.

'What about this one?'

It was the mugshot of me.

'I guess that was in a restaurant. I was having lunch with The Sarge and trying to persuade him to photograph the TAL girls.'

'You sure?'

'It must be because that… ' I pointed to the picture of the roller-skating waitress's cleavage, 'is one of the waitresses.'

'And this?'

There was no mistaking Thalia's bosom and I had a flash memory of her thrusting it towards the Sarge the afternoon we all got well sloshed down at Canary Wharf to celebrate the meeting with his Fashion Editor.

'That's Thalia,' I admitted.

'Thalia Leonard,' said Sell, as if for the record and I nodded. 'And can you say when that was taken?' he went on.

'About a month ago, down at Canary Wharf, I told you about that.'

'And the one of you and this – waitress?'

'Maybe a week before that. Hey, and she really was a waitress.'

'And the one of Wolfgang Mansfeld?' This from Stokoe in the tone of a man climbing back on his hobby horse.

'I have no idea. Honest.'

I tried to keep my face blank. There was no point in trying to look honest. These guys were professionals.

'You never saw Eugene Sargeant and Wolfgang Mansfeld together?'

'No. I had no idea the Sarge knew him. Christ, I didn't know him, I just saw him a couple of times.'

'So, why do you think Sargeant took a picture of him?' Stokoe pressed.

'How should I know? He was a photographer, he took pictures.'

I had a sudden thought. They weren't asking the right question.

'Sargeant seemed to be a bit of a tit man,' Sell cut in, deliberately changing tack.

'You mean these?' I indicated the cleavage shots on the table.

'And others. We found a lot of others at his flat.'

'He worked in fashion photography,' I shrugged, 'and it seems a healthy enough obsession. I can think of worse. It was his job and probably nice work when he got it.'

'Which is why you wanted him to photograph your TAL girls, right?' Sell was working round to something.

'Yeah, I told you. I don't know that many top-notch fashion snappers but I'd run across The Sarge in the past and I knew he had contacts with the tabloids, so I asked him if would do a spread on the TAL operation. They're not my girls, by the way. I work for them.'

'So you say. You're just the driver, the messenger boy, right?'

'Right.'

'Yet here you are fixing up photographers and newspapers and acting like some sort of agent for them. Or should that be pimp?'

I refused to rise to the 'pimp' reference, rolling with it because Sell was getting further and further away from the question he should have been asking.

'Look, the concept they have, the way they work, it's a good story and nobody had picked it up. I was just trying to get them some publicity, help the business along.'

'You've got a stake in their business?'

'No.' That was true, well, not a financial one.

'So, out of the goodness of your heart you fixed them up with Sargeant and his newspaper down at Canary Wharf.'

'Yeah, got it in one.'

They looked as if they believed me; then again they could have had a very greasy fried breakfast in the police canteen.

'And did Sargeant do a spread on them?'

'No, he never got back to me on it,' I said. 'He took some staging shots down at Canary Wharf but he didn't get to fix up a proper shoot before... well, before—'

'Before someone ventilated his brain with a long, sharp object, technically known as a knife, on Friday night,' Stokoe said, almost airily.

I thought that this was the cue for the, 'Can you establish your movements?' line of questioning, but Sell steered us back to the photographs. I had a nasty feeling I knew what was coming. And it was dangerous but I couldn't see a way of avoiding it.

'You're saying that Sargeant never got around to taking pictures of these TAL girls?'

'That's right.'

'No, it's not.'

'What?'

'We've found lots of photographs of your three ladies, several films' worth, round at Sargeant's flat. When did he take them?'

'I have no idea. Honest.'

'Why did he take them?' asked Stokoe, as if smelling fear on me.

'I don't know,' I said, feeling my voice rise a notch towards frantic.

'You can't think why Sargeant would be photographing your girlie friends – your models – without you knowing about it?'

'No I can't,' I blustered.

Of course I could; the bastard was going behind my back to cut me out of the commission we'd agreed. And what galled me was I hadn't asked for that much.

'Would you be willing to take a look at them for us, maybe identify some places, tie down some times for us?'

They looked at me expectantly but they knew the answer wasn't in doubt. It was my way out.

'Yes, I'll help,' I said wearily.

And then Sell got around to asking the question I had been dreading because in answering it I would not be getting out at all but getting in, and in deep.

'But what about these photographs?' Sell began to shuffle the black and white prints in front of me into a pile. 'You're on this film and yet you said you didn't remember this being taken. How do you think Sargeant took them?'

He left the pile so that the head and shoulders mugshot of me was on top, looking up at me accusingly.

'When you found him,' I said carefully, 'was he wearing a tie?'

19.

Now

Eugene Vincent Sargeant lived – had lived – in a two-bedroomed flat, one of twelve in a two-storey block built of brick and concrete in a style the architects would probably call Post-War Expediency, without specifying which war. An estate agent would have trouble talking them up unless they found a potential buyer who just had to live within a drunk's stumble of Whitechapel High Street, Aldgate Station and the (alleged) sites of two of the Jack the Ripper murders, if, that is, they agreed with the post-modernist theory that his score was at least ten.

There were six doors, each leading to a ground floor flat and to a staircase up to the one above it. All of them had security lights and it was obvious in daylight that none of them worked. Three of the windows to the front of the block were boarded with plywood. Some had been replaced with reinforced wire mesh glass. At the roadside, behind a broken street light and a burnt-out litter bin, was a sign saying Hanbury Green, which someone had taken a lump hammer to. I could guess how they had felt. The whole place looked like somebody's idea of sheltered accommodation for the elderly in the unimaginative and innocent early Sixties.

Which of course was exactly what Hanbury Green was. The Sarge – he was known as Vince around here – had moved in to look after his widowed mother. When she had died, he had sort of inherited the flat from the local council even though as a fit, single, employed (and well-paid) male, he could hardly have been on any council's priority list for sheltered housing. But then, he was a good old East End lad and was probably related to half the residents in the block, not to mention half the members of the local council.

I got all this from my driver. He was a policeman, so he knew these things.

Our driver. DS Stokoe had insisted we visit The Sarge's flat in a police Vauxhall complete with uniformed driver. I had offered them a lift in Armstrong but they had declined, telling me to leave him where he was round the corner from Dirty Dick's pub. I had said it was just as well that black cabs never got parking tickets, but they did not seem impressed.

Stokoe was quite happy for me to ask the driver questions. For my part, it gave me a chance to show how little I knew about The Sarge and where he lived.

'Does he have relatives around here?' I asked the back of the driver's neck.

'Bloody hundreds,' came the answer. 'You'd think every dodgy garage from here to Dagenham had a Sargeant involved in it. Oh, sorry Mr Stokoe, no offence.'

'None taken,' growled Stokoe next to me. 'Two of his cousins identified the body, didn't they?'

'That's right… er… Sarge.' The neck in front of me reddened. 'Phil and Duane, from Stepney. They used to drink with Vince down the Mile End Road of a Sunday lunchtime, big family tradition. They said they knew something was up when he didn't show down the pub this week. We thought it better to get them in rather than trouble the old dear downstairs.'

'What old dear? Downstairs where?'

I glanced at Stokoe to see whether I was allowed to ask this, but he was busy looking out of the window.

'Vince's Aunty Julia,' said the uniformed neck. 'She lives in the flat under Vince's, but she's nine-tenths blind and eleven-tenths senile. We didn't want to put her through it. In fact, we don't think it's sunk in yet. It was her home-help, who does a bit of moonlighting as a cleaner, who found him. Here we are. That's it on the corner, upstairs right, number twelve.'

I wasn't sure what I had been expecting. There was a uniformed policeman loitering at the front door, but otherwise, no sign that anything out of the ordinary had happened. No massed hordes of media hounds blocking the garden path; no streamers of POLICE tape to cordon off the area; no cars with blue lights flashing; no helicopter gunships packed with snipers hovering overhead.

Stokoe flashed some ID at the guard cop and we trooped upstairs. Even inside The Sarge's flat, nothing looked unusual or out of place. There wasn't even a chalked outline of a body on the floor, which disappointed me, but then again there wasn't any blood or gore in evidence, which was a relief.

The living room was kitted out in stark bachelor Gothic. A four-seater black leather sofa stood opposite a huge television rigged for cable and satellite. Against a wall was a drop-leaf table and one chair. On the table was a carton of sea salt and bottles of Tabasco and hot Jamaican sauce. You got the impression that The Sarge didn't do much entertaining.

There were two black steel shelf units, one holding an expensive

CD set-up with a rack of at least fifty CDs, the other acting as a book-shelf displaying complete sets of everything written by Terry Pratchett and Robert Rankin, barring notes for the milkman. The only other things in the room were the framed photographs dotting the walls. They were all black and white and most seemed, at first glance, to be shots of London streetlife; a tourist here, a pretty girl there, a derelict asleep in a box in a shop doorway, a pair of lovers groping under a streetlamp somewhere.

'You can see where the struggle took place,' Stokoe was saying.

'Er… what?'

I hadn't noticed anything out of place. By my standards this was a neat and tidy gaff. We could have been in an Ikea showroom.

'Just there, end of the sofa. We reckon the victim was sitting down when he was stabbed. The marks on the carpet are where his heels dug in when he spasmed. He died hanging over the sofa arm. You can see the stain on the carpet round that side, though he didn't bleed much. Don't you want to look?'

I shook my head.

'No? Well, there wouldn't be much point, would there? You're not a forensic scientist, are you?'

'No,' I croaked.

'Not even curious?' Sell asked, smiling.

'I'm not here for this,' I said.

Stokoe walked to the far end of the sofa and positioned himself, arm raised as if holding a knife above his head, ready to strike downward. It was the classic melodramatic Victorian pose from the penny dreadful magazines. We were, after all, in Ripper country.

'So what am I doing?' he snapped at me.

Playing games, I thought. But it was time to stop playing along with them.

'You're telling me that The Sarge knew his killer,' I said, staring him down.

He relaxed from his *Psycho* pose.

'Go on,' he said.

'The Sarge was sitting down. He'd let somebody in – must have, as you would have mentioned if there had been any forcible entry. And it was somebody he knew well enough to relax while they went in there.' I pointed to the door behind Stokoe. 'What is it? Kitchen Bathroom?'

'Bathroom,' said Sell automatically.

'So, he lets somebody in, they chat, the somebody blags him that they need a piss. He sits down to wait, they come out of there with a carving knife and do the business.'

'Carving knife? Who said anything about a carving knife?' Stokoe may have relaxed from his murderer act but he was still wired, his eyes boring into me, his head cocked like a gun dog as if listening for me to make a mistake.

'I was thinking kitchens, places where you have knives. If it's a bathroom that makes it worse because the killer brought the knife with him, went into the bathroom and came out stabbing. That means they'd planned it.'

Stokoe stared at me. Somewhere to my right I could hear Sell breathing.

'Very good,' said Stokoe quietly.

If that had been an audition, I sensed I had passed.

'So, was he wearing a tie when he copped it?' I asked.

'No he wasn't,' said Sell.

'You didn't think it was going to be that easy, did you?' added Stokoe, and he was smiling again.

'No, not really,' I said wearily.

We found it easily enough in the top drawer of a pinewood chest in the bedroom. The drawer was devoted to socks, boxer shorts, silk ties and secret cameras. Well, one secret camera anyway, carefully fitted into a permanently-tied knot in a screamingly loud yellow and black dotted tie. Goodness knows how I'd not remembered it. If I had worn it, people would have said I looked like a Dalmatian with jaundice. As soon as I had seen the close up of Thalia's cleavage, I had remembered the way The Sarge had fumbled with his tie that afternoon down at Canary Wharf. I had put it down to a simple and understandable nervous reaction, not thinking he was into a private version of Candid Camera.

'Don't touch it, sir,' said Sell, lapsing into professional courtesy by mistake.

He picked up the tie as carefully as he would handle a stunned snake and held it to eye level whilst flipping open a plastic evidence bag.

'This looks like the little bugger, guv'nor. East German spy camera, a classic buttonhole job. Takes a seven-shot disc film. And –' he screwed up his eyes, 'it's empty. Looks like a dead end.'

Stokoe sat down on the bed, crossed his legs at the ankle and folded his arms.

'You had yourself going there for a minute, didn't you, Mr Angel?'

'I don't know what you mean,' I said churlishly.

'Oh, come on, you thought there was a good chance poor old Vince Sargeant had done the happy snap job on his killer, didn't you?' He was enjoying this. 'No chance, sunshine. Things like that just don't happen in this universe. Sorry to dash your hopes there, Sherlock.'

'At least I worked out how he took the other pictures.'

'We were there, Sherlock, we were there. Well, as soon as you mentioned meeting Sargeant in a restaurant. Even you would have said if he'd produced a Box Brownie over the prawn cocktail. You didn't, so he took your mugshot without you knowing it. Unless he'd hidden a camera in the restaurant, that meant one hidden about his person so he could get up close. Those things don't come with zoom lenses, you know.'

'You've seen one before?' I asked, not really interested, just giving myself time to think ahead.

'Usually find them built into briefcases,' said Sell. 'You can pick them up at any security equipment shop, even mail order.'

'I didn't think of the tie, I admit,' said Stokoe, but not in a way that suggested he would lose any sleep over it. 'And the Scene of Crimes boys missed it last night. But we would have got to it eventually. It tells us one thing, though.'

I shouldn't have said anything, I should have let him tell me. But I couldn't resist it.

'That The Sarge got as close to Wolfie Mansfeld as he did to me, which was like close, in-your-face close.'

Stokoe looked at Sell, his mouth a silent 0 as if impressed.

'*Very* good. You're going to be a real asset to us, Fitzroy. I can call you Fitzroy, can I?'

'If you must.'

'Good. You can call me Detective Sergeant.' he said and Sell sniggered, as he must have done countless times before.

'Doing what?'

'Looking at Vince' s collection for us.'

'What collection?'

'Not his fucking CDs, that's for sure,' cracked Sell. 'My colleague here has first go at them,' said Stokoe. 'And it's quite a collection. Vince has a freezer full of them in the kitchen – serious. Going back to *Brothers In Arms*. Collector's items, some of them. Was it his hedge against inflation or was he just an anorak? Who cares? No, I want you to go through his dark room, flip through his photographs for us, see if you can pick anybody out for us.'

'His photographs?' I said dumbly.

'Mostly negatives, actually. Bleedin' thousands of 'em.'

Vince, as I was beginning to think of him now he was dead, had converted the second bedroom of the flat into a dark room and had installed a deep Butler's sink, either rescued or stolen from a Victorian town house redevelopment. Not that he would have done much of his own film processing. Most professionals use outside image labs these days, as only they can afford the computer scanning gear that lets you touch up even the grottiest print. Vince would probably just have developed his own black and white work or maybe printed up the odd sheet of contacts. The main purpose of the dark room was to serve as a large, light-free filing cabinet for negatives and as I wasn't prepared to count them, I accepted Stokoe's guestimate that there probably were 'bleedin' thousands' of them.

There were a dozen or so rolls of film, 35 mm and a square format I didn't immediately recognise, hanging by bulldog clips from three lengths of wire hung over the sink, but the bulk of them were stored in a metal cabinet. The films hung there vertically from a coat-hanger system of wires, each one weighted at the bottom and marked at the top with a white label on which was written a four-digit number to identify the job. Some films had the number and then a slash and a single digit to show that a job had taken more than one film.

I switched on a light box, the only piece of equipment in there I knew how to use, and took a film at random from the filing cabinet. I had no idea what I was supposed to be looking for and Stokoe had not offered much help, saying simply, 'Anything you recognise.' The first film seemed to be devoted to a group of female Japanese tourists feeding pigeons in Trafalgar Square. I recognised Nelson's Column but I didn't think that counted.

For twenty minutes I gave myself eyestrain sliding negatives across the light box. Some strips made no sense at all, some were of models on catwalks with several shots taken from the rear which suggested that Vince had not been exclusively a breast man. Four rolls featured a BMW coupé parked outside Canary Wharf and two showed it strapped to the deck of a Thames barge passing in front of the House of Commons. Then finally I found something that I recognised.

It was a strip of 35 mm numbered 4821 and though I couldn't be a hundred per cent sure, because of the smallness of the negs, the subject was a group of three women sitting side by side on metal-frame chairs. As the setting was an office of some sort and the women were looking not at the camera but at something or someone to the right of the frame, I guessed they must have been the shots Vince had taken in the office of his Assistant Editor (Fashion), whilst I was waiting for him down in the atrium of Canary Wharf.

What had he called it? Not so much a meeting, more an audition, the Ass Ed (Fash) testing the TAL girls for their media value.

I picked up strip 4821 between finger and thumb and went back into the living room to report to Tweedles Dum and Dee.

Stokoe was sitting on the sofa at the other end from where The Sarge had been stabbed. Sell was standing in the kitchen doorway with a mobile phone to his ear as if waiting for an answer. Stokoe was tapping an untipped cigarette against a thumbnail but making no attempt to light it.

'Found anything?'

I handed him the strip and told him what I thought it was. He held the strip up to the light, the unlit cigarette between his lips, his head moving left to right.

'Make a note, Steve,' said Stokoe absently. 'Print up contacts of everything numbered 4821 and above. Take them to the nearest happy snaps place if you have to.'

Sell grunted an acknowledgement and fumbled out his notebook, the phone still jammed into his neck.

'You've narrowed the timeframe for us,' Stokoe said to me. 'That could be useful.'

As I thought about that, Sell muttered into his mobile then switched it off and slipped it into his pocket.

'Call out, guv. We're expected.'

Stokoe rolled up the strip of film as he levered himself off the sofa.

'Gotta go, duty calls. It's been a pleasure, blahdy-blahdyblah. We'll be in touch.'

He held out a hand, showing me the door.

'That's it?'

'For now,' he said. 'We'll be in touch, don't leave town, all that stuff. Oh, and don't be a stranger if you think of anything useful.'

'Hang on, hang on,' I yelled desperately, 'I've got a question.'

'He's got a question,' Sell repeated.

Stokoe shook his head and made a big play of pulling the sleeve of his jacket back and looking at his watch.

'Get on with it, then, we haven't got all day.'

I bit my tongue to stop myself saying that was precisely the impression they had given me since I met them.

'Look, you just ordered prints from all Vince's films *after* 4821, which I just identified for you.'

'Nothing wrong with his hearing, is there, Steve?'

'Pardon, guv?' Sell hammed it up.

'That means you're only interested in stuff he's shot after he met the TAL girls,' I pressed on.

'So?'

'So, you have a connection between TAL and Vince's murder, or you just think you have?'

'It's one line of enquiry,' said Sell officially.

Stokoe looked at me as if he had only just noticed me in the room. He was still toying with his unlit cigarette and I was sure he was going to blame me if he succumbed to temptation.

'I'll go better than that,' he said, eventually. 'I think we do have a connection and a strong one. You see, from what we've found out about the late Mr Sargeant, you know, talking to neighbours and relatives and such, he wasn't much of a ladies' man.

'Oh, sure, he took lots of pictures of totty and had probably seen more Class A naked flesh than your average family butcher, but when it came to *relationships*–' he said it like it hurt '– he was a bit naff. Suddenly, he starts to take an interest in three particular young ladies and then he ends up dead.'

'That's a bit thin,' I said, knowing it was but also knowing there must be something more.

'Add in the fact that last Friday night, Vince's aunty in the flat below tells us he had a female visitor, and the plot thickens.'

'You mean the blind, senile aunty?'

'That's the one, but she ain't deaf and she swears a pair of high heels went up those stairs last Friday night about eleven o'clock. She was dead chuffed that Vince had pulled at last.'

'That's still thin. You're really taking her seriously?'

'I am. And so should you.' He reached out with the roll of film still in his hand and tapped me lightly on the nose. I flinched. 'Because it means we don't suspect *you*.'

And they never really had.

'We have statistics on our side as well, guv, don't forget,' said Sell, moving to open the flat door. 'The vast majority of knifings done indoors are down to women. Seems second nature to them somehow. If it's outside on the street, or at a football match or in a schoolyard, then it's usually young lads messing about. If it's in a kitchen or a parlour, it's a woman.'

'Parlour?' growled Stokoe as he pushed me gently to the door. 'Where did that come from, Detective Constable?'

'My Cluedo set, guv. You know, Colonel Mustard in the parlour with a Kitchen Devil.'

'Ho, ho, ho. I'll remember that one.'

I bet myself he would, then, as we were trooping downstairs, me in a policeman sandwich, I thought of something rather important.

'Wait a minute, I need to know something.'

'Join the queue, sunshine,' said Sell from below me.

'No, listen. Please.'

We stopped on the stairs. Sell looking up at me and Stokoe looking down, both deadpan.

'You said – or you— Well, one of you said, back at the nick in Bishopsgate, that you knew I'd be in Dirty Dick's today. You knew where to pick me up.'

Stokoe frowned, then reached into his trouser pocket and produced a one pound coin which he handed to Sell right under my nose.

Sell took it with a big grin.

'Told you he'd remember, guv. Said he was sharp.'

'Yeah, yeah,' said Stokoe. Then to me: 'Amy May identified you from those black and white photos we showed you. She told us you'd be in the pub.'

Suddenly, I had a hundred questions I wanted to ask, but none of them would get a straight answer from these two. I had to try one though.

'How did you know to ask Amy?'

'We don't have to answer that,' said Sell ominously.

'Can't see the harm,' said Stokoe. 'We knew about the three girls visiting the newspaper, Vince's fashion editor told us. She said he was concentrating on them rather than doing other jobs for her, which peeved her a bit. Mind you, she's the sort that's easily peeved. And when we found Ms May's address in Vince's wallet, we nipped round to see her.'

Vince had Amy's address; and I didn't.

I was still thinking of that as we hit the street where the police car and driver were waiting by the kerb.

'You don't mind finding your own way home, Fitzroy, do you?'

Before I was really aware of it, Sell was in the car and Stokoe was standing there shaking my hand in full view of the neighbours. The jungle drums were spreading the news through the East End before he'd relaxed his grip. That was my street-cred down the storm drain.

'We've got to get on. Important conference, that sort of thing. Don't worry, we'll be in touch. We know where to find you.'

Even the awesome implication of *we know where you live*, which had always upset me, seemed to flow over me. And then the cop car had pulled away and I was left with an urge to turn and look at Hanbury Green and count just how many curtains were twitching.

But I had enough to worry about. I hoofed it to Aldgate East and hopped a tube to Liverpool Street, coming out of the Bishopsgate exit just as the homeward-bound commuters were filling up The White Hart, Hambledon Hall and The Railway, mobile phones beeping everywhere, the ether jammed with lies to husbands and wives about yet more delays to Great Eastern services.

I gave the Bishopsgate police station a wide berth and walked by Dirty Dick's without going in, though I could have murdered a pint or four.

Around the corner, there was Armstrong parked where I had left him on double yellow lines. There was a parking ticket in a plastic envelope under the windscreen wiper.

In my case, they had made an exception.

20.

Then

The morning had started as every other morning that week, with about seventeen attempts to get Amy on her mobile, while Springsteen wove in and out of my legs, reminding me – painfully – that I had temporarily forgotten my resolve never to walk around the flat barefoot when he was there.

I tried to kick him away, missed as usual, but thought it wise to put something on before he broke the skin. I chose a pair of new Nikes, a present from Amy to go with a white Paul Smith T-shirt, which was also a present from her but not one of her 'free samples'. It must have changed my luck, as Amy's phone picked up on the next try, just as I was lacing up the left shoe.

'Hi, it's me.'

'Hello, you. What's up?'

'Nothing, just ringing for instructions, invitations to lunch, that sort of thing. I'll even offer to listen to any sexual fantasies you might have.'

'Sorry, lover, I'm up to my ears in it. I've got meetings all morning and I'm supposed to see a supplier in Nottingham this afternoon.'

'Busy girl. You really should— Sod off!'

'What?'

'Sorry, kiddo, not you. Springsteen. He's missing you.'

He probably wasn't missing her at all but he had taken a fancy to the trainers she had bought me and was busy chewing his way through the lace to the right shoe.

'Nothing I can do about that today, Angel, but I was going to call you.'

Well, that was something. I sat down on the edge of my bed, content to let Springsteen destroy the lace.

'Moklis Ali wants to see you about something,' said Amy, which was not exactly what I had been expecting.

'What? A delivery?'

'No, nothing to do with TAL and I don't think it's one of your little freelance jobs for Mujib either.'

So she knew about them. Wrists suitably slapped, but she didn't sound too put out.

'So what's going down?'

'No idea. Moklis rang and asked me if I could get to you and fix a meet with him. A pub called Dirty Dick's, lunchtime today. Early, around twelve. Is there really a pub called Dirty Dick's?'

'Yes there is. It's quite famous. I know where it is.'

'Now why did I ever doubt that? Listen, lover, got to go.'

'But when… ?'

'I'll try and ring you late tonight, OK? Bye. Don't forget to feed the cat.'

'He's already eaten,' I said into a dead phone.

That was how I had come to be in Dirty Dick's, ordering a pint of Young's Special whilst waiting for Moklis Ali, just before noon.

I had only managed to moisten my top lip with the head of the beer – was still waiting for my change – when the two detectives closed in, asked me if my name was Angel and whether I would mind joining them for a chat at Bishopsgate nick, which was only just down the street.

By the time I had told them I knew perfectly well where it was and started to ask them why they wanted me there, we were through the black oak doors and out into the sunlight. They hadn't laid a finger on me; we just seemed to move by osmosis.

From the corner of my eye I saw Moklis Ali and Roshan Ara rounding the corner of Brushfield Street. When they saw me flanked by my two young, well-dressed minders, they froze.

I ignored them, turned away and went to help the police with their enquiries.

21.

Now

I screwed up the parking ticket and dropped it on the floor as I climbed into Armstrong, kicking it around a bit until I had my feet on the pedals. I'd find it when I needed it.

My prime concern was Amy.

I took the mobile from where I had stashed it behind the sun visor. I had done that before going round to Dirty Dick's that morning, as I had always felt that mobiles going off in pubs was never really on; a bit like smoking in church.

I called Amy on the memory.

'The Vodaphone you have called may be switched off. Please try later.'

'Bugger, bugger, buggery, double bugger,' I shouted, bashing the phone on Armstrong's steering wheel.

I tried the TAL office and when there was no answer there, I almost snapped the damn thing in half. When it refused to snap, I banged my forehead on the steering wheel instead. That hurt, so I didn't do it again.

As I started the engine I looked around just in case anyone had been watching me. It could have put them off hailing a taxi for ever.

I drove back to Stuart Street in a blur, operating on instinct rather than to any sort of plan.

I was certain I would be seeing Stokoe and Sell – those cheeky comedic cops – again and they had hinted that it might be a house call. So the one useful thing I thought I could do was make sure there was nothing embarrassing there for them to find. That would mean finding a new hiding place for my spare passport (in case the worst came to the worst) and the driving licence that still had me living at a non-existent address in Southwark. Then there was the fridge full of smuggled French beer and some substances which, while not exactly Class A drugs, might be seen as hostages to fortune. I didn't worry about the pirate videos and CDs; everyone in London has one, whether they know it or not.

Outside Number Nine I followed the old Brixton maxim: What do you do if you see a spaceman? – Park the car, man. Though at that time of an evening, parking wasn't the problem it would be later. I scanned the street for strange cars as I locked Armstrong, telling myself it wasn't paranoia and they really were after me.

In fact, somebody was already there waiting for me.

I had one foot in the house, the key still in the lock, when Fenella's door opened and her head appeared at the top of the stairs.

'Oh, Angel, it is you. You've got a visitor.'

I almost stepped straight back out but Fenella gave me a long, slow wink and her eyebrows shot up and down.

Amy.

I was taking the stairs two at a time and almost breathing in her face when she whispered, 'I wanted to make sure you were alone.'

'What?'

'I thought I'd better keep this one out of sight in case you turned up with Amy, but I'd no idea you'd be this long. You'd better get her out of here before Lisabeth gets home.'

'Fenella, what planet are we on? Who?'

By this time I was level with Fenella's door and could see over her shoulder and into her flat where Roshan Ara was getting up from a scatter cushion in the middle of the floor.

'I'm sorry, Angel, but I have to see you,' she said, looking as if she was about to burst into tears. But then, I'd had Fenella's camomile tea tool and knew how she felt.

She was wearing a navy blue TALtop, open deep at the neck and drawn in around her breasts to reveal three inches of bare midriff above the belt which, unnecessarily, held up skin-tight black jeans. Stiletto heeled sandals added a couple of inches to her height but she still managed to look younger than she was.

'And I'm sorry I missed you at lunchtime, but I was unavoidably delayed,' I said. 'You'd better come on up.'

She bent over to pick up a shoulder bag from the depths of the scatter cushion and I noticed that both Fenella and I were admiring the rear view she presented. I was admiring the workmanship that had gone into the fine cut of a pair of fake jeans. I wasn't sure what Fenella was looking at, but when she caught my eye, she blushed and glanced guiltily at her watch.

'Thanks for the tea,' said Roshan.

'Watch out for the cat,' Fenella said with a watery smile.

I let Roshan Ara get two steps up the next flight before I handed her the key to my flat.

'Here, let yourself in, I won't be a minute. Oh, and watch out for the cat.'

'I like cats,' she pouted, taking the keys.

'Be afraid. Be very afraid.'

I caught Fenella's door just as it was closing and pushed my face into hers.

'Has anyone phoned for me today?' I hissed.

'No. Why are we whispering?'

'Never mind. Are you sure?'

'Yes. I'm not totally stupid.'

'One other thing – why did you want Roshan out of there before Lisabeth came home? Is it because she's Asian?'

'No,' she said, surprised but not shocked at the question. 'It's because she's so attractive.'

Fair enough. Maybe she wasn't totally stupid.

'Those were policemen we saw you with this morning, weren't they?' she asked as soon as we were in the flat.

'Yes they were.'

There was no point denying it and I was busy scanning the furniture trying to spot Springsteen's latest ambush site.

'What did they want?'

'To make life difficult, like they always do. Listen, have you heard from Amy today?'

'No. Now will you tell me what they wanted?'

'Why?'

If I hadn't started to take her seriously it was because I had noticed Springsteen snaking around the corner of the kitchen door, coming up on her from behind.

'Because we need to know.'

She had her fists clenched down by her thighs. She wasn't kidding.

'They wanted to ask me about somebody I know. Knew. It's somebody who died recently. I was helping them. Now, why the need for you to know?'

She relaxed slightly. Bad move. Springsteen slid behind one of the hi-fi speakers.

'They didn't mention us?'

I obviously didn't take that in, so she tried again with more pitch in her voice.

'Did they mention us? Me, Moklis, Mujib? Any of us down at Brick Lane?'

'No they didn't,' I snapped.

Well, they hadn't mentioned anybody by name and anyway, I was feeling quite indignant by now. It was me who had suffered the third-degree for five hours and was I getting any sympathy?

'You're sure?'

'Sure I'm sure.' Springsteen was on top of the CD player now, gaining height. 'Now, what's this all about?'

She breathed out deeply, stretching the TALtop; then her nose twitched and her bottom lip quivered and, suddenly, she was burying her head in my chest, her fists bunched up under her chin.

'I thought it was because we were coming to meet you and you'd taken them out of there before we arrived so they wouldn't find out,' she sobbed.

I put my arm around her and steered her away from the hi-fi until the back of her legs hit my one and only comfortable armchair and she had to sit down. My sweeping her away meant that Springsteen had to check his pounce at the moment of take off. He overbalanced, wobbled, and then plummeted head-first to the floor. He landed perfectly and flicked his tail as if saying that was what he had meant to do all along.

I dropped to my knees in front of Roshan and held her fists in my hands.

'I didn't understand a word of that. Look, the cops wanted to ask me about a guy called Vince Sargeant, who lived in Whitechapel.'

I looked her in the eyes but she did not react to the name.

'It was a guy I knew, a photographer. He died last Friday.'

Still no recognition.

'That was all they wanted out of me. Now what's your problem?'

I thought it better not to mention Stokoe's little homily on the increasing use of heroin around Brick Lane, nor Sell's speciality of investigating gang wars between Roshan's mob and the Turks in Islington. There was no point in upsetting the girl.

Her upper body shuddered with another deep exhalation and she said, 'It's about the Turks who are pushing drugs.'

Oh no.

'We've captured one.'

Oh shit.

'Thanks for sharing that, Roshan, but I don't think I want to know any more,' I said, releasing her.

I looked around but Springsteen was nowhere when I needed him.

'You've got to help,' she pleaded, reaching for me.

'No I don't.' I staggered to my feet. 'I've got enough problems of my own. More than enough. I've got other people's shares as well. I've bought bulk to get the discount. When it comes to problems, I've shopped early for Christmas.'

'But you've got to help.'

'Help you do *what*?'

'Tell us what to do with the man they caught.'

'How should I—? Just a minute. When did you *catch* this guy?'

'Yesterday.'

'You mean as in twenty-four hours ago? Yeah, I thought so. Did you invite him for nan bread and a couple of curries and then suggest he sleeps over? No? I didn't think so. In that case, it's called kidnapping and it's got nothing to do with me and you're well and truly on your own. Now I'll pretend I—'

'But you've got to help,' she repeated, as forcefully as before. It didn't look as if I was wearing her down. Springsteen could have helped, but seemed quite happy to let me stew as he sat himself down and began to lick the end of his tail.

'Why me?' I tried, putting real desperation into my voice.

'We couldn't think of anybody else.'

'Oh, *brilliant*. Fucking A. Don't softsoap me, give it to me straight.'

'Amy said you'd help.'

'She did? When?'

'Late last night... early this morning... Moklis and me, we went to see her and she said—'

'You went to *see* her?' She nodded, holding back a tear. 'At her place?'

'Yes. We—'

'You know where she lives?'

'Moklis does.'

Something struck me and it should have been a brick.

'How did you know where I lived?'

'Mujib Ur Rehman knew. As soon as you started to work for him, he made sure he found out. I think he probably had someone follow you.'

Great. It was getting so that you couldn't even trust your local fashion forger and sweatshop owner.

'I had to come here,' Roshan said between gulps of air. 'When we saw you with those policemen, we thought they must know.'

'They don't, but that doesn't mean others don't. I told you, they wanted me about something else, nothing to do with you. But it does involve Amy. Tell me where she lives.'

'I don't know,' she sobbed.

'You went there. I must get to see her.'

I grabbed her by the shoulders as if to shake some sense in to her, but I was too late. She'd found some on her own.

'I couldn't tell you, exactly. Moklis knows, he drove us.' Her defences were suddenly up. She was confident again and I should have seen it coming.

'Will Moklis tell me?' I asked, my stomach already beginning to sink.

'Yeah. Sure. If you come and help us.'

22.

Now

They said his street name was Nosey, though this was more likely to be a corruption of a Turkish name such as Nusret, rather than a reflection on any personal habit. Dealers like him, operating on enemy turf, are rarely users themselves.

He wasn't over the moon at the situation he was in, but then he wasn't foaming at the mouth and climbing the wall. He was either young and stupid enough not to be scared, or young and smart enough to know that if the Bangladeshis had been going to do him any serious damage, they would have done it by now.

They had him in a small room two floors above and somewhere to the back of the camera shop off Brick Lane. At least I think we were still in the same building but I couldn't be sure as the labyrinth of fire-trap staircases, half-turns and split levels, no natural light and few working light bulbs had disorientated me as effectively as a blind-fold. The atmosphere was damp with the warm steam of washing machines and the faint scent of machine oil. At one point we had walked through a room in which three elderly women sat on an ancient leather sofa watching Zee TV on a wall-mounted digital stereo television. There was no other furniture in the room and the lights probably didn't work, but they had cable.

Moklis had been waiting for us in the shop, nervous and red-eyed. He had the decency not to be able to look me in the eye. Mujib Ur Rehman appeared in the doorway to the back and simply said, 'He's up here,' and we followed him in single file.

Nosey was sat in a corner, knees up to his chest. At first I thought he was untied, only held there by the threat of having to pass the three old ladies in the next room to escape. I knew how he felt. He would have to be a thousand per cent braver than me to interrupt their afternoon viewing. Then I spotted the rope which bound his ankles just above a pair of black trainers, leading off to an ancient radiator. So far they were sticking to tradition. How can you take a hostage if you don't have a radiator to chain them to?

Then I spotted their own variation on the theme. Nosey's hands were not free at all, the thumbs had been tied together with what looked, in the gloom, like cotton – metres of it, tightly bound as if on a reel. I suspected that his circulation had gone hours ago.

'He had these in his pockets,' said Moklis from behind me.

I was glad somebody had said something as I was well stumped for polite conversation.

Moklis was offering me a plastic Harvey Nichols carrier bag. I resisted the temptation to ask if it was an original and looked inside. It contained maybe fifty twists of greased paper. I didn't want to handle them and I didn't have to open one and test it on the tip of my tongue. Only amateurs and television scriptwriters do that. I knew a £25 wrap when I saw one.

'He was selling them on our streets,' said Mujib quietly. 'Out in the open, touting for business. To our children. We have had enough. We took him off the street.'

'Who did?' I asked.

Nosey was staring at me as if trying to place me.

'Some of the men,' said Moklis. 'Fathers. They've started to patrol the area.'

'Isn't this a fairly extreme sort of Neighbourhood Watch?'

That didn't get an answer.

'So, now what?' I tried. 'Where do I come into this?'

Mujib shrugged and pulled at his beard.

'I persuaded them to ask you to talk to him,' Moklis said falteringly. 'Get a second opinion, before they did anything stupid.'

'I don't know what good me talking to him is going to do and if you're worried about stupid, you're too late.' I looked at their faces and saw not an idea between them. 'Has he had anything to eat?'

Mujib, Moklis and Roshan all shook their heads. Good. We were agreed on something.

'Is there anything to eat here?'

'Of course there is,' snapped Mujib, affronted.

'Then get it.'

Mujib glared at Roshan but, give her her due, she held her ground and he had to stomp off himself.

'Go help him,' I said, taking the carrier bag from Moklis. 'Both of you.'

I tried to estimate the length of the rope that held Nosey to the radiator. It wasn't easy in the gloom, the one window was boarded up with hardboard. I played safe and stayed a good metre out of kick range and sat down cross-legged on the floor facing him.

'I'm here to get you out of this,' I said for openers.

'Who the fuck are you?' His voice carried no trace of fear and wouldn't have been out of place on the terraces at an Arsenal match.

'I'm a sort of negotiator, I suppose, but don't think for one flea-bite of a moment that I'm offering to swap places with you. My radiator-hugging days are over, though I cannot dispute that they were, in context, quite a formative experience.'

He looked at me as if I had flipped.

'You're fucking mental,' he concluded.

'Spot on, Nosey, me old mate, I must be.' I put on my most inane grin. 'If I wasn't I wouldn't be here, so let's cut to the chase, shall we? These very nice, normally law-abiding citizens here have something I want.'

I followed his gaze and held up the carrier bag.

'No, not this. Something else. I get it if I help them sort you out. They don't want you here, but they don't want you out on the street selling naughties to their kids. Now let's put our heads together and work out a deal.'

'Call the fucking cops,' he snarled.

'That's one option,' I agreed.

'Pay me for my goods and I'll disappear.'

'Buy you out? I don't think so.'

'I'm out of pocket. I've lost a day's trading.'

'No, we're drifting here. There must be another way.'

'Can't think of one,' he said coolly and started to stare at the ceiling.

'Well, the good news is… ' I drew it out, 'neither can I, so I'll just have to leave you to their tender mercies.'

'They won't do anything to me,' he said, still looking up, 'not now. They've no balls.'

'I hope you're right, Nosey, I really do.' I was pretty sure he was. 'But if you're wrong, it'll be your balls dangling in the back of one of their cars instead of furry dice. What's your family name?'

He didn't fall for it.

'Fuck off.'

'Would that be one of the Islington Fuckoffs?'

There was a footstep behind me but I had already picked up the scent of fresh herbs and curry coming up the stairs. Roshan Ara stood over me holding a large soup dish and a plate which was overlapped by a stuffed nan.

'Fresh meat curry,' she said.

'Fuck off,' said Nosey.

I uncurled my legs and stood up, taking the dish from her. 'Thanks,' I said, 'I'm starving. Haven't eaten all day.'

I sat on the bare board stairs to eat the curry. The others stood and watched me. Behind us, Zee TV still blared out. From below came the throb of washing machines and the buzz of an occasional sewing machine. The curry was good and I said so several times, just for the sake of something to say.

Eventually, Mujib rattled something off in Bangla and Moklis answered him with his hands up in classic defensive pose. Mujib shook his head and stamped downstairs.

'He doesn't think you can help,' said Roshan.

'He's not wrong,' I said, balancing the dish on my knee and wiping it with the last of the nan bread whilst weighing up the odds on there being a second helping.

'You must have some ideas,' Moklis said.

'Why?'

'Amy said you would have. Said you were resourceful.'

Oh she did, did she?

'Let Nosey go; flush the stuff down the toilet. That's it, that's the bottom line.'

'He'll be back tomorrow with another supply of heroin,' Moklis said seriously and deliberately, as if he had actually been thinking through my suggestion.

'You're right there.' I didn't add that Nosey would probably be able to put his prices up and they would be paid by his regular customers worried about the temporary failure of supply.

'There must be an alternative,' said Roshan.

'You could kill him and put his head on a spike outside the town hall in Islington if you think it would do any good.'

'That's what Mujib and the others want to do,' said Moklis, deadpan.

'I wasn't being serious.'

'No, you know what I mean. They want to beat him up and leave him on the street somewhere. Outside a police station maybe.'

'I do know a policeman who might just be willing to listen to you on this one,' I said tentatively.

Even knowing Stokoe and Sell for less than a day, I was pretty sure that they would listen and then probably wet themselves laughing.

'No police. Don't you know anyone else?'

'Such as who?' I held up my empty dish and Roshan took it. There was no sign of a refill. 'The Samaritans? I'm just a musician.'

'Nosey is Turkish. Don't you know anyone in the Turkish community?'

'Don't you? Apart from heroin salesmen, that is.'

Moklis switched to Bangla, aimed at Roshan but definitely about me from the tone. I can recognise insults in most languages.

'That's not fair—' Roshan began, counselling for the defence.

'Hold on,' I said, 'I have an idea.'

And I had.

I had told Stokoe and Sell that I knew Turks just like I knew Bangladeshis; just part and parcel of living in London. But I did know one specifically, who was in the music business, albeit on the sidelines. He was certainly not a friend, not even a friend of a friend, but I knew a man who knew him. I pulled my TAL mobile phone out and punched in the number of Boot In recording studios and waited for a satellite to bounce my signal from outer space down to Curtain Road, just the other side of Liverpool Street station.

'Thank you for calling Boot In Recording, Remixing and Reviving Studios. If you wish to talk to sales, press 2. If you— Yeah? Hello? Who's this?'

Good as gold was Danny Boot. You could always rely on him not to be able to resist answering a ringing phone. He never had been able to keep a secretary and it seemed as if he was going through answerphone systems at a rate of knots.

'Danny? It's Angel.'

'Angel? Angel who? Used to know an Angel, played brass. Set up a meet for him with a really useful new talent. Guy called Topher, the total money when it came to ideas, a real fizz sparkler, the next Mr Creativity. But what happens? Jerko Angel doesn't show.'

Oh no. Topher was the guy I had been waiting for in the Hog In The Pound that night, weeks ago, when I had run into Amy, Lyn and Thalia.

'He never showed, Danny, honest. I was there.'

'He says he showed,' growled Boot. Then, quieter, 'But he does admit it was after midnight and the pub was shut.'

'Yeah, right. When does he appear on *Mastermind*?'

'Watch this space, Angel-man, that kid's going places, but not with you, so don't try—'

'Listen, Danny, I wasn't ringing to apologise.'

'Oh. Well, that's all right then.'

I sighed to myself. I had often suspected that Danny was two sandwiches short of a picnic and I certainly wasn't going to tell *him* what I had in the Harvey Nichols bag between my feet.

'I'm trying to track down Ritchie Fortune, used to run Box Pop, the tour managers. Remember him?'

'I do, he doesn't.'

'What was that, Danny?'

'I know who you mean, but he's not in the biz any more. He wound up Box Pop last year, just does the family business now.'

'What's the family business?'

'I don't know. Kebabs?'

'Restaurants? Does Ritchie still operate out of that restaurant up west?'

'I guess so. Hey, why not try Yellow Pages?'

'I would, Danny, but you're cheaper. Bye.'

It didn't make sense, but it would worry him.

'What was that all about?' asked Roshan as I folded the phone.

'It's a long shot, but there is somebody I could have a word with if I can find him and if he'll listen. And I'm not saying it will do any good.' I hefted the bag of heroin wraps. 'I'll need these.'

Moklis and Roshan eyeballed each other.

'OK, let's go,' he said.

'What's this "us" shit? *I'll* go, but first I've got to see Amy.'

Roshan said something in Bangla and Moklis came back at me: 'No, we do this first, *then* I'll show you where Amy lives.'

'Thanks a bunch,' I said, staring down Roshan.

Ritchie Fortune had run a company called Box Pop which had put together (boxed) tours for bands in the UK and Europe. He was the man who found the lighting gear, the generators, the trucks, the drivers and the Techs – technicians, or what in happier days were called roadies. I had only met him once, when I had been trying, for devious reasons, to track down a touring heavy metal band called Astral Reich.

If Danny Boot was saying Ritchie was out of the music business, it didn't surprise me. The scene had changed and the number of big tours being cobbled together these days were few. Ritchie had always run things from the family restaurant, the Fortuna, and if he had gone into that then the music business' loss was the kebab industry's gain.

The Fortuna was hidden away off Great Titchfield Street, near the BBC. When I had last been there, the entrance foyer had doubled as a takeaway but that appeared to have gone, to be replaced by chintzy purple curtains and subdued lighting inside, a string of red lights, stolen from a cheap Christmas tree, surrounding the door to make it look like one of those stargate things you have to go through at airports (and some of them are so sensitive now that foil-wrapped condoms set them off).

I parked Armstrong pointing down Great Titchfield Street (Rule of Life No. 277: always park in the direction of easiest escape) and told Moklis to get out. He refused.

'Look, you can't come in with me, right?' He nodded. 'So you'd prefer to be picked up by a couple of beat coppers sitting in the back of an empty taxi?'

'OK, OK. I'll be across the street,' he conceded, opening the near-side door.

'Leave that,' I said.

He didn't argue on that one and pushed the carrier bag through the partition and I stuffed it down by my feet, palming some of the wraps into my jacket pocket while doing so.

'What do I do if you're not out in half-an-hour?' Moklis asked so seriously I almost giggled.

'Take the night bus.'

I got through the Fortuna's security arch of pretty lights without setting off a metal detector. Not that they had one. They didn't need one, not with a *maitre d'* like the one they had.

He was wider than he was tall and totally bald. He rolled towards me like an eight-ball with eyes. He probably had X-ray vision as well, to check out customers' wallets. He certainly didn't think I could afford the *cebic*.

'Sir?'

He said it in such a way that I almost looked over my shoulder to see who he was talking to.

'Good evening. I'm early. There should be a reservation, name of Angel.'

He bowed slightly and in the same movement turned his back on me as he consulted the restaurant diary on a lectern near the till. His dinner jacket strained across his shoulders like a black cloud. If I had been sitting down, he would have blocked out the light.

'I'm sorry, sir, no reservation.'

He wasn't sorry at all. He'd clocked my Nikes, jeans and the leather jacket which was not so much distressed as paranoid, and hadn't liked what he saw.

'But there should be. Table for six at eight. My secretary should have rung. Name of Angel, BBC Drama Department?'

It might have been the dropping of the BBC name or just the prospect of six covers on a quiet night. Whatever, I suddenly had a table and he was showing me through.

I remembered the restaurant as being bigger on the inside than appeared possible from the street. Going upmarket had lost it a few tables, which had made way for potted palms and a small circle of dance floor. The posters on the walls advertising belly-dancers explained that and I could detect Ritchie Fortune's hand on the commercial tiller there. Belly-dancing was catching on. Not among men as spectators but among women as participants, having discovered that it was more fun than aerobics and burned off more calories (and developed better muscle control) than the salsa.

'Would you like a drink while you wait?' the *maitre d'* asked as I sat down at the head of a table for six which was almost as long as he was broad.

'Just a beer, please.'

'We have Efes, Heineken, TAG, Bitburger, Cobra, Tiger, Giraf, Tusker, Rolling Rock or Screaming Beaver.'

'Mmm, tricky choice. I'll have an Efes. When in Rome and all that.'

He grunted, shoved a menu into my hands and bowled off.

I scoped the menu, surprised to find that *cebic*, a whole spit-roast lamb, was actually on. I was impressed by the *uskumru dolmasi*, as you don't see mackerel much any more, the butterflied aubergines and the quaintly-named *kadinbudu kofte* – lady's thigh rissoles. The last time I had been there, the choice had been much simpler, just liver cooked any one of twenty-eight ways.

A red-coated waiter brought my beer and I looked around the restaurant as I drank.

Ritchie Fortune had run his Box Pop business, and no doubt several others, from a table at the back of the restaurant. He still did, though it took me a minute to spot him, even though the place was not a quarter full.

He had put on a few pounds, had his hair cut short, swapped his John Lennon circular frames for a pair of tortoiseshell Armanis, and the Whole Earth T-shirts had given way to a single-breasted Paul Smith suit. But it was Ritchie Fortune and even if I hadn't recognised him, the portable computer – smaller than a laptop – on the table in front of him would have been the give away.

There was no point in hanging around. If I was going to get thrown out, I'd rather it got done, so the rest of the evening was my own.

'Mr Fortune? Ritchie?' I tried as I hovered over his table.

He didn't look up from his mini-computer.

'I know you?'

I had no doubt that he had seen me come in.

'You might remember me from Box Pop days. My name's Angel—'

'Wait.'

He held up a finger, still not looking up, and typed rapidly on the keyboard with a motion that reminded me of someone using a finger bowl after a particularly troublesome crab in black bean sauce.

A minute went by, him looking at the tiny screen. A minute is a long time when you're standing in the middle of a Turkish restaurant being ignored.

'Trumpet player,' he said, and I realised he was reading from the screen. 'Based in Hackney. Worked for Boot In on a couple of backing tracks. That the one?'

I was impressed and nodded vigorously but when he still didn't look up, I said, 'Yes.'

Then he read off the phone number of the house in Stuart Street and I was not so much impressed as worried.

'That you?'

'It's a friend's actually,' I lied. 'That's pretty impressive.'

'It's a tool – and a toy. I just like to keep my hand in, but I'm out of the music business, Roy Angel, I'm in the hospitality industry. So, unless you've a complaint about the food, please go and enjoy your meal.'

'I need a word, Ritchie, just a moment of your time.'

'My time is precious.'

'It's important.'

'To you or to me? I'm a *very* busy man.'

He had raised his voice slightly and that may have been a signal, or there was a some body language I missed, but I felt the approaching presence of the lateral giant in the dinner jacket.

'If you typed "Nosey" into your computer, would it come up with anything?'

'Sit down,' he said, without missing a beat.

I did so, taking the chair nearest the wall so I had my back against something solid which wasn't the *maitre d'*. I found myself at eye-level with the navel of a belly-dancer pictured in full flight, her hips a blur, on a circus size poster in a cheap plastic frame.

'One of your regulars?' I asked, when Ritchie concentrated on ignoring me.

'That's what I do, these days,' he said. 'Import export. Food, beer and belly-dancers straight from the Boyuglu.'

'And some of them are women?' I asked and he cracked a smile at that.

Maybe he was impressed that I knew that the Boyuglu was the red light district of Istanbul and that Turkey had the highest proportion of transvestites in Europe. I hoped he was.

'So, what's this "Nosey" business?'

'You know who I'm talking about?'

'I might.'

'OK, let's say this Nosey is a market trader dealing in certain specialised products. Or he was, until yesterday when he went out of business.'

'Permanently?'

'No,' I said carefully, 'just temporary, but his stock has been – shall we say – impounded.'

'Where is he?'

'You could say he's been impounded as well.'

'And what has all this got to do with me?'

'Probably nothing. I'm stuck in the middle of it, trying to negotiate a way out. A peaceful way out. There's enough bad blood already.'

'Still don't see what this has got to do with me. I don't know this Nosey.'

'Fair enough, but you probably know somebody who does.'

He nodded his head slightly at that. Flattery usually works.

'Tell me who to talk to,' I went on, 'or tell me how to put the two sides together, that's all I'm asking. I'm just the messenger in all this.'

'Regular little UN peace-keeping force, aren't you? So what if I can put the word out? Why should I? And what's in it for you?'

'Nothing in it for me, just repaying a favour. There's trouble brewing and that's not good for business. Is that a good enough reason for you?'

'It's not my business.'

'It's not mine either.' I reached into my pocket and produced one of the heroin wraps I had liberated from Nosey's stash. I held it with my thumb in the palm of my hand as if I was finessing a fifth ace and put my arms on the table. Ritchie could see what I was holding but no one else in the restaurant could, even if anyone was looking.

Ritchie saw it and knew what it was, but said nothing. I wondered if he thought I was rigged with a wire.

'I'm prepared to return Nosey's stock as an indication of good faith,' I said, off the top of my head.

'In return for what?'

'Peace in our time? I don't know. A moratorium on trading in certain areas?'

'Brick Lane for example?'

'Be a start.'

Ritchie put the middle finger of his right hand to his mouth and tapped on his teeth with the nail, loudly. It quickly became very irritating and I wished he smoked instead. Whilst he was still tap-tapping, I slipped the wrap back into my pocket.

'Was that the entire stock?' he asked eventually.

'No. The rest is close, though.'

'How close?'

'Ten minutes away.'

He gave his teeth a final tap; decision made, deal done. If only I had known what the deal was, I would have relaxed.

'Get it.'

He lifted a finger and the *maitre d'* appeared at our table. Ritchie spoke in halting Turkish, giving the impression he was not comfortable in the language. He probably hadn't been further east than Dover but I wasn't about to raise the issue.

'Bring it round the back,' he said to me, 'down the alley to the kitchen door. Ugor here will go with you.'

'Then what?' I asked, not sure I wanted an answer.

'Then we'll see.'

There was nowhere to go but with the flow.

With Ugor – was that Turkish for Igor? – breathing down my

shoulder blades, I strolled as casually as I could towards the door, wondering what I was being set up for. Was it really a good move to hand over Nosey's stash to Ritchie without any sort of guarantee? What sort of guarantee could I expect? What was Ritchie going to do with it? Why was I worrying? I didn't want it. Just how fast could Ugor run?

For no more than one second I thought about slamming Armstrong's door into Ugor and cutting out of there. But the door would only have bounced off him or, if I had managed to get behind the wheel, he would have overturned the whole cab before I got the engine warmed up.

So I unlocked the door and reached in for the Harvey Nichols bag, scanning the street for Moklis and hoping he had the sense to stay in the shadows. Then I relocked the door and followed Ugor into the alley down the side of the Fortuna.

Ritchie was waiting for us in the rectangle of light from the kitchen door and when he took a step into the alley I could see he was holding a metal ice bucket and there was a clear glass bottle rolling around inside it.

I didn't get a chance to think that one through. Perhaps my brain got as far as registering that this was a pretty odd place for a party, but that was about it. Ugor was suddenly behind me, over me, throwing me flat-faced against the wall and my forehead and my nose and my lip and my chest all hurt at once. He put his weight into crushing me against the wall; I tasted brick dust and would have screamed if I had been able to breathe. I was being squashed by a giant medicine ball, but a ball with hands which were somehow between my chest and the wall, pulling my T-shirt up and running across my skin like giant spiders. And then they were over my buttocks and kneading the insides of my thighs and all the time I was flat against the wall because whenever he changed position there seemed to be another unyielding part of him holding me in place.

Suddenly, the pressure relaxed and I was able to peel myself off the wall like a cartoon character, leaving pieces of lip and skin stuck to the bricks. I staggered back a pace and rocked on my heels, trying to assess the damage and waiting for the pain to kick in. I felt the carrier bag being removed from my hand. For some reason I had held on to it while Ugor frisked me.

'Sorry about that,' said Ritchie, then added: 'No, I'm not.'

'That's OK,' I slurred, tasting blood. 'You had to be sure.'

I dug a tissue out of my jeans and held it to my lip. With the fingers of my other hand I explored my forehead and nose to find patches that felt like sandpaper, bits of grit flaking off me like dandruff, but at least the nose didn't feel broken.

Ritchie was looking inside the carrier bag.

'How much do you want for this lot?' Ritchie asked, without looking up.

'*Nussing*,' I said, or at least that was what it sounded like through my lip; it seemed to have ballooned to three times its normal size. And to think, some people paid good money for collagen implants when this was so much cheaper. "*s-not f'r-sale.*'

'So I can have it, can I?'

'It's no good to me.'

Ritchie had put down the ice bucket and now he bent over and removed the bottle. It contained a clear liquid but there was no label on it.

'It's no good to me either.'

As he spoke, he emptied the wraps from the carrier bag into the ice bucket, then took the cork out of the bottle and sprinkled the liquid over them. He handed me the bottle and I took a sniff but either it was odourless or my nose wasn't working. I put my bloodied Kleenex to the neck of the bottle and tipped some of the liquid over it and dabbed it on my lip. The stinging pain was worse than anything Ugor had done and I shook my head to stop myself fainting.

Ritchie smiled at that, then busied himself tearing a match from a cheap book printed with the name Fortuna and a fake crest of arms. He struck the match and dropped it towards the bucket, but it was out before it got halfway there.

He sniffed in annoyance and struck another.

'If you want a job doing—' I muttered.

As the match flared, I reached out with the tissue I had held to my lips. The spirit on it caught immediately and I dropped it quickly into the ice bucket. There was a quiet *whoof!* and flames shot almost two feet up into the air, reflecting in Ritchie's glasses like a tiger's eyes.

As we stood around the pyre I reached into my jacket and pulled out the three or four sample wraps I had lifted. I threw them into the bucket and poured in some more of the clear spirit, boosting the flames.

It seemed to be the right thing to do by Ritchie.

'I'll take that as a gesture of good faith,' he said. 'We know where we stand now, don't we?'

'Do we?'

'Send Nosey home. Can you do that?'

'Maybe. I can at least suggest it.'

'Just do it, or see it's done. Tell him to go home, make sure he gets that message. I'll make a few calls.'

'To whom?'

'Never you mind. Nosey'll find a new sales area, that's all I can do.'

'Will there be any recriminations?'

'If Nosey is still in one piece, probably not. They're not good for business, though I can't guarantee that. Just like I can't guarantee nobody else will move in on his patch.'

'Fair enough,' I said and I raised the bottle in a mock toast to him, then took the smallest of sips.

I strained every nerve ending to stop myself choking and wondered if I would ever taste anything other than aniseed again. Then I handed the bottle back to Ritchie.

'Good juice, isn't it?' he grinned.

'Don't get any on your clothes,' I said.

23.

Now

'Are you sure this is the place?'
'Of course I'm sure,' snarled Moklis, 'I'm not stupid. Look, there's her car.'

Her car? That bright red, less-than-a-year-old BMW Series Five convertible? I didn't even know she could drive. Mind you, I didn't know she lived in Hampstead either. She'd told me Stoke Newington and her flat was always a mess. Moklis had brought me to a Victorian mansion sheltered from a quiet mews by a five-bar gate, two oak trees and the heavy scent of money long before you got to the very obvious burglar alarm systems.

'This can't be her place.'

When Moklis had told me the address I had blanked him. What the hell? I wasn't a real London cab driver, not one that had done the Knowledge and knew every street after a two-year diet of London A-Zs instead of corn flakes for breakfast. So I had taken him along for the ride and he'd been willing enough.

He had waited for me to emerge from the alley by the Fortuna and get into Armstrong before he had shown himself. I had no idea where he had been hiding or how much he had seen of the little Viking ritual with the heroin wraps. He was keen to know what had gone down and so I had told him everything was cool. In the dark and riding in the back of Armstrong, he couldn't see my face, which was good because I didn't want to spook him, but I caught the odd flash in the rear-view mirror – enough of a view to expect some spectacular bruising by the morning.

When he had swallowed my version of events I handed my phone to him and told him to ring Mujib Ur Rehman and arrange for Nosey to be released, and released unharmed.

'Just like that?' he had asked and I'd said exactly like that. If he passed on the message that Nosey was to 'go home', then Mujib and his vigilantes wouldn't see him selling anything stronger than Lucky White Heather down Brick Lane. Just like that.

'Here it is.'

'It can't be.'

'Go and ring the doorbell, then.'

'Right, Mr Smart-Arse, I'll do that, but you'd better be right. Make yourself useful and ring Mujib again. Try and talk to Roshan. Make sure they've let Nosey go.'

'What if they haven't?' he asked, worried.

'I have absolutely no idea and couldn't care less. I'm on my time now and I've got enough problems to worry about.'

I climbed out of Armstrong and strode up to the house. There was no point in beating about the bush, and looking furtive in this neighbourhood was asking for trouble.

The BMW wasn't the only vehicle in the short driveway. Behind it, hidden from the road, was a 250 cc motorbike complete with carrying pannier. It was the sort of bike a Hell's Angel wouldn't be caught dead on, but a motorbike messenger could use it to good effect in and out of the traffic. With a luggage box that size, it could have belonged to a pizza delivery guy. Or a woman.

There were lights on but it was impossible to see into the downstairs rooms as the windows had both blinds and curtains. The front door had a light behind it and I could see another glass door leading into a hall. I rang the doorbell and instantly an overhead security light came on, drenching me in bright light. From the road it must have looked as if I was being beamed up to the mothership. Question was: were the aliens friendly?

'Look up, please,' said the aliens and I almost died on the spot.

Of course I obeyed orders before realising that there was a video screening set-up. Not that I could see the voice box or the camera, because of the light, but then I didn't have to.

'Angel,' said the chief alien, 'what have you done to your face?'

'It's been one of those days, Amy,' I said into the light. 'Can I come in?'

There was a loud metallic click and the door flicked open electronically. I don't know why I was surprised, it was the sort of security lock you saw on hundreds of office doors. I'd just never seen one on a detached Victorian villa in Hampstead before. But then, I wasn't a burglar.

I stepped up to the second door and looked for a handle.

'It's an airlock system,' said Amy through the intercom. 'You have to close the outside door before that one opens.'

I hadn't seen *that* outside a British consulate overseas (and I wasn't exactly a welcome visitor there either).

The doors double-clicked and there was Amy wearing a white TALtop, something I hadn't seen before, arranged so the sleeves were long and the neck round, underneath a pinstripe trouser suit.

'Angel, sweetie, you look like shit.'

'Don't soft-soap me, give it to me straight,' I said, reaching for her.

'But you're wearing the jacket,' she said, slipping her arms around me.

'And the T-shirt,' I said and I could have added the trainers too. All were 'free sample' presents.

'You've ripped it,' she said suddenly, her hands sliding over my chest to get me in a hug.

I felt her fingers explore a hole under my left armpit. That must have been Ugor's doing.

'Sorry,' I said, burying my face in her hair whilst thinking that a real Paul Smith shirt wouldn't have ripped that easily.

'You do look like shit,' said another female voice and I knew it couldn't be Amy. She wasn't wearing shoes, so her mouth was buried in my chest.

It was Lyn, wearing biker's leathers, arms folded across her chest, a hand-rolled cigarette drooping from the fingers of her left hand.

'Did the police do that?' she asked and as she did, Amy lifted her head to get a better look at the damage and caught my lip on the way.

'Ow! No they didn't, why should they?' They had plenty of ways of frightening me. 'I got this on Amy's recommendation.'

'Come and sit down, you,' said Amy. 'I'll clean you up while you tell us.'

She took my arm and when I hissed 'Where have you been?' she just shushed me and steered me into a living room into which you could have fitted my entire Stuart Street flat. The furniture in it was probably worth more than all the furniture in the Stuart Street house.

'Sit there,' she said, easing me into a leather armchair big enough for both of us, 'while I get something out of the medicine chest.'

'Best offer I've had all day,' I lisped. 'Only offer I've had all day.'

There was no sympathy from Lyn, however.

'What do you mean you got thumped on Amy's recommendation?' It wasn't so much a polite enquiry after my health as an interrogation.

'She told your bloody suppliers down Brick Lane that I was a hostage negotiator in a previous life and in between heading off a gang war and leaping tall buildings, I sort of ran into a wall.'

'What the bloody hell is he talking about?' Lyn shouted over her shoulder as if I wasn't there and it was like she was watching a politician on the television.

'Your friendly sweatshop emporium,' I pressed on. 'You know the one: Mujib Ur Rehman PLC, branches in New York, Milan, Paris and Brick Lane. They've found themselves in the middle of a big drugs marketing exercise and decided to do something about it.'

'Like what?' Lyn perched on the arm of another armchair and

drew deeply on her roll-up. It either contained some really good grass, or her hands were shaking.

'Like taking one of the dealers off the street – literally. They turned vigilante and lifted a Turkish kid called Nosey. They've been holding him above the shop since yesterday.'

'Were you able to help?' Amy asked, striding back into the room, holding a small bottle and some wads of cotton-wool.

'I think so, but I can't be sure. It'd probably be safer to avoid Brick Lane for a while if you get the urge for a late-night vindaloo or... *Jesus!* What's that?'

Amy had splashed something on to the cotton wool and applied it to the cuts and grazes on my forehead. It stung like fury and a strange smell assaulted my nostrils; it was like being back in wood-work class at school.

'Tea-tree oil,' said Amy, 'don't be such a baby.'

'It's been a busy day.'

'Tell us about it,' Lyn snarled. 'And it's down to you.'

'I thought it might be,' I sighed, 'but just for the record, I'd like to know how you work that one out.'

'It was you who introduced us to that creepy photographer and now he's got himself killed, we're being hounded by the police.'

'Join the club. They think there's a connection with TAL.'

'What? They think we killed him?'

I was tempted to ask what all this 'we' business was.

'They think there's a connection. TAL was down as one of The Sarge's jobs, so they've got to check it out.'

'But he never got round to taking any photographs.' Lyn looked around for an ashtray and settled for a brass coal scuttle by the York stone fireplace. 'He was all mouth and trousers if you ask me.'

I watched Amy's expression carefully but she refused to meet my stare, concentrating instead on screwing the top back on the tea-tree oil.

'Is that what you told the police?' I turned back to Lyn.

'I told them I'd only seen the man once, that day down at Canary Wharf when all he could do was drool down Thalia's tits.'

'Did they ask anything else?'

'Not really. They snooped around the office a bit but didn't seem to find anything to trouble their tiny minds.'

'Was it Stokoe and Sell?'

'What's that?'

'It's an estate agent's. No, they're the two coppers who turned me over this afternoon. Fancy themselves as a double act.'

'I got a pimply youth, looked like he was on a Work Experience course, called Smith or Jones or something like that. And a police woman called Betts, though *he* called her Betty. She was all right, I suppose. She was the one who found the dexies in the old fag-hag's desk. Didn't say anything, though.'

'Dexies?' Amy almost dropped the tea-tree oil.

'Dexfenfluramine,' I said automatically. 'It's an antidote for alcohol craving and for treating obesity. You used to be able to get it on prescription, though you can't now. It's hardly chasing the dragon.'

'How do you know this?' Amy's eyes widened.

'She was taking slimming pills. So what? I saw her popping them once in the office. Where is she, by the way? And do you always call her "fag-hag" behind her back?'

'It's usually "slapper" to her face,' snapped Lyn. 'Or "bitch queen",' Amy added.

'Slag.'

'Witch.'

'Steady on,' I said, 'let's not get personal.'

Lyn stared at me.

'But she really is a witch. Didn't you know?'

I didn't know Lyn rode a motorbike. I didn't know Amy lived in a quarter of a million quids' worth of middle-class security. I didn't know why she had been avoiding me all week. I didn't know that the Sarge had been named after Gene Vincent. I didn't know he carried a spy camera inside his tie. How in heaven's name could I be expected to know that Thalia was a witch?

'You mean she's a wholefood freak, knits her own yoghurt and weaves her own tofu, that sort of thing?'

'No, she's a witch.'

'You mean a pagan, tree-worshipper, communer with Mother Earth, that type?'

'No, she's a witch. Spells, incantations, rituals, blood sacrifices at midnight. That sort of witch.' Amy shook her head. 'No, OK, maybe not that last bit, but she took it seriously.'

'She wanted to handfast you,' said Lyn.

'Isn't that rude?' I asked innocently.

'It's the witches' equivalent of a wedding ceremony,' Amy said sharply. 'Joining hands together.'

'Oh,' I said, trying not to look disappointed. 'But why are you telling me this?'

'Because we can't tell the police.'

'Why not? I'm sure they've heard worse.'

'We promised we wouldn't tell anyone,' said Amy seriously, 'unless she said we could.'

'And we have no idea where she is,' added Lyn.

I studied Lyn and wondered if she would roll me a smoke. Then I looked at Amy and tried, by psychic infiltration, to get her to offer me a drink. On both counts I appeared to be losing my touch.

'Since when? I mean, when did you last see her?' I asked, knowing I would regret it.

'Yesterday,' said Lyn.

'Day before,' said Amy simultaneously.

'Before the cops called?'

They both nodded.

'Where does she live?'

'Notting Hill. She has a flat but she's rarely there,' said Amy. 'I had to give the police her address, but I've tried to call her a dozen times. No reply. And she doesn't have a machine.'

'If they want her, they'll find her. Did they ask you what you were doing last Friday night?'

'I told them I was round your place,' said Amy. 'Lyn was at home.'

'Alone?' I asked Lyn after a beat.

'Yes,' she said with a sneer. 'I was surfing the 'net if you must know.'

'Do we have any idea where Thalia was last Friday?'

That was received with total silence, then Amy put her hands on her knees and massaged her kneecaps with slow, strong fingertip movements that would have put a fastidious spider to shame.

'As it was one of her lunar cycles, she was probably off at one of her retreats,' she said quietly.

Now I really was out of my depth.

'What are you saying? Because it was her time of the month she just disappears like a hermit monk?'

'No, you ignorant pig,' snapped Lyn. 'Not that sort of cycle. It was one of her lunar cycle things. You know, like Venus being in Capricorn or the sun being in conjunction with Mercury, that sort of shit. It was part of what she believed in. When the planets were right she'd piss off into the country and do some stuff.'

'What sort of stuff?'

'I don't know, do I?'

'Any idea *where* she went?'

'No.'

'I think it was Kent,' said Amy, and now Lyn and I were staring at her.

'Why?'

'Well, Dover actually. She used to come back with duty-free cigarettes sometimes.'

I almost burst out laughing at that.

'That's a bit tenuous isn't it? I mean, why wasn't she popping over to France on the hovercraft? A quick black mass on the beach at

Calais and you've still got time for a bloody good lunch before zipping round the hypermarket for the fags and the Algerian brandy for the folks back home.'

'Don't take the piss out of our partner.' shouted Lyn, jumping to her feet.

'I doubt if she went over the Channel,' said Amy, motioning to Lyn to calm down. 'She hated water and boats.'

'A seasick witch? What about the Channel tunnel? Why not put the broomstick in the guard's van and—'

'I won't tell you again,' Lyn growled.

'I'm sure she didn't get further than Dover,' Amy soldiered on. 'The cliffs there, they have some special meaning for people like Thalia. They got a witch in to bless the Channel tunnel when it opened. I read about that. And she would have said if she was going to France – or she would have brought something back other than cigarettes. Someone there supplied her. There must be tons of duty-free fags floating around Dover.'

There were millions floating around Hackney, if you knew where to ask, and it was reckoned there was no legal, tax-paid rolling tobacco south of Birmingham these days, but I kept that to myself.

'OK, OK, so she may or may not be in Dover if the planets are lined up the right way. Does that get us anywhere?'

'No it doesn't.' Lyn zipped up her leather jacket and picked up a crash helmet from behind her chair. 'And I've had enough for one day.'

'You OK with all this?' Amy asked her.

'I am. Will you be all right?' With him, she left unsaid.

'Yeah, it'll be cool,' said Amy, forcing a smile. 'See you in the office tomorrow. Let's make it business as usual whether Thalia turns up or not.'

Lyn made to put her crash helmet on and I suddenly remembered Moklis outside sulking in the back of Armstrong.

'Do me a favour, Lyn. Moklis is outside in the back of my cab. Just tell him not to panic, will you? I'll catch him in a minute.'

She flashed me her killer look and I wondered what I had said.

'Tell him your fucking self.'

That shut me up and left Amy to make polite 'I'll see you out' noises, though in that house you probably needed Securicor to see you out through the airlock doors.

'What? What did I say?' I asked her when she returned.

'Forget it, she can be a right moody cow some times.' She put her arms around me. 'I suppose it was Moklis told you where I lived?' she said into my ear.

'Is it a problem?'

'No. I'm glad you came round, I've got a present for you.'

'Not more free samples?' I said as she broke away.

'Sort of.'

She picked up a large brown shoulder bag from where it had been dropped on what looked like a genuine mahogany coffee table and opened the front flap. From it she produced a tissue-paper wrapped parcel.

'I'm beginning to feel a bit guilty about accepting all this stuff,' I said weakly, thinking that apart from my socks, everything I was wearing had come from Amy.

She unwrapped the parcel in front of me and something floated to the floor. It was a red silk stocking. Then another and she still seemed to have two or three silky red flimsy things in her hands. She held one up and shook it out. Four long suspenders dangled from it.

'Er... this one's for me, I think,' she said, trying hard to keep a straight face. 'But I thought you might help. I'm not very good with stockings, you see.'

'Don't worry, I am,' I said. 'But I'd better nip out and tell Moklis to get a mini-cab, otherwise he'll be outside all night.'

'Do it now,' she said, her voice dropping a tone.

'Yeah.'

I could wait until the morning to ask her why she had been lying.

24.

Now

True love may be blind, but good sex sends you cross-eyed.

Amy woke up the third time I said her name and told her that the coffee I had made her was going cold. She mumbled something and crawled diagonally across the big double bed to reach for it, the bedstead, a genuinely old brass and metal affair, creaking and swaying as if it might collapse. I had faith in it, though, after what it had gone through during the night.

She slurped some coffee, smiled sweetly at me and then kicked at the duvet which had her in a bear-hug. Then she frowned.

'Why am I wearing only one stocking?'

I pointed with my coffee mug to where the other red stocking was knotted to one of the brass knobs on the bed head.

'Oh, yeah,' she said to herself. 'Now I remember.'

She sniffed at her coffee and then sniffed the air in general.

'I borrowed your mint and thyme shampoo when I had a shower,' I explained.

'Oh. That's OK. You found the kitchen too.' I sat down on the edge of the bed.

'Had to. It seems like it's the maid's day off. Quite a place you've got here.'

She slurped more coffee and I realised she was giving herself some thinking time.

'I didn't think you'd be comfortable with this place, if you're wondering why I never told you about it.'

'Hey, what? Fan-assisted oven, walk-in freezer, ice-machine, large screen digital TV, power shower, bidet, personal computer, Internet, worry-free security system… hell, I could hack it. Whose is it?'

'Just how long have you been up and around?' She was smiling, but not with her eyes.

'Five minutes,' I lied.

'Well, if you must know, it's mine. My first husband thought it would be the ideal place to bring up a brood of nice middle class kids. We disagreed – about the kids not the neighbourhood. When we split, I got the house and the payments.'

I wondered if I should ask her to explain *first* husband, but the hairs on the back of my neck told me not to.

'You never said.'

'You never asked. I didn't lie to you.'

'You lied to Lyn last night,' I shot back, looking for the reaction to this rapier thrust of interrogation.

She didn't bat an eyelid.

'What? About where I was last Friday? So, big deal. I was doing stuff here on the computer, clearing some work before I spent the weekend with you. It's none of her business.'

'The cops won't see it that way. What did you tell them?'

'I kept it vague, just said I'd spent the weekend with you.' She reached out a hand towards me. 'I wouldn't have mentioned you, but they had a picture of you.'

I took her hand and held it gently, but kept an eye on the one that held the coffee mug.

'Let me get this straight. The cops came here yesterday?' She nodded. 'After you'd rung me about Moklis and his little problem?' Another nod. 'You identified me and told them where I would be, didn't you?'

'What else could I do? They didn't seem very bothered. They were here and gone within ten minutes. They just said it was routine enquiries about your friend the photographer.'

'Then it couldn't have been the SAS,' I murmured.

'What?'

'Stokoe and Sell. They were the two detectives who grilled me yesterday afternoon. I was there for bloody hours.'

She squeezed my hand. 'If they have something on you, then it was a good thing I said we were together. I gave you an alibi.'

'I don't think I need one,' I said, 'and we may hear no more about it. The cops are just checking out everything they come across. They must have found something at The Sarge's place to link him with TAL and you and Lyn and Thalia.'

'Such as?'

'I don't know. Expenses, diary entries, work notes, photographs. Something like that.'

'Photographs?' Her expression did not change but the grip from her hand tightened.

'Like the one they showed you. The black and white one of me. And The Sarge had the films he took of the three of you, when you saw his Fashion Editor.'

'Oh yes, I'd forgotten about them.' Her grip relaxed.

'I can't work out how Sarge got a snap of old Wolfie, though.'

Amy disengaged her hand and swung her legs out of bed.

'I'd better get undressed and ready for work.'

She flashed me a stunning smile over her shoulder.

'Wolfgang,' I persisted. 'You know, the Nazi in the attic. Lyn's personal Führer. How did The Sarge get him in the lens?'

'I don't know,' said Amy, padding towards the en suite bathroom.

'Did you identify him yesterday, when they showed you the pictures?'

'No,' she said without looking round and she closed the bathroom door after her.

I was weighing up whether or not to go in hard: bang on the door, demand she come out, take her by the shoulders and shake her until she told me what game she was playing. But then the doorbell rang.

Amy opened the bathroom door, which she hadn't bothered to lock, and stuck her head out.

'Get that, will you, Angel-love? It'll be the police. They said they'd be back.'

*

There were two of them, a young male Detective Constable and a stocky policewoman who, from the way she parked her feet, had only just come out of uniform.

I struggled with the door locks to let them in and they said they wanted to see Miss May. I told them she was getting dressed. They asked me who I was and I said I was her boyfriend. They asked my name and made a note of it in a little black book with an elastic band to keep the pages in place. No, I didn't live here and they asked my address. I told them Detective Sargeant Stokoe already knew it. This seemed to ring a bell with them but they didn't pursue it.

Instead they asked if I thought Amy would mind if they looked around and I said no, go ahead.

The policewoman went straight towards the kitchen and the CID man and I stood and shuffled our feet and cleared our throats. I heard the sound of cutlery being rattled in a drawer and then the dishwasher being opened and I knew what she was looking for.

'Shall I go and see what's keeping her?' I offered, jerking a thumb to indicate upstairs.

'I'm sure she'll be down in her own good time, sir,' said the detective.

That worried me as well. They did not seem at all worried about me being there and couldn't think of anything to ask me, even though I had volunteered that I was involved, through Stokoe, in their investigation. They were also suspiciously relaxed about Amy. If I'd been her I would have been out of the bathroom window, down the drainpipe and legging it by now.

The policewoman appeared from the kitchen and shook her head at her colleague. So she hadn't found a knife.

'Sorry to keep you waiting,' Amy announced, sweeping into the room.

She wore a short red felt skirt with matching jacket, a white shirt with a narrow black tie and black opaque tights. She carried a pair of red high-heeled slingbacks in her hand.

'Please,' she said, all expansive and totally in control. 'Why don't we all sit down and be comfortable?'

She sat down herself and pulled her shoes on, turning her feet and giving us all an unselfconscious flash of thigh.

'There's no need for you to hang around, Roy.' She smiled at me, her charm dial on 10. Then, sweetly, to the male detective, she asked, 'Is there?'

'We don't need Mr... Angel, is it? But if you want him to stay...'

'That's not necessary, is it Roy? You go on, I'll catch up with you at the office later.'

I was being dismissed, and I didn't like that.

I had a sneaking suspicion that I had served some sort of purpose, but I couldn't work out what.

I ought to stay and guide her. She wasn't aware of what Stokoe and Sell could do or what they knew.

'Bye then, catch you later,' I said.

25.

Now

I pointed Armstrong towards the Finchley Road and headed for Swiss Cottage, Baker Street and the West End. As I drove I sniffed my T-shirt and decided it would have to do. I didn't want to go back to Hackney just yet. With my luck, Roshan and Moklis would be camped on the doorstep wanting a recipe or career guidance or something. Moklis had been hacked off enough last night when I had turfed him out of Armstrong and told him to find his own way home. Come to think of it, though, he did owe me ten quid for his cab fare.

But right now I had to make some time for myself. I needed to think what I would say to Stokoe and Sell when they next decided to jerk my chain, as they surely would. I had to try and work out what Amy was doing, why and to whom. I had to try and guess what The Sarge had been up to, as I surely didn't have the full picture yet. And most importantly, I had to get something to eat.

Dino's would do, just down North Audley Street. It's next door to a posh Italian restaurant (which is actually good fun when Lazio are playing Juventus on television and you can remember which of the waiters supports which team) but does one of the best fried break-fasts for less than a fiver in town. And by the time I got there it was after nine, so the early shift had left their newspapers lying around and I didn't have to buy one.

I wasn't really expecting to find anything in the national papers about The Sarge and I didn't, not even a line in the rag he had mostly worked for. There might have been something on the radio or on the local TV news last night, but I had been busy last night. It's always the way. It has to be a really outstanding murder these days to make the front page, and only then if the cops want it to.

But what *did* the cops want? I thought about this all the way through a second round of toast and half a sausage.

Stokoe and Sell, who had bounced me around, seemed to be pursu-ing their own agenda. The Sarge's murder seemed like just an excuse for them to get out and about and throw their weight around. For them, it was probably a welcome break from filing the ninth burglary report of the day or taking statements from the entire fifteenth floor of a tower block where the lifts hadn't worked since Punk died, or whatever it was they did to earn a crust in between bodies.

I knew I would get a flash of inspiration if I just worked at it. Clear the mind, focus on the problem at hand and concentrate, breathing deeply all the time sucking in gobfuls of air and holding it until the lungs ached, then releasing slowly, counting to ten.

Alternatively, I could order another *cappuccino*.

I had just caught the waitress' eye – Gabriella, just twenty-three and training to be a nanny and looking remarkably chipper considering she had been on her feet since 5.30 a.m. and her hair smelled of bacon – when the mobile phone chirped in my pocket. I had turned it on when leaving Amy's house and promptly forgotten about it.

But it wasn't Amy, it was Lyn ringing from the TAL office.

'Where are you?'

'Having breakfast.'

'In which country?'

'Not far away, actually. Down the other end of Oxford Street. Why? What's up?'

'Oh, nothing much,' she drawled. 'Apart from one of my partners going walkabout and the other being questioned by the police and me having a business to run, nothing. I've got some stuff to go down Brick Lane, so I'd really appreciate it if you could drag your carcass in here.'

I rubbed a hand over my chin and realised I could do with a shave, not to mention a change of underwear from Stuart Street. I couldn't put off going back East for ever.

'Be with you in half an hour,' I said.

In fact it took me double that. I wasn't going to break sweat for Lyn, someone who wouldn't pee in my ear if my brain was on fire, so I stayed for another coffee. But then the traffic around Seven Dials when I got there was gridlocked and frustrated drivers were already leaning on their horns.

Eventually, the traffic edged forward and when Armstrong was level with one of the fruit and veg street stalls, I opened the window and asked the stallholder what the problem was.

'Some dickhead loading a van,' he said, standing on his toes to look over the jigsaw of cars and vans. 'It's OK, he's on the move.'

'Cheers, mate.' I pointed to the tray of Granny Smiths he was holding. 'Apples look nice. Let's have one.'

He walked over to Armstrong and selected a shiny green example and dropped it into my hand.

'That'll be 80p, guv.'

I blanched – no wonder people bought their vitamin-C at the chemist's these days – but found a one pound coin and passed it out to him.

'Sorry, guv, just opened up. Haven't got no change,' he said with a fixed stare and a sick grin.

'That's OK, keep the change.'

He went back to his stall with a spring in his step. I had made his day.

I had the apple in my mouth so I could change gear as I came up to the Seven Dials roundabout, the traffic crawling forward but still the occasional horn blasting out. The venom of the real cab drivers seemed to be reserved for a small white Ford Escort van coming from the right, its engine revving wildly.

The van driver was gripping the wheel and staring madly, determined to bulldoze his way out of there and down towards Covent Garden. It was Star Trek from Printer Pete's and although I couldn't lip-read accurately at that distance, I was confident that what he was shouting to himself, over and over, was, 'Warp speed! Warp speed!'

I took another bite of the apple and watched him go, then started hunting for a place to dump Armstrong, shaking my head at the inconsiderateness of civilian drivers in London, just like a real cabbie would.

Lyn was alone in the TAL office, sitting at her word processor with a box of computer disks in front of her. She was still wearing the biker's leathers she had at Amy's.

'You're late,' she said without looking up. She pressed a button, something whirred and a disk ejected. She plugged in another.

'The traffic was a bitch. Any sign of Amy?'

'No, not yet, and I'm not holding my breath. It's over there, by the door.'

She didn't look at me once, but then I had grown used to that from Lyn.

There was a parcel on the floor by the door. It was oblong, about two feet long and wrapped in thick brown paper. I bent at the knees to pick it up and was grateful I did. It weighed a ton and I could easily have had a claim for an industrial back injury. I eased off and looked at the address instructions written in thick felt-tip pen. All it said was: *Rehman. For collection by Satinex.*

Something made me turn my head to find Lyn glaring at me from across the office. I realised that my sixth warning sense had been triggered by her eyes boring into the back of my neck. For a second there, it was really spooky.

'Got a problem?' she said, looking back to her screen quickly.

'Problem, no. Hernia, maybe. What's in here?'

'Fabric samples. Got to go back to the manufacturer. When you can spare a minute, that is.' She continued to peck furiously at her keyboard.

'It's urgent, is it?'

'Yes. I said I'd get it over there before I split for the weekend.'

'Going anywhere nice?'

'Just away. Away from this place. Away from you, if you ever decide to do what you're paid for.'

Suddenly, almost on cue, there was a thump on the ceiling from the floor above, as if someone had moved a heavy piece of furniture. Lyn looked up at the noise as well.

'The rally's started early,' I muttered to myself, bending-again and gripping the parcel.

'What?'

'Nothing. Do you know what time Amy's coming in?'

'No I don't. And give me a ring when you've delivered that, so I can push off early.'

'*Jawohl, mein Führer*,' I said quietly, staggering under the weight of the fabric samples.

Me and my big mouth.

*

It took ages to get over to Spitalfields and the traffic didn't really thin until I was almost in Brick Lane, where it didn't so much thin as disappear. The whole Bangladeshi enclave was unusually quiet, not a BMW illegally parked outside a restaurant anywhere to be seen. And on the street corners, pairs or trios of young Bangladeshi men just standing around, smoking, watching. Neighbourhood Watch or Early Warning Line, it was difficult to tell.

I kerb-crawled by the photographic shop to check for signs of life. It seemed to be open, so I parked and humped the parcel from where I had thrown it on the back seat.

Moklis didn't offer to help me with the door and his lips curled back from his teeth when I said hello. I guessed I wasn't his favourite person.

'Delivery for Mujib from the TAL girls,' I chirped. 'How's tricks?'

'It was 1 a.m. when I got back last night,' he snarled. 'I couldn't get a cab.'

'Then you didn't need that ten quid I loaned you, did you?'

He ran a hand down his face and blinked his eyes rapidly. 'It was three o'clock before I got to bed.'

'This is my fault?'

I thumped the TAL parcel down on the counter.

'Yes it is. When I got back, they questioned me for hours.'

'Who did?'

'Mujib and some of the elders.'

'Did they let Nosey go?' I had a sudden panic attack. What if they'd ignored my advice and just disembowelled the guy to be done with it?

'Of course they did. Roshan insisted on it once I phoned her, but they wanted to be sure that there would be no revenge taken by the Turks.'

'Hence the vigilantes out on the street today,' I said and he nodded agreement. 'Yeah, well, nothing is guaranteed, but we did what we could. You know it was the only thing we could do. What other options did we have?'

'I've been thinking, though.' He raised a finger and aimed it at me as if he was going to lecture me. He was. I'd seen that gesture before in my life – all of it.

'How do I know you saw *anybody* in that restaurant last night? I never actually saw you do a deal with anyone. Never heard what you said. You went off with the drugs and then you came back and said it was sorted. You could just have sold the drugs and pretended to talk to someone for us. Kept the money for yourself.'

Bugger. I had never thought of that.

'Would I do that to you? And if I did, would I be back here now, playing messenger for TAL? Give me a break, Moklis me old mate. Has anything happened?'

'Not yet,' he said uncertainly, and I couldn't blame him. He knew as well as I did that if there was trouble – even if it was only Nosey back on the street with fresh samples – it would come after dark.

'There you go, then. Now give this to Mujib would you? I was told it was urgent.'

He looked down at the parcel.

'It's not really. The Satinex people don't collect until Monday. You can take it upstairs to him.'

'No, I'll let you. For a start, I'd get lost up there and then old Mujib would only want to thank me for all my efforts sorting out his problems on his territory. And that would take time and lavish hospitality and I've got to get home and have a shave, feed the cat, do the laundry, stuff like—'

Moklis saw the fear on my face.

'What is it?'

'The cat,' I said slowly. 'I haven't fed the cat since— Oh, my God.'

*

It was quiet; too quiet.

I went up the stairs sideways, my back against the wall, remembering to avoid the steps that creaked. My eyes flitted from the landing to my flat, to the next flight of stairs up to where Inverness Doogie and Miranda lived, and then downstairs again to where I had left the front door ajar in case I needed a fast track exit.

I hugged the wall again as I approached the door of Flat Three, my keys held out like a gun in front of me. The key was less than two inches from the lock when my heart stopped.

'I've fed him,' said a voice.

'*Jeeesus* Christ but you made me jump, Fenella.'

'You must have a guilty conscience,' she said, stomping up the stairs towards me.

I checked for the obvious signs. Yes, racing heart, sweating hands, rapid uncontrolled eye movement; all the dead-giveaway signs of a guilty conscience.

'I've had a lot on my plate,' I said weakly.

'And now you've got this,' she said, halting in front of me, one hand on her hip, the other holding a piece of paper right in front of my nose.

I focussed on it and saw it was a till receipt for £9.27.

'What's that?' I asked warily.

'It's what you owe me for Springsteen's breakfast. He was howling so much we couldn't sleep, so I decided to feed him. I won't tell you what Lisabeth wanted to do to him.'

I could guess. Springsteen may be a different species, but he was a male and Lisabeth wouldn't have made an exception just because he wore fur.

'So, you bought him some tins of cat food, right?'

'Not exactly. I knew you had lots of tins in the flat and I assumed you'd come back *eventually*, so I thought I'd get him a treat as he sounded so lonesome. And that meant I had to go into a butcher's for you, so I want my money back. It was horrible, having to look at all that stuff.'

I dug out my wallet and removed a ten pound note.

'What did you get him for £9.27?' I asked as I handed the note over to her.

'I don't know, I just pointed. I could hardly *speak*. I think the man said it was T-bone steak or something.'

'Thanks, Fenella. I'm sure he enjoyed it. Did you cut it up for him?'

She started to blush.

'He... er... didn't actually give me a chance.' She turned her wrist over and I could see three lengthy scratch marks down the back of her hand.

That's my boy; always scratch the hand that feeds you.

'I don't know what he did with the carrier bag,' she said as she turned to go downstairs. 'The last I saw, he was dragging it through the cat-flap.'

Oh, dear. If he'd had to unwrap his own breakfast, he would be really hacked off.

I found the plastic bag in the kitchen, the bedroom and in the shower. It had been shredded more effectively than if it had gone through an office shredding machine and no one piece was longer than five inches, or wider than two. He seemed to have vented his anger, though, as Springsteen himself was collapsed across my bed, his distended stomach rising and falling with each feline snore.

I tiptoed into the bathroom and locked the door, deciding on a wet shave with a razor I'd only used once (although Amy had also used it once) rather than my Braun battery shaver. Cats hate electric razors. There must be something in the sound they emit that triggers a race memory in them. Something to do with a visit to the vet, maybe.

I was halfway through when the mobile phone went off in the pocket of my jacket. The jacket I had left in a heap on the floor of the bedroom.

I got there on the third ring and found myself transfixed by the stare of one fearful yellow eye.

Springsteen hadn't moved a muscle apart from opening that one eye and he was still a good two metres away on the bed. But I was naked to the waist, hands slippy with shaving foam and armed only with a semi-blunt plastic disposable razor. It was no contest, so I grabbed my jacket, dragged it out of the room and slammed the door.

I answered on the sixth ring and it was Amy.

'Angel? That you?'

'Yes,' I yelped, having almost put my eye out with the razor whilst trying to open the phone and get it to my ear with one hand. My other hand was on the bedroom door knob and I had no intention of letting go.

'Are you all right?'

'Fine. Look, I'm really glad you called. I wanted to say—'

'I'm in the office,' she interrupted. 'Have you seen Lyn this morning?'

'Yes, she called me in to do a job.'

'Do you know where she is?'

'No. She said she was going away for the weekend, though.'

And she had told me to call her, but I'd forgotten.

'She's gone,' said Amy, but after a pause which convinced me there was someone with her, prompting her perhaps.

'I told you, she said she was going away for the weekend. She was trying to slip off early.'

'I think it's more permanent than that,' she said. 'You'd better get down here.'

26.

Now

When I got there, they were having a picnic.

To be fair, Amy wasn't eating, just pacing the office drinking from a plastic bottle of Volvic. But Stokoe and Sell had made themselves at home, leaning back in chairs with their feet up on Thalia's desk which was covered with greaseproof paper, sandwiches, fruit, pots of low-fat yoghurt and plastic spoons. They may have been slobs, but they were calorie-conscious slobs.

'Come on in, Fitzroy,' Stokoe bellowed jovially. 'Join us, feel free. I think there's a salt beef and a – what's that one, Steve?'

'Crab mayo',' said Sell, still chewing. 'Or it might be salmon and pine nuts.'

'Oh, yeah. Didn't like them. Whatever's left, Fitzroy, help yourself. Bloody good grub you get round here. Better than we're used to.'

'I'll pass, thanks,' I said.

Amy walked over to me and stood at my side, her hand fumbling for mine so that when we faced the two policemen we were side-by-side, together, a pair, an item. Maybe an alibi.

'They've come about Lyn,' she said.

'What about her?'

Stokoe looked at Sell and Sell looked at Stokoe and they went into their act.

'Do you see her here, boss?'

'Can't say that I do, Detective Constable. It must be a bit stressful to work in this place. First the one with the funny name disappears, now the one with the attitude does a runner too.'

'She was here this morning,' I said, looking at my watch. 'Three hours ago, sitting over there. What's up? Trying to set a new record for police response to a missing person's case? According to *The Big Issue*, you have to have to have been sleeping in a packing case down by the Embankment for three years before you guys will even fill out the forms.'

'I think we have a cynic among us,' Stokoe said grandly.

He swung his legs down from the desk and stood up. He looked around the office at the piles of fabric and boxes of shoes spaced out across the floor.

'You got VAT receipts for all these, Ms May?'

'They're free samples mostly, or promotional—' Amy started but I squeezed her hand.

'You're not interested in VAT receipts, are you, Mr Stokoe?'

'No, I'm not, Fitzroy, I'm just making conversation.'

'You're not really interested in Lyn either, are you?'

He looked down at Sell.

'I told you he was sharp, didn't I?' Then to me: 'No, I'm not. It's her boyfriend I'm after. Wolfgang Mansfeld, the Nazi in the attic.'

I realised that all four of us were looking up at the ceiling.

They hadn't even needed me to go over there, although as the last person to have seen Lyn that morning I suppose I had some sort of curiosity value. Perhaps it was Amy wanting me there as a security blanket, which was a nice thought and possible as she had not come across the SAS team before.

But Stokoe and Sell were simply there waiting for a warrant to search the Web 18 offices upstairs. They were in no hurry to tell us why and had shown only a passing interest in Lyn. When I tried to describe what she had been doing at her desk earlier, Amy had logged in to her computer and after fifteen minutes or so she had announced that nothing was missing, or at least nothing to do with the TAL business. Was I sure she had been downloading files on to disks? How would I know? My computer illiteracy is fairly comprehensive, so I wasn't actually sure the thing was turned on.

'Maybe she was just surfing the 'net,' I said, trying to bluff it out.

'We're not on the Internet here,' said Amy.

'I'll bet they are upstairs,' said Sell but Amy didn't respond.

A phone rang and I automatically went for my pocket, so conditioned was I becoming. But it was one of the land-lines on Lyn's desk and Sell answered it without hesitation.

He grunted a couple of times then hung up.

'Warrant's here. They're getting the gear out of the car now.'

'Good,' said Stokoe. 'Fancy helping us smash a door down, Fitzroy?'

Of course they didn't smash the door down; they had a civilian in brown overalls and carrying a briefcase instead. There was a uniformed policeman as well, who handed Stokoe some papers and then Stokoe told the civilian, 'Get on with it, Clive.'

We were on the stairs outside the Web 18 office. Clive put down his briefcase, opened it and took out what at first sight I thought was a cordless phone. When he levelled it at the door lock, I knew what it was and I wished Star Trek had been with us so he could have said, 'Phasers on stun,' or similar.

Two fine wires extended from the end of the lock gun and Clive attached them to the terminals he had exposed in the keypad lock, after prising the plastic cover off with a screwdriver. He pressed a button on his set and a liquid crystal display began to flash. I had never seen one of these in action before, though I once owned (briefly) a mechanical lock gun which could get you into a Saab faster than a thirteen-year-old joyrider.

'Might have known,' sighed Clive, showing the read-out to Stokoe. 'Could have saved me a house call. It's eighteen, eighteen again. No imagination, these bleeders.'

'Sorry for the call out, Clive,' said Stokoe. 'We'll take it from here.'

He reached for the keyboard and pressed 1,8,1,8. Then he took a pound coin out of his trouser pocket and handed it to Sell.

'I didn't think they'd do it twice, Steve, you win.'

'You've come across Web 18 before?' I asked.

'Web 18, Column 18, Action 18, Forward 18, they're all the same. It's like a signature or a trademark, the "18" bit that is.'

'What, like Club 18-30?'

'Don't be silly, Fitzroy. It means the first and eighth letters of the alphabet.'

'A and H? AH?'

'Adolf Hitler,' said Amy softly.

'Full marks, Ms May. At least you seem to be catching on.'

The door clicked and Stokoe pushed it open with the flat of his hand.

'Do you want me to sweep the place?' Clive the civilian asked in a bored sort of way.

'No need,' said Stokoe surveying the empty office. 'I think some-body's done that for us.'

I peered over his shoulder and had to agree with him. Apart from some basic pieces of furniture, the Web 18 office was empty. It could have doubled as a photograph in an advertisement for Office Space To Let.

'You cut along, Clive,' said Stokoe, all authoritative. 'And you go and make sure nobody nicks the petty cash from downstairs while we're up here.'

For a minute I thought he was talking to me, but when the uniformed constable started downstairs I relaxed and tried to look cool.

Our footsteps echoed on the bare floorboards as we trooped in. I remembered the sound of thumping on the ceiling that morning when I was downstairs with Lyn and wondered if I should mention it.

'They've done a runner,' said Sell before I could volunteer anything. 'Behind on the rent, you reckon?'

'They left that.' Stokoe pointed to a computer and screen with a connected printer on a bare desk by the window. 'Can you hack in?'

'Beyond me, guv,' said Sell, rooting through a wastepaper basket. 'Doesn't even seem to be any rubbish worth sifting.'

'How about you?' Stokoe asked Amy.

'I can do a letter, the accounts and a bit of mail-merge, but I left most that stuff to Lyn,' she said.

'Fitzroy?'

'Couldn't even turn it on.'

'Then I'll have to have a go myself, won't I?'

He pulled up a chair, turned on the power and then the computer and settled himself like a poker player at the high-roller table while it warmed up.

'Of course, we don't know his password, so I'll have to use mine.'

'Yours?'

'Well, my twelve-year-old boy's actually. He taught me how to do this. Now let's get a line.'

Amy and I watched over his shoulder and when the computer made a ringing noise like a telephone, I automatically reached for the mobile in my pocket, stopping myself just in time. I sent myself a mental e-mail to get a grip on myself.

'We're in. Now, let's find a search engine to hook up to. This one's as good as any.'

His hand clicked on the mouse control. I wondered why 'mouse' when 'spider' seemed so much more appropriate when scanning the world wide web.

'Of course we can't know what Wolfgang was surfing but you never know your luck. Here we go.'

He typed in 'Nazi' and clicked on 'Search'.

None of us spoke then for what seemed like ages. We just read from the screen.

```
Nazi
Top 10 of 36915 matches. View Titles only.
70% Shalom Shalom
We have a Biblical duty. God hates fags, fags
hate God, jews send fags, aids cures fags.
68% Nazi Marching Songs
67% Revisionist Truth
Summary:In a clever attempt to disguise the
subterfuge, the figures for Jewish losses were
```

```
inflated to nearly double, though now in a
much smaller ratio to non-Jewish victims.
67% New World Order
Summary:Unemployment in Germany now 4 mil-
lion. Turks take our jobs. Repatriate now.
66% Action This Day
Summary:The virus is everywhere. Instate a Bu-
reau of Prisons now.
65% Gare de L'Est
Summary:First strike. The tide will turn.
64% The Master Race In Outer Space
Summary:Base on the moon. Remember 1945.
Coloureds, ragheads and wogs be warned.
64% Re. To The Bigot
Summary:Go stick your thumb up your Nazi ass
racist fuck.
62% News and Media
Current events. Dateline NBC - Canada, a haven
for Nazi war criminals?
61% Society and Culture.
Gay nazi page. (More Like This)
Organisations: Skinheads.
```

There were incomprehensible Internet references and signatures, the one I liked best was *http://www.tim.html*, which was the guy with the thumb-and-ass advice. I worked out that html stood for 'hate mail' and that 'tim' – if that was his name – had sent his message at 11.33 Eastern Standard Time. Apart from that, it was all anonymous, strangely remote and very frightening.

'Have you searched for Web 18?' Amy asked.

'Yes, we've run that but it didn't turn up anything except that it's part of a genuine address for a real estate agent in Colorado,' said Stokoe Then he tapped the screen with a fingernail. 'No, that's the interesting one.'

I screwed up my eyes to read the screen where his finger was.

'The "Gare de L'Est" reference?'

'Yup. He's used that one before. We've been tracking it for some time. It was in French originally, which made it stick out like a sore thumb as 85% of the Internet is in English. But they must have liked the name because they stuck with it.'

'What does it mean?'

'It's the station in Paris from where they deported the jews during the war. It first came up in the context of the French National Front trying to introduce a law encouraging people to inform on illegal immigrants. You see, Fitzroy, you can learn a lot on the Internet.'

'Sure, all human life is there.'

'I wouldn't say human sometimes, and they do get everywhere. There's a page running which tells you which politically unsafe bookshops not to shop at. Not just here but everywhere in Europe, the States, Australia. Turns out the reason the bookshops are deemed politically unsafe is because they sell copies of *The Diary of Anne Frank*, which they class as "subversive fiction". Then there's the White List. Ever heard of the White List?'

'Do I really want to?'

'It's a points system for football teams. The only ones that qualify for the White List are teams which have never fielded a black player.'

'That's not possible,' I said, thinking fast.

''Fraid it is.'

Stokoe named two Premiership sides and five or six from the lower divisions.

'That explains why they've never won much,' I said. 'But it's something I wouldn't have picked up on in a month of Sundays.'

'That's because you go with the flow in life, Fitzroy. These sad fuckers don't. Still… ' he flipped a switch and the screen faded, 'this isn't helping us much. Anything, Steve?'

Sell was leaning against the door jamb of the small kitchen at the end of the office.

'Coffee making gear, nothing else, guv. Nothing to say what they were doing up here.'

'They were stuffing envelopes,' I said and they all looked at me.

Stokoe swung around in his chair and folded his arms across his chest.

'Do tell us, Fitzroy.'

'Tell me why you want to know first. Why the warrant? Why the search?'

Stokoe flashed a glance towards Sell who responded with a what-the-hell shrug.

'I told you we've had our eye on Wolfie Mansfeld for some time. He's connected to Ms Lyn Buttress and *she's* one of the usual suspects in the investigation of the murder of Eugene Sargeant. Do we need a better excuse to roust the Nazi bastard? Well, actually we've got two because not only are we sure he's involved in printing inflammatory literature, but our colleagues in Europe reckon there's a strong link between the heroin coming in from Germany and this Gare de L'Est group. That good enough for you?'

'You don't suspect Lyn of The Sarge's murder?' I knew I was pushing my luck.

'No,' he said slowly, 'not her.'

I tried for eye-contact with Amy but she avoided it.

'OK, then. I came up here once, just to piss them off really. Lyn had been on my case all morning but when the boyfriend snapped his fingers, she went like a puppy. So I just thought I'd jive them. Never got through the door, but I did see in. Lyn was helping him collate paper and stuff envelopes. Looked like they were doing the parish magazine.'

Stokoe exhaled loudly.

'We should have come earlier, Steve.'

'I did say, guv—'

'Yeah, yeah, I know. And now we've missed him.'

'Why?' Amy had recovered the power of speech.

'Because he did a runner from his digs this morning, paid up the rent and left. We had him spotted at Victoria getting on the Eurostar for Paris.

'Was Lyn with him?'

'Can't be sure, Ms May. If they were travelling together they would have got on the train separately and met up later. They'll be somewhere in the Channel Tunnel by now. Pity. We could have had him picked up over there if we'd found he'd been downloading this sewerage and circulating it.'

I cleared my throat nervously.

'I might be able to help you there.'

27.

Now

On the hectic drive over to Southwark through the thickening afternoon traffic, I asked Amy two questions.

'When I asked you how you'd ever found Mujib Ur Rehman's set up, you told me Lyn got it from a directory on the Internet. That was really Wolfgang's directory, wasn't it?'

'I suppose so,' she said from the back of Armstrong.

I checked my mirror as we approached Blackfriars Bridge. The police car carrying Stokoe and Sell was right behind us. It was almost as if I was giving them an escort.

'That night I first met you – met the three of you, in the pub when I judged the Leg Competition – afterwards, there was a taxi, a real one. Thalia got in but Lyn wouldn't. Went on the night bus instead. Where does she live?'

'Shepherd's Bush.'

'And Thalia is Notting Hill, so it would have made sense them sharing. Except the cab driver was a black guy, wasn't he? And last night I asked her to talk to Moklis outside your house and she told me to go fuck myself. She's got a big problem with coloured people, hasn't she?'

'Yes, she has.'

And probably jews, gypsies, gays, Christian Scientists and sociologists as well, I thought.

Then I asked a third question.

'How long have you known?'

There was no answer to that.

28.

Now

'No, it's not bleedin' convenient,' Peter shouted, which was the least cool thing he could have done in the circumstances. 'It's Friday afternoon and we're cleaning down and shutting up for the weekend.'

'Sounds to me to be the perfect time for a little look round, sir,' said Stokoe politely. 'We could wait for a warrant to be sent over, though, if you prefer.'

Peter looked out of the window of the print shop to where Armstrong and the police car had parked so that the entrance to the narrow loading bay was completely blocked. There was no way Peter's white van was going anywhere and we were already inside, having simply walked in as two of the staff were leaving.

The place was indeed closing down for the day; none of the machines were working and there were only three brown-coated staff in view, finishing off a job on a manual guillotine. One of them was Star Trek, who was nervously avoiding my eye.

Peter took a huge plug of orange bubblegum from his pocket, unwrapped it one-handed and stuffed it into his mouth. He was buying himself thinking time.

'Just what is it you're looking for?'

'Anything to do with a company called Web 18 over in Seven Dials, sir. I believe you did work for them.'

Peter glared at me.

'This down to you, Roy?'

'Absolutely, Pete.'

There was nothing Peter could do to scare me, or at least nothing that would scare me as much as what I had seen on Web 18's Internet.

'Don't know who you mean,' he said to Stokoe. 'We print all sorts of things for loads of people.'

Stokoe gave Sell the nod and Sell moved off, floating among the machines, hands in pockets, peering into the waste bins stationed around the shop floor. Amy moved to my side, close but not touching. Stokoe sat himself down on a three-foot pile of crown-size sheets of paper.

'Oh, I think you'd remember the sort of printing you did for Web 18 if you put your mind to it. It's Mr Sokolowski, isn't it?'

Peter blew a bubble of gum in my direction but I ignored him. I hadn't told Stokoe his surname, I'd not known it.

'Actually, I know it is because I put in a few calls on the way over,' Stokoe went on. 'There was that little incident of the Obscene Publications Act charge, wasn't there?'

'Not proven,' Peter snapped.

'Interesting case, though. Would have been the first for obscene video covers. That was a foreign customer as well, wasn't it? Danish? Or was it Dutch?'

'Like I said, I don't know what you mean,' he maintained with a set jaw. 'Am I going to need a brief, Roy?'

I was surprised he was asking me for advice. I wouldn't have blamed him if he hadn't spoken to me at all, me arriving with the law as I had. But then again, I hadn't expected Peter to be so awkward. If I'd had to put money on it I would have thought it a good bet that he would have rolled over on Web 18 and told Stokoe what he wanted to hear within five seconds. He was like that – a natural born coward. The only reason I could come up with as to why he was stonewalling was that he was frightened of Mansfeld and Web 18 in some way. Or perhaps he was frightened of something he had done *for them*.

Depends what you've been doing for Web 18, Peter,' I said. 'And whether you've got any of their stuff here.'

'Never heard of them,' he persisted.

'That doesn't exactly tie in with our information—' Stokoe started, but I overrode him.

'Oi! Star Trek!' I shouted, pulling out my wallet. 'Was it you dropped that twenty quid round at Web 18 this morning?'

He saw me tugging notes from the wallet and that was as long as it took for him to put his foot in it.

'That's logical, Captain,' he said, starting towards me, holding his hand out.

Sell moved in on him and flashed his ID. Star Trek's brain worked at warp speed.

'The stuff's in the Security Room. The boss has the key on his desk.'

'Shit,' said Peter under his breath.

'Can I have my twenty quid now?' asked Star Trek.

There were over fifty boxes of printed paper stashed haphazardly in Peter's Security Room. Peter claimed he had no idea what was in any of them. He had been helping out a client with a storage problem. There was no way anyone could prove that he had actually printed any of it and as it was sitting in a locked, secure room, it wasn't being distributed, was it?

No one answered him. As far as I was concerned, that was a problem for Stokoe and Sell, but they, like Amy and me, were drawn to the boxes of printed sheets with an unhealthy fascination.

Each box contained at least 500 sheets, some double-sided. Some had grainy illustrations which I guessed had been downloaded intact from the Internet. Some were just word-processed text and even a cursory glance suggested they were translations from another language. Some sheets had been set out on a desktop publishing unit to give the impression of a newsletter or a very sick parish magazine. There were cartoons of a type I had seen in history books at university – cartoons that would have made Julius Streicher blanch.

We spread the boxes out across the floor. The technique was clear. Pages could stand alone as flyers or, as some proudly proclaimed in the top right-hand corner, 'background briefs'; or several could be clipped or bound together as a magazine. Either way, they made gruesome reading.

Not that you actually needed to read beyond the headlines. There was nothing there I hadn't overheard on a train, or in a pub, or on a Party Political Broadcast or at a football match, and usually more cogently, if as distastefully, expressed.

'Nowhere near six million jews had perished in the Holocaust.' Well, not according to some guy in the engineering department of a north-west American university and he had a copy of a 1939 *Baedecker* to prove it. There were four million people unemployed, which was probably true, and four million jobs held by guest-workers which I doubted was anywhere near true. Still, the implication was that the arithmetic was inescapable and there was only one possible, if not final, solution to the problem.

There were bogus statistical tables on immigration into the UK in an article which then progressed on to the fertility rates and breeding capabilities of various ethnic groups. A similar piece, which looked as if it had been taken from an academic journal, was headed by a logo of an American eagle and prophesied that the US population would be 108% Hispanic by the year 2015, or at least that's the way I read it.

Then there were the lists. Now, most people have enjoyed hours, sometimes days, of harmless fun compiling stupid lists: the ten best movies; the hundred best albums; the top twenty jazz solos ever (any instrument); the order in which *The Magnificent Seven* were shot; music you should never be seen dancing to – anything Portuguese, anything John Travolta danced to before he did *Pulp Fiction*, anything by a gay icon, and so on; ten greatest goals; that sort of thing. Maybe not tasteful and certainly not useful, but generally harmless.

But the Web 18 lists were not harmless. There was the one Stokoe had told me about – football teams (nearly all British) which had never fielded a non-white player. Then there were golf clubs that operated restrictive membership policies (eight pages of them) and then pubs and bars across Europe that offered rooms for hire for 'Debating Societies'.

And there were lists of shops, thousands of them, described variously as Tactical Supplies, Militaria, Outbackers, Rough Survival or just Survivalist (plus other things in languages I didn't understand) from Little Rock, Arkansas to Sydney in Australia, via Manchester, Amsterdam and Athens. A truly world-wide web, which had after all been originally a military concept (I knew that much) and that was the impression they were trying to create. I guessed that half the shops on the list (a) didn't know they were on it, and (b) sold nothing more dangerous than a lead model of a troop of Napoleonic cavalry.

Oh, sure, there were some who would have Bowie knives on display in the children's section and some in the US where you could probably buy a battle tank by mail order. But by lumping them all together Web 18 was presenting a picture that would comfort its followers and impress the easily impressionable. Look at us, it was saying, we must be right – we have branches everywhere.

'I think I've seen enough,' Stokoe announced.

I certainly had. Amy was crouched near a group of boxes which contained sheets in French, German and Dutch. Maybe she was an interpreter at the UN in her spare time. I'd be the last to know.

'They're nothing to do with me, I'm just storing them,' said Peter hopping from foot to foot. He had been unnerved by the silence in which we had examined his bizarre archive. 'There's no law against storing things.'

'They'll think of one, Peter,' I said and Stokoe grinned at that.

'If you're only storing this stuff, you'll have no objection if we remove it, will you?'

'No, no problem with that,' Peter said quickly.

'And no objection to signing a statement for us to the effect that these – documents – are the property of Web 18 and were left with you by Wolfgang Mansfeld?'

Peter looked at me, wide-eyed, hoping for advice, anything.

'Do it, Peter,' I said. 'Boldly go, for once.'

He weighed up his options for about a minute, which gave him time to run through them all at least twice. Then he nodded his head and said, 'OK.'

'Then we've got enough to get Wolfie-boy pulled,' Stokoe said to Sell. 'Take a quick inventory and a verbal from our good friend Peter here. I'll be out in the car on the radio.'

'Do you need us any more?'

It was Amy. Stokoe seemed to have forgotten she was there.

'Not at the moment, Ms May. We know where to find you if we do need you. Thanks for all your help.'

I thought that a bit rich. I mean, they didn't know where to find Thalia or Lyn and what help had Amy provided? It was me who had given up Printer Pete. But then, there's no gratitude in this world any more.

I kicked idly at one of the boxes as I made for the door of the Security Room but Amy held me back, her hand on my arm. She made frantic face signals to indicate that she wanted Stokoe, Sell and Peter to leave first. Then she repeatedly jabbed a finger downward to the box at her feet.

I picked up the top sheet. It was in German and looked to have been badly photocopied from a technical magazine of some kind. As I scanned the single page, I picked out about one word in five, getting the impression that it was something to do with electronics. Then I came to some chemical symbols and I mentally switched off.

'What?' I said and she shushed me.

'What?' I said again, in a whisper.

'How good's your German?' she whispered back.

'I'd never starve or go thirsty but this is too dense for me.'

'It's a How to Build an Incendiary Device leaflet,' she hissed.

'Yuk!' I gagged, holding it with finger and thumb and dropping it back into the box. 'They got that off the Internet?'

'There's some pretty weird stuff out there.'

'Then we did the right thing. As they say, *Surf Nazis Must Die*.'

'It might not be funny,' she hissed.

'What?'

'That parcel you delivered to Mujib's this morning, what did you say it was?'

'Something for Satinex. Returns of fabric samples is was Lyn said, I think.'

'Satinex call at Mujib's on Mondays.'

'Yeah, Moklis said. So what?'

'So, it wasn't that urgent.'

'Lyn said she wanted to get away... ' My whisper tailed off.

'A tad suspicious, perhaps?' she smiled patronisingly.

'I didn't... Look, it *was* fabric samples. I carried the damned thing. It was floppy, you know, flexible. It was heavy, mind you.'

'How big?'

'About like this.'

I held my hands about half a metre apart, then I mimed about a quarter deep and half a metre wide.

Amy bit her lower lip, looked me in the eyes and shook her head slowly from side to side.

'But—?'

She put a hand on my chest and talked low and fast.

'You asked me how I found Mujib's factory – OK, sweatshop. I told you Lyn got it from a directory on the 'net, right?' I nodded foolishly. 'Now what if that was one of Web 18's directories? What if it was from a page put up by this Gare de L'Est group? It wouldn't be their version of the Good Fashion Guide, would it?'

She removed her hand and stepped over to another of the open boxes and plucked out a handful of sheets of paper. The printing was small and in French, most of it a long double column of single line addresses. The introductory text was headed: Centres of Illegal Economic Activity.

'No, it's not a recommendation,' I said, more to myself than to her. 'It's a target.'

29.

Now

We fluffed our way out of the Security Room and across the floor of the print shop where Sell was writing in a notebook as Peter spoke, emphasising each word with body language which said with every nuance, 'It wasn't me, guv.'

I had my arm around Amy's waist, her head on my shoulder, the back of her hand up against her face as if wiping away tears, her chest heaving. She was sobbing, 'How could she?' as we walked and I was making all the right, 'there, there,' noises and looking at Sell and making faces as if to say, 'Women, eh?' We hadn't rehearsed it, not even discussed it. We just did it and it got us out of Peter's place to the cars.

Stokoe was half-in, half-out of the passenger seat of the police car, talking into a radio. He spotted us when we were about two metres from Armstrong.

Amy and I kept moving, me pantomiming all the time. She's upset, I'm taking her home, you know where to find us, you don't need us any more, do you?

Stokoe was still on the radio when I sat Amy in the back of Armstrong and made to shut the door, still acting as if I was consoling her. As soon as she was in the cab and out of his view, her expression changed to stone hard.

'Get in and punch it,' she said.

We were going over Tower Bridge, lights on against the dark, and I was trying to listen to the local news with one ear, whilst keeping the other open for the distant sound of fire engine sirens. I even scanned the night sky for any sign of the twin-engined aeroplane, the Spy In The Sky, which brought you the traffic news. Surely the plane would be able to spot an explosion in the Brick Lane area, but as usual, it was never around when you wanted it. The pilot was probably over the other side of town leading weary and unsuspecting drivers into four-hour tailbacks on the Westway just to boost the road rage statistics.

Amy, on the other hand, was taking the easy way out and being practical.

'Have you got your mobile with you?'

'Yeah. Good thinking.' I pulled the phone from my jacket and handed it to her through the sliding partition. 'I was just about to ring ahead and warn them.'

We came off the bridge and I was negotiating the traffic around the old Royal Mint site when the phone came back through the partition, hit the dashboard and bounced on to the floor.

'When did you last put this thing on the fucking charger?' she yelled.

Oh shit.

There was no time to find a phone box. Most of them were inside pubs and I just knew that if I'd suggested that, Amy would have deliberately misconstrued it and then we would have wasted more time while I had the mobile removed by surgery.

So I pushed on, shouting at the traffic and leaning on the horn and relying on the fact that when a taxi honks you, you get out of the way – unless you're a bus or another taxi of course.

I did a double-back through a side street to get round Aldgate station and immediately ran into trouble. There were cars parked on both sides of the narrow street, leaving just enough room for one vehicle to thread its way through. The only problem was that the vehicle in front of Armstrong was a green Transit van and it had decided to stop halfway down the street.

A girl wearing green overalls jumped out of the driver's side and sprinted round to the double doors at the back. She opened them to reveal the back of the van stacked deck to roof with boxes of plants. She began unloading them two at a time and carried them to the pavement, piling them on the kerb between the front bumper of a parked BMW and the rear lights of an ancient Renault.

'Bugger the bitch, bugger the bitch!' Amy swore and I heard her grab for the door handle.

'Stay here,' I said, slipping Armstrong into neutral and flinging my door open, 'and look pregnant.'

By now there were three cars behind Armstrong so there was no way I could reverse. The girl from the van spotted this as well.

'Don't give me no grief,' she shouted over the noise of running engines. 'I've got to get this lot stashed for the flower market. More than my life's worth.'

'Come on, lady, you're totally stuffing the Queen's highway,' I shouted back, grabbing three of the cardboard trays from the Transit.

'Don't crush them, them's my net profit. I've got a living to make, you know.'

'So do I, darling.'

We passed between kerb and van and I dumped my trays on the hood of the BMW.

'Yeah, yeah, yeah,' she said, loading up again. 'Everyone 's in such a bleedin' rush these days.'

'Tell me about it, lady. I've got a seriously pregnant mum-to-be in the back of my cab, just about ready to pod.'

'Oh, shite-in-a-bucket,' she said as we passed again. 'Get the last four would yer? I'll nip round the block.'

'Won't somebody nick them?' I shouted over my shoulder as I dumped another three trays on the BMW. The windscreen was no longer visible.

'If you can't smoke it, they don't grow it round here,' she said. 'Get going. Come down Columbia Road on Sunday and I'll get you a bunch of fresh for the mother.'

'Cheers, love.'

I had my hands under the bottom of the last four boxes as she climbed behind the wheel and gunned the engine. I lifted the boxes just as she drove off, leaving me in the middle of the street.

I planted the boxes on the roof of the BMW and ran back to Armstrong as a door opened down the street and somebody yelled, 'Oi!'

The Transit van was at the end of the street, indicating right, its back doors swinging wildly as I found first gear. It had disappeared by the time I got into second and then we had a clear run at Brick Lane.

'There are lights on in there,' I shouted through the passenger divide as Armstrong careered by Moklis' camera shop.

'They work all hours,' Amy yelled in my ear. Her hand came through and gripped my shoulder. 'Pull up! Stop! What're you doing?'

'Getting out of the way, ' I snapped, 'in case we need the fire brigade to get through.'

That wasn't strictly true. I had no intention of letting Armstrong II get caught in a blast, if there was one. And if there was, we might need some intact transport urgently.

'So where's the nearest fire station?'

'Christ knows. Old Street? I dunno.'

I steered Armstrong up on to the kerb on the the corner and killed the engine.

'They'd never make it in time, not with the traffic,' she said as we piled out. 'That's why they would have timed it for now.'

'Timed what? There's nothing to say—'

We were running back down the street now, Amy pulling ahead.

'I hope I'm wrong but if I wanted to cause maximum—'

Thirty metres away the glass in a second-storey window above the camera shop cracked like a whip and a cloud of smoke seemed to punch large shards out into the street, shattering and tinkling as they landed. From the shattered window came a whoofing sound and tongues of flame flicked out like snakes' tongues tasting the air.

And we were running *towards* this?

We were going in through the shop when we ran into Moklis coming out of the back. He was staggering, a long cut on his forehead dribbling blood down one side of his nose, and he blundered into the back of the counter.

Amy grabbed the front of his shirt and brought his face down to hers. Even I could see that he couldn't focus properly on the floor let alone Amy.

'How many are there back there?' she asked him.

'I can't see—' he said, holding his hands away from his eyes.

'Where's Roshan Ara?' I tried.

'Light. White light. Can't see— I fell down the stairs—'

'Leave him,' I said to Amy and for a second I thought she was going to hit me. 'Point him at the door and push him out. He'll live.'

Then I was into the rabbit warren that was the back of the building and to my right was a staircase with smoke seeping and curling around the landing like early morning mist. The smoke stung my eyes and nostrils but I shut out those senses and concentrated on my ears. From upstairs, somewhere beyond the smoke, came the crackling of the fire and then a cough, then another.

I felt Amy up close behind me. She pushed me in the small of the back.

'Come on, there's somebody up there.'

'Wait.' I put out an arm to stop her lunging up the stairs. 'Listen.'

'What?'

'Through there.' I pointed down the dark and winding corridor where Moklis had once led me to meet Mujib Ur Rehman. 'Sewing machines.'

'Fuck! They're still working.'

'Is there a fire escape that way?'

'What do you think?'

'Them first.'

As I ran I could hear Amy's heels clacking on the bare floor behind me. Her red power suit jacket and short skirt were hardly practical examples of what the smartly-dressed firefighter was wearing these days, but she wasn't complaining.

I turned left into an even darker corridor but Amy said, 'No, here,' and pulled me up a set of three steps and down another wallpapered alley. Then I bounced off a damp wall and we were bursting through a door and I was colliding with a still warm washing machine, but I didn't have time to swear as Amy was putting her shoulder to another plywood door and the noise was such that I wouldn't have heard myself.

Amy screamed and I yelled, hopping on one leg and rubbing the other which had caught the edge of the washing machine.

There were sixteen women in the room, sitting at banks of sewing machines putting the finishing touches to the latest batch of TALtops. They were either enjoying the work or needed the money badly. Maybe they were just deaf from the drilling of those awful jack-hammer needles. Either way, they didn't turn a hair.

Amy grabbed the first Bangladeshi woman by the shoulders and the look on her face was such that I was sure she hadn't been at all aware of us bursting into the room. What chance had she had of hearing a bomb go off next door?

Amy screamed at her, got literally in her face, but all she got back was fear and incomprehension. The Bangladeshi woman second in line only reacted to the fact that the first woman's machine had stopped sewing in a straight line. She hadn't even noticed Amy screaming at and grabbing the woman next to her.

We had more chance of clearing the room by explaining it with finger puppets to each one of them individually and so I resorted to one of my long-standing philosophical maxims and thought: Stuff this for a bunch of soldiers.

I looked up at the cracked and stained ceiling, following the track of the power cables which hung down to each machine. The mother cable ran the length of the room and I followed it to where it hit the corner behind me and came down the wall about three feet to an ancient black bakelite fuse box just above a metal sink with two taps and a draining board. I might have known those old friends water and electricity would go together in a place like this.

There was one big trip switch and I tripped it. The lights went out and the whine of the machines trailed off like a departing swarm of bees.

The silence may have been golden, but it lasted no longer than it took for the women to draw breath. Then they started screaming.

At first they screamed at the darkness, so I flicked the trip switch up again and the lights came back. Two of the women stopped screaming and immediately hit the foot pedals of their machines.

Amy wrenched the garment – it was a TALtop – from the machine of the first woman she had grabbed and waved it above her head, shouting: 'Quiet! Quiet!', until the renegade machinists recognised her and stopped.

Then they all started screaming again because they were looking at Amy, or rather behind her, at a plume of grey smoke coming out of the corridor as if it was auditioning for *Ghostbusters*.

Amy started shouting at them again, but there was no way she would win this time. They all knew there was one way in and one way out, and that was where the smoke was coming from. They began to push back their chairs and stand up and clutch each other, totally ignoring Amy and me. Didn't they appreciate we were trying to save them? Still, if you want a job done well—

I jumped to the metal sink and turned both taps on full, the squealing and rumbling of the plumbing lost in the female scream-fest. Then I caught the TALtop Amy was waving about her head like a demented bullfighter and pulled it and her over to the sink, scrunching up the material and ramming it under the spouting water. I made kneading motions as if I was showing her how to make bread and she caught on and took over, squashing the TALtop to absorb more water.

I pulled another TALtop from the second machinist and showed it to her and the other women and waved them to follow me over to the sink. I pushed the second TALtop under the water and pulled out the first, sodden one, working the neck open and thrusting it over Amy's head. Using the drawcords for the waist, I tightened it around her head, mouth and nose, so that only her eyes showed. Then I pushed her to the smoking doorway.

'Go! Lead them out!'

By then the women had caught on and were tearing the tops from their machines and rushing for the sink. I almost got trampled on, although one of them had the foresight to rip open a pack of finished, white, TALtops and hand one to me.

It was a kind thought. I had seen the way the dye had come out of the blue one I had dressed Amy in and knew that she'd kill me if we ever got out of this.

She'd never get that blue stain out of her red felt jacket.

30.

Now

'So the building was on fire when you ran into it. Is that right, sir?'

'More or less,' I said wearily.

'We don't normally recommend that, sir,' said the Senior Fire Officer.

'I can see why,' I said, 'but you just had to be there.'

I nudged Amy and her head flopped against my shoulder.

'Come on, don't Bogart the oxygen.'

She handed me the cylinder and I fitted the plastic mask over my face, drawing in deep, chest-burning draughts.

'You don't have a pint of lager about your person by any chance?' Amy asked the fireman.

'You seem to be recovering,' he grinned. 'I'll be back in a minute. Just got to check on the others.'

When I could breathe without my throat hurting, I took the portable oxygen cylinder from my face and turned it off.

'Do I look a mess?'

We were sitting on the edge of the pavement down the street from what was left of the camera shop. We were only a few feet from Armstrong but that was where the Fire Brigade had taped the street off and now a crowd of rubber-neckers had gathered around him to gawk.

Amy stretched out her legs into the road. Her black tights were ripped in several places that hadn't been fashionable for five years. The heel of her left shoe was missing and her skirt had a hole burned in it over the left thigh. But it was above the waist where the most spectacular damage had occurred. The TALtop she had used as a smoke mask had seeped blue dye into the shoulders of her red felt jacket and through on to her white shirt, not to mention on to her cheeks, throat and neck, though I didn't think she'd realised that yet.

'Yes, you do,' I said, putting an arm around her.

She pulled down the neck of her shirt and peered down. 'Oh, bloody hell, I've got blue boobs. Look!'

She turned into my chest so I could.

'Mmm. Different,' I agreed, noticing that my hands were blue from where I'd soaked the first top for her. 'That could take some serious scrubbing.'

'How's my hair?'

'Smells as if you've done a double shift down the flame-grill Burger King, but otherwise not even singed.'

'You too. Good idea using these.'

She pulled the white TALtop over my head. I had forgotten it was there, the last of its dampness cool and comforting around my neck.

'I never thought of marketing these as some sort of firefighter's kagool.'

'You will.'

I smiled into her eyes and tried not to giggle at the blue dye on her cheeks as our lips got closer and both of us tried to moisten them without the other noticing.

'Now there's touching, don't you think, Steve?' said a voice above us.

'Hello again, Mr Stokoe. What brings you here?'

'DC Sell and an unmarked Ford Mondeo actually.' He rocked on his heels, his hands in his trouser pockets bunching up the folds of his raincoat. 'But you don't want to hear my witty banter, do you, Fitzroy? It's been a busy day for you one way and another. You must be shagged out.'

'Maybe not quite yet,' sniggered Sell beside him.

'Now, now, Steve, that's no way to talk about our local hero.' He nodded towards Amy. 'And heroine, of course. We have to treat them with velvet gloves, Constable, heroes like this. No nasty questions for them.'

'Just get on with it,' I said dismissively, patting my pockets for cigarettes I knew weren't there.

'No, I'm serious, Fitzroy. You are a hero, according to all the assorted lowlife DC Sell knows around here. The building was on fire when you ran into it, right?'

'So the Fire Chief said,' I said, spoiling his next few jokes.

'Well, that takes balls – pardon my French, Ms May, because I'm including you in this. Running in like that with no thought of personal safety and then leading those women out... How many was it?'

I made no attempt to answer, but he had been asking Sell.

'Witnesses told the Fire-boys it was anything from thirty to fifty, guv. Funny thing is, none of 'em seem to have stuck around, not even to say thank you.'

'There's gratitude for you. Still, quite something, bringing them all out through the smoke like that. But then to go back in again – alone this time, I believe?'

Amy nodded. I had left her to look after the machinists and

Moklis, still unable to see properly, when I had realised that Roshan Ara had not emerged. I had found her upstairs, her denim jacket smouldering between the shoulder blades, her face black and her tongue out. She was crawling along the landing, dragging the unconscious Mujib Ur Rehman behind her.

'That was something to see, by all accounts, and the first fire engine on the scene did see it, so you've got a witness. Wish I'd seen it. You coming out of that towering inferno with that young girl on your arm and that old geezer slung over your shoulder.'

'I only did it because I thought the TV cameras would be here by then.'

'And they're still not, are they? So your Good Samaritan act will go unappreciated by the wider world. What a shame, eh Steve?'

'Very sad, guv.'

'Still, you'll get your reward in heaven no doubt, Mr Angel. Now simply isn't the time to ask you if you saw anything when you just happened to arrive here, is it?'

'Such as?'

I knew I shouldn't have asked and Amy thought so too if her grip on my thigh was anything to go by.

'It's just that this Mr Moklis Ali, who runs the, shall we say, camera shop there; he says he's sure he heard something like a window smashing. This is before you showed up, of course.'

'So?'

'So he went upstairs and walked into a blinding flash. Sent him blind – it's only temporary though. The Fire-boys are sure it was some sort of magnesium or phosphorous-based incendiary device. He, this Moklis character, blunders out of the room and goes arse over tip down the stairs only to run into you. We were just wondering whether you saw anything in the street before you wandered into all this. Somebody on a motorbike, maybe? Somebody doing a drive-by perhaps?

'You see, we think this might have been a racially-motivated attack. We were just wondering how the device got inside. We did find these inside.'

He reached inside the poacher's pocket of his raincoat and produced a couple of sheets of paper. They were crumpled but suspiciously unsinged, though clearly recognisable as Gare de L'Est leaflets on do-it-yourself urban terrorism.

When I had last seen them, Amy had been clutching them as we had left Peter the Printer's place.

'Didn't see a thing, Mr Stokoe,' I answered after a pause. 'Like I said, the building was on fire when I ran into it.'

*

I kept my arm round Amy's waist as she hobbled towards Armstrong on her one good shoe.

The crowd of rubberneckers had dispersed and gone home. There was probably something really good on TV. I didn't blame them. It hadn't actually been that impressive a fire. Lots of smoke from smouldering bales of fabrics and boxes of melted trainers, but no explosions or anything. The fabric of the building hadn't suffered, apart from the windows popping and in fact it now blended in nicely with some of the uninhabited properties down the street.

Round on Brick Lane itself, the Balti houses were firing themselves up for the Friday night trade, traffic was moving, the Fire Brigade were winding up their hoses.

Mujib Ur Rehman, Roshan and Moklis were all carted off to hospital for observation, though all three vocally resented it, especially old Mujib who had many observations of his own to make on the National Health Service. He only went quietly when one of the paramedics said he could go private and they would give him a bill for his insurance company.

'Fancy a curry?' I asked Amy as we reached Armstrong.

'Oh, my sweet Lord,' she gasped, catching sight of herself in Armstrong's wing mirror. 'Why didn't you tell me I looked like this?'

'OK then, a takeaway.'

'Not even that until I've had—'

'Angel.'

It was a quiet interruption from a tall, bespectacled man who had stepped out of the shadows in front of Armstrong. I took him in with one glance and a white Mercedes sports car with no lights on with another.

'Hello, Ritchie,' I said, opening the rear door for Amy.

Ritchie Fortune looked over my shoulder, then over his shoulder, and when he was sure there were no uniforms of any sort around, he took a step forward and put a finger on Armstrong's bonnet. Just his right index finger, like he was making a point.

'Just want you to know,' he said softly, 'I've asked around and this is none of my people's doing.'

'I know that, Ritchie.'

He pursed his lips and tilted his head.

'Do they know that?'

'Yes, they do. They're not going to blame your lot.'

They might blame me, but they wouldn't be out looking for revenge in Islington.

'So everything's cool, then?'

'For now.'

He nodded his satisfaction at that and started across the street.

The lights were on and the engine revving in the Mercedes before he got to the passenger door.

'Who was that?' asked Amy as I climbed behind the wheel.

'Community Relations Officer,' I said.

31.

Now

'Come *on*, Fenella, shake a leg.'

The door opened and Fenella parted the hair in front of her eyes like a curtain.

'It had to be you, Angel, didn't it. It's Saturday morning, you know. I'm entitled to a lie-in.'

'Fenella, sweetie, you're unemployed. I know you go back to bed every morning after Lisabeth's gone to work.'

'Shush!' She held a finger to her lips and closed the door a smidgeon in case we woke the sleeping dragon. 'I suppose you're scrounging breakfast again?'

'No. Actually, I'm… Have you got anything to spare?'

'I've got some snail cakes,' she said over a yawn.

'What?'

'Croissants. We used to call them snail cakes when I was little.'

From the way the extra large West Ham (away strip) shirt was hanging on her, I think she meant *young* rather than little, but I let it pass.

'That'll do. Any chance of four?'

'Good thing I bought extra, isn't it?' she said sleepily.

She turned and walked to her kitchen and I eased the door open wider so that I could watch her retreating figure. The West Ham shirt had the name, as they all do now, of a player across the shoulders. In Fenella's case it was that of an expensive Rumanian winger who had lasted about a month before being sold on. That meant Fenella would have got the shirt cheap. From the way she moved in it, though, she might get a game herself.

She returned and handed me four croissants in a cellophane bag.

'Any butter?' I smiled sweetly.

Without changing her expression, she produced her left hand from behind her back and handed over a pack of slightly-salted.

'Thanks. Jam?'

'We're on a diet,' she said tersely.

'Don't worry, I think I'm OK for jam,' I said, remembering that I had borrowed some earlier in the week.

'I'm so glad. What have you done to your hands?'

'Ah, yes, that's what I came about. Have you got anything for removing stains?'

'What sort of stains?'

'Blue ones... Oh, I see. It's fabric dye.'

She pinched her chin with thumb and forefinger.

'Saponaria leaves swished up in water are supposed to be good. They turn all soapy and it would be ever so kind to your skin.'

That sounded just the thing for Amy's stains, which were in a far more sensitive place than mine. I had also choked at the idea of suggesting she used my Jif kitchen scourer and a pan scrub.

'Good call, sweetie. Can I borrow some of this... whatever.'

'Saponaria, but I haven't got any. Lemon juice might do.'

'Can I—?'

'But I'm out of lemons.'

'Gee, thanks a bunch.'

She made to close the door, yawning again.

'You might try Jif kitchen scourer and a pan scrub,' she said.

'Won't that hurt?'

'Get a friend to do it. It'll still hurt but you won't notice so much.'

I was shocked.

'Really, Fenella, who told you that?'

'Lisabeth.'

*

We hadn't done anything about the stains, or anything much else, when we had finally made it back to Stuart Street. We managed a cold beer each and I made a half-hearted attempt to calculate how much food there was in the fridge, but gave up when I saw Amy's eyelids start to droop.

Sleep is the natural consequence of, and antidote to, delayed shock. The discovery of what Lyn and her boyfriend Wolfgang had been up to, the frustration of the drive from Southwark, the fire and then Ritchie Fortune turning up out of the dark, had all taken their toll.

Within five minutes of sitting down and kicking off her one-and-a-half shoes, Amy was fading and only mumbling answers to my inane questions. I caught her bottle of lager as it slipped from her hand, then I peeled off her jacket and tucked her legs up on to the sofa.

My jacket fell off me as I stomped into the bedroom and when I was within range I let myself fall forwards on to the bed. I had a brief recollection that Springsteen had to leap out of the way before I hit the duvet and I knew I would pay for it later, but I was asleep before I bounced.

It took three cups of coffee and Fenella's croissants to get Amy's engine started the next morning.

Once she was fired up, though, she moved like a blur and, of course, it was all my fault. How could I have let her sleep in her clothes? What was that brown stain on her dress? Why hadn't I told her that her hair reeked of smoke? Why in God's name had her breasts turned blue?

We hit the shower together, me armed with a plastic bottle of Jif cleaner.

While Amy used my hairdryer I sorted out some clothes for her. She'd told me casually to burn the ones she'd been wearing and I said it looked as if somebody already had.

I dug out a pair of denim deck shoes which just about fitted her, thanks to some thick white sports socks that I'd bought on a fitness binge and only worn once. She raised an eyebrow at the pair of seer-sucker trousers I produced and I don't think she believed me when I said they had been a mistake by the mail order people. And when I offered her one of her own TALtops, still in its packaging, she asked how many other free samples Mujib had given me. I told her just that one, working on the theory that she wouldn't think of looking in the big drawer under the bed.

'It'll have to do, I suppose,' she said, flicking her hair with a brush in front of the bathroom mirror, 'until you drive me home.'

She had worked the drawstrings on the TALtop so that it was round-necked (to cover up the still pink scrub marks) and tied at the waist just above the trousers. I thought she looked good, but I would say that.

'Once I've changed I'll treat you to lunch, OK? We've got some catching up to do.'

I said 'yes' to both offers, but as it turned out, our timing was way out.

We made it as far as Armstrong. I had even got the key in the lock. Then they appeared, parking an unmarked Rover three spaces away.

'Oh, no,' I said under my breath. 'Good morning Mr Stokoe, Mr Sell.'

They both consulted their watches in a well-rehearsed move.

'Hate to be picky, Fitzroy,' said Stokoe, 'but it's afternoon. Can we have a word with the two of you?'

'We were just going over to Amy's place to—' I started.

'I don't think that's a good idea, do you, guv?' said Sell.

Stokoe didn't answer him. He just said, 'Inside.'

'Have you picked up Lyn and Wolfgang?' I asked them as soon as we were back in my flat. 'Is that what this is all about?'

Stokoe settled himself in my one good chair. Sell sat on the arm of the sofa and leaned over to stroke Springsteen who had wandered in to conduct his own investigation. It would serve him right.

'The French police got them both in Paris last night. They went on separate trains but Wolfgang made no bones about giving her up to the *flics*. Seems he's quite happy to put her in the frame for anything he can.'

'Bastard. Poor Lyn,' said Amy, but not all that convincingly.

'Charges are being drawn up as we speak—'

'Bloody Nora!' screamed Sell, clutching his hand.

'That'll teach you to be nice to animals, Steve,' said Stokoe with a big grin as Sell sucked the slash wounds on his wrist. But I noticed he moved his legs out of Springsteen's majestic path across the room and into the kitchen.

'Though it does mean that we can't link them to your fire last night,' he went on.

'Does it?' I didn't like the idea of it being *my* fire one bit.

'They weren't in the country when somebody threw that device through the window.'

'Is that how it started?'

'Can't think of any other way.' He paused, as I knew he would. 'Can you?'

'Nope.'

'Still, we've got enough on Wolfgang with what we found at the printer's. He's been very cooperative. The two of you have been very helpful. But no, it's not.'

'Not what?'

'Not what this is all about.'

I looked from one to the other, then at Amy. She looked as confused as I felt.

'Then what is it all about?'

Stokoe nodded to Sell, who took his hand away from his mouth before speaking.

'Thalia Leonard was arrested by Kent police at around 10 o'clock last night. She escaped just after 7 a.m. this morning.'

It took a lifetime for it to sink in. It was in fact perhaps a minute.

'Arrested for what?'

I should have noticed then that it was me who had to ask, not her friend and business partner.

'Suspicion of the murder of Eugene Vincent Sargeant, eight days ago,' said Sell as if he was reading from a notebook in court.

'How long have you had her in the frame?'

'Interesting question, Fitzroy,' said Stokoe. 'Most people would have said no, not her, couldn't be, wouldn't harm a fly, all that stuff. You just wanted—'

'You've had her tagged all along, haven't you?'

'From the off.' Stokoe smiled wickedly.

'You might have said something when you pulled me,' I complained.

'Would we have got to Wolfie Mansfeld if we had?'

'You'd have found a way. That was all you were after, wasn't it?'

'I made no secret of it. I told you I had my speciality, people like Wolfie. This investigation was a good way to stir things up, see what came out of the woodwork.'

'While the real detectives stitched up Thalia.'

'Hardly stitched up. We knew Sargeant was interested in the TAL girls. Lyn Buttress had an alibi for last Friday night. She was at a National Front meeting in Barking with Wolfie. We know. We had one of our blokes there undercover.

'Ms May here, her alibi checked out watertight... '

Alibi? She didn't have one except for me and she hadn't been with me.

'So that just left Thalia Leonard, we just couldn't find her. Funny name, that, Thalia. Irish is it?'

'Where did you find her?' Amy asked slowly.

'Down in Deal, near Dover, as we thought.'

'She was hiding in a sort of safe house,' said Sell, 'but once the local Plod started rounding up the usual coven members, they soon—'

'Excuse me?' I jumped in. 'Coven?'

'As in witches,' said Stokoe as if he was explaining the way to Big Ben to a tourist. 'There's quite a ring of them down there, something to do with the White Cliffs, like in the song. Most of 'em are harmless of course, but some of them go a bit over the top.'

'Over each other, more like,' Sell chipped in.

Amy had said Kent, even mentioned Dover specifically. But she'd said it to me when Lyn was there, not to the cops.

'No doubt there was a certain amount of lewd behaviour—'

'Shagging.'

'Very well, Detective Constable, shagging. No doubt there was shagging involved in Miss Leonard's particular version of black magic. We don't know for sure and nobody seems keen to offer too many details down in Deal, but I think it's a fair bet that was what drew Vince Sargeant down there.'

'I'm sorry?' I heard a clicking noise which was probably my jaw dropping. 'The Sarge was in this... this coven?'

'Shouldn't think so, not for a minute, but he certainly went down to Deal at least twice, at night. We checked with a mini-cab firm he used. He didn't have a car, you see, used to get a car and a driver and sometimes he'd charge it to the newspaper. We're tracing the drivers he used but I reckon he was following Thalia Leonard.

'When he spotted her taking off her clothes and dancing round a bonfire chopping the heads off black and white chickens or whatever it is she did, then he whipped out his Box Brownie and ran off a few snaps. He was a photographer, you know. In fact, you helped us there, because those films you identified round at Sargeant's place showed us that there were four or maybe five films missing from his filing sequence. Whoever killed him took them.'

'Hang on, hang on, this won't wash.' I shook my head, to clear it more than anything else.

'Is he gonna debate it, guv?' Sell grinned.

'I do hope so, Steve. You know I love a good debate. Go on, Fitzroy, spit it out.'

'Look, from what I know of my brief acquaintance with Thalia,' – I hoped they noticed the *brief* – 'she was not the sort of woman who would be worried about somebody taking pictures of her without her clothes on. I would have said she was more likely to have asked for a set of ten-by-eights.'

'You might be right, Fitzroy. Maybe she didn't care for herself and everything we've heard about her so far tells us she wasn't what you'd call a prude. But what about photographs of the people with her? Her followers, if you like.'

'Followers?'

'Oh, yes. She was something of a priestess in the weird circles she moved in, or so we hear. She's recruited one or two interesting people into her coven. You know, the odd MP, a sprinkling of BBC producers, a minor film star, a couple of members of the House of Lords, that sort of thing. This is just rumour at the moment, but if it was half-true, and young Vincent got them on film, wouldn't that give her a motive – protecting her coven?'

I couldn't think of anything to say. Even if I had, it would have been near-impossible with my jaw somewhere down around my knees. I turned to Amy, floundering, but she was eyeballing Stokoe. It was almost as if I wasn't there.

'You said she'd escaped,' she said to Sell.

'My colleague did not lie, I'm afraid.' Stokoe leaned forward and clasped his hands together on his knees. 'Some very sloppy station house police work is to blame and questions will be asked down in Deal, I can tell you.'

Sell couldn't resist telling us the details.

'The duty officer took in her breakfast instead of waiting for a policewoman. She was naked and… ' he caught Amy's glare, 'and doing things to herself… '

Stokoe took over as Sell began to blush.

'She seemed to be having a good time, so the duty officer was off guard. Maybe he even thought about joining in; who knows? He's not saying, but what he does admit to is that she cold-cocked him with a left uppercut any heavyweight would have been proud of. She pulls on her clothes and legs it, jumps over the front desk like a hurdler and vanishes. But that's another piece of the case against her.'

'What is? Seducing a sleeping policeman?' It came out before I could think.

'Ho ho, sleeping policeman, very good Fitzroy. No, the fact that she was left-handed. Forensics now say that Vince Sargeant was killed with a left-handed stabbing motion. Miss May here and Lyn Buttress are both right-handed.'

I took a deep breath in through the nose, then a top-up one, held it and let it out through my mouth slowly, counting to ten in my head – just like the counsellors tell you to do.

'Now hold on, while I get this straight. You've got a prime suspect, a motive and some circumstantial evidence, right? Well, apart from the fact that you've mislaid your prime suspect.'

'She was spotted in Dover a couple of hours ago,' said Sell, defending his professional pride. 'We'll get her.'

'She was digging in the garden of an empty house, funnily enough,' Stokoe chipped in. 'A neighbour called it in and then described her to the hilt.'

'What for?' Amy said.

'We don't know. She got whatever it was, though. A passport? Stash of cash? Her bank account hasn't been touched since Wednesday. Have you got any ideas?'

'No,' she said quickly.

'Whatever,' I resumed my flow. 'Your prime suspect isn't us, is it? And you've got Lyn and Wolfgang, so why are you here? Why not just leave us alone?'

Stokoe put on his hurt expression. It was one I doubted he had ever used sincerely.

'Only here to warn you, that's all. If Thalia Leonard was unstable enough to kill once, not to mention seriously damaging a policeman this morning, then she's dangerous. And she's on the loose.'

'Dangerous? Why tell me? What have I ever done to her?'

Stokoe looked straight at Amy.

'I wasn't talking to you, Fitzroy,' he said.

32.

Now

'In your own time,' I said gently. 'Whenever you're ready.'
I was tactful, I was considerate, I didn't bully. Inside, I was screaming: We Have Ways Of Making You Talk, and measuring up her fingernails for the sharpened matchsticks.

We were in a Chinese restaurant and such was the state I was in, I couldn't for the life of me remember what it was called this week. It was local, though. We hadn't strayed far from Stuart Street since Stokoe and Sell had left us that afternoon.

We had gone shopping – locally – for clothes for her and cat food, a bottle of Wild Turkey and a pack of cigarettes for me. She had picked out two polo-neck shirts, a pair of jeans and new underwear in the time it took me to choose which brand of cigarettes I wanted. The shoes took longer though, and she ended up buying two pairs – the first two pairs she'd liked in the first shop we'd visited – two minutes before the stores closed.

And all the time, we had hardly spoken except for the usual banalities exchanged between regular couples out shopping every Saturday.

Give her time, I had said to myself.

Time to get her story straight, I thought to myself.

It was time. Over the Mongolian lamb and the *Mah-Po* bean curd, it was now time.

I had to start.

'They never said anything about the picture of Wolfgang.'

Amy dabbed at something with her chopsticks.

'The Sarge had taken a picture of Wolfgang. The cops showed it to me the other day, but they've not mentioned it since.'

I was still being calm and not really thinking about hitting her with a bottle of Tsingtao beer at all.

'He had pictures of us all,' she said moodily.

'What?'

'Don't stop me,' she said, which I thought was a bit rich. 'Your friend Sargeant followed us. All of us. Me, Thalia and Lyn. He took pictures. That policeman, Stokoe, was dead right; probably doesn't know how right. Thalia was playing with some very odd people. Some of them connected or at least well-known faces.

'Sargeant followed her down to Deal or Dover – I don't know exactly where – and photographed a ceremony, a pretty sick one.'

'How sick?'

She looked up from her bowl.

'It involved killing a cat.'

That was it. I was joining the pro-hanging lobby first thing Monday.

'Go on.'

'He recognised some of the faces, knew he had a story. That was his big scoop. The pictures of Lyn and Wolfgang drinking with some skinheads and doing Nazi salutes, they were less commercial.'

'He was blackmailing you?'

'Us.'

'Did you pay?'

'A down payment he called it. One thousand in cash. It can't be traced.'

'Each?'

'No, just me. I thought I could stall him. I never said anything to Lyn and he wouldn't have dared go near Wolfgang with a deal like that. Thalia must have taken matters into her own hands.'

Or into her left hand anyway, I thought.

Then I had a more serious thought.

'You said all of you. What did The Sarge have on you?'

She smiled then.

'Where do you think I've been recently?'

'Avoiding me?'

She smiled again, put down her chopsticks and took my hand in hers. It must have felt like putty.

'No, just busy. I've been in meetings with people.'

'If you're in a meeting you're not with a customer,' I quoted back at her.

'Yes, yes, I know. But this was important. I'm selling the company to one of the big High Street chains – I can't say which yet – but it's involved some fairly nifty footwork since all this blew up.'

I sat back, fumbled out a cigarette and lit up. Amy glared disapprovingly but said nothing, picked up her chopsticks and carried on eating.

'You mean it wouldn't look good if one of your partners was up on a witchcraft-related murder charge and the other was busy fire-bombing the East End?'

'Something like that.'

I finished the cigarette in three draws and stubbed it out before I spoke again.

'On the other hand, if one of your partners was up on a murder charge and the other being held for inciting racial hatred, then that's two partners less to consult about selling the company, isn't it?'

She reached out again and this time stroked the back of my hand.

'It sounds harsh, I know, but there is a lot of money at stake, more than I'd ever dreamed of. It would be the big time for me and the company. High Street distribution, quality control, marketing, distribution nationally. And I think I want you to be a part of it. We are good together. We fit well.'

'Hah! What's all this "we" business all of a sudden?'

'I mean it.'

'I'm not even your alibi for the night The Sarge was killed, am I?'

She shrugged.

'I told the police I was with the chief executive of one of the large department stores, but made them promise not to tell anyone. It was true; they checked it out.'

'Did you tell your partners you'd given The Sarge a grand in blackmail?'

'No.'

'But you told them about the pictures The Sarge was selling, didn't you?'

'Just Thalia. She had to know about them,' she was almost pleading.

'But you didn't tell her – them – that you were planning to sell the company, did you?'

She shook her head.

'So you wound up Thalia and let her go?'

'Oh, come on, I didn't think she'd go this far.'

Something else struck me.

'And you'd known about Lyn's little hobby for some time, hadn't you? She was easy to set up, wasn't she?'

'It was only a matter of time. I had spotted the police watching Wolfgang and the Web 18 office. Good God, you're not defending what she's been doing are you?'

'No,' I said slowly, thinking. 'No, she deserves what she gets.'

And Thalia, the cat-killer, was beyond the pale too. But in truth, I wasn't worried about either of them.

'You told the cops where Thalia was, didn't you?'

She didn't answer. Cool as anything she flagged a waiter who brought a pair of hot towels on a plate and cleared away the debris of the meal. Amy wiped her fingers on one of the towels and then dabbed her lips daintily.

'Thalia will have worked that out, won't she?' I said. 'And now she's on the loose. No wonder you've been looking over your shoulder all afternoon.'

'So have you,' she said, and it was true I had. 'But I can't think why. The police will pick her up. As long as we stay here we'll be OK.'

That 'we' again.

'After all,' said Amy, 'she doesn't know where you live.'

33.

Now

Good sex sends you cross-eyed. Regular good sex destroys both the long and short term memory. I am convinced of this. That Sunday morning I woke up and for a good fifteen minutes, didn't have a care in the world. Then Amy woke up, rolled over and smiled at me.

Which smile was this one? Was it the businesswoman cutting her partners out of a deal, or the professional helper of the police? Was it the confident her-own woman who knew she could make a man look at her legs, but only if she wanted him to, or the unselfconscious girl who didn't mind eating fish and chips in the back of a delicensed cab? Was it the naturally secretive female who hadn't mentioned a house in Hampstead and an ex-husband? Or the lover who had already decided we were a good fit and that was all there was to it?

'*Goooood* morning,' she purred.

'Is it?' I said, playing it cool. Her hands moved under the duvet.

'It is now,' she said.

I forgot what I was worrying about.

'So, what do normal couples do on a Sunday morning in Hackney?' she asked as we finished breakfast.

'Are we a normal couple?' I asked, probably sounding more doubtful than I had meant to.

'OK, there are two of us, it's Sunday and we're in Hackney. Shall we start from that base? I wouldn't want to rush anything.'

I realised diplomacy was called for.

'Right then, let me think. We could start the day with some frenzied sexual activity.'

'Done that.'

'We could lie in bed until lunchtime reading the Sunday papers until the pubs open, then.'

'Do you have the Sunday papers delivered?'

'No, I usually read them down the pub.'

'Is that it then? Is that all there is to do in Hackney until the pubs open?'

'Of course not,' I lied, then had a brainwave. 'Do you like flowers? You know, plants, foliage, that sort of stuff. Grows in the country all the time.'

'What are you talking about?'

'The Columbia Road flower market. We could walk round there, it's not far and it's quite a sight.'

If you liked green stuff you couldn't smoke, that is.

The East End has always had a tradition of street markets, not just for fruit and vegetables or cheap clothes, which you could find anywhere, but specialist ones dealing only in antiques, or animals for domestic pets (now gone), or, like Columbia Road on Sundays, flowers.

I had never been clear just how many residents of Hackney, the majority of whom live in high-rise tower blocks, used the flower market but lots of people came in to it and nobody seemed to mind. The plants themselves didn't do much for me. I couldn't tell the difference between the trays of lobelia and the trays of begonia. I didn't want a bay tree trained as a standard, why should I? Bay leaves came in little jars from Mrs Patel's open-all-hours shop. Why would I want a harvest of them? And I simply wouldn't know where to put an ivy on a topiary frame, although I could envisage getting a few ideas if I'd had several drinks and Lisabeth was in the room. The oriental poppies sparked a bit of interest, but I realised they weren't that sort of poppy.

But if the main product of the market was of little interest, the market itself was fascinating. Good markets always are, whatever they're selling. The traders make it, a bit like a good landlord can create a brilliant atmosphere in the roughest of pubs.

And the Columbia Road traders were top whack good at their jobs.

'Pelargonium, five pound a tray. Do better, lady, see if you can.'

'Parsley, tarragon, mint, basil, you name it, it's 50p. Surprise yourself, take twelve mixed for a fiver.'

'Marguerites in pots, £1.50, and no you can't drink 'em, you grow 'em.'

'Summer bedding, darling? Or would you like some plants instead?'

I loved it: the banter, the blag. These guys were good and they were shifting some gear. Both sides of the road were lined with shoulder-to-shoulder stalls, the space in between jammed with a heaving, floating mass of customers, most of them spending money very freely.

A woman in a fur coat and more jewels hanging from her than was sensible in this neck of the woods, was handing over a wodge of twenty pound notes to one trader and saying loudly, 'It's the white Volvo over there, if you wouldn't mind.'

An old boy, probably a retired stallholder, was acting as banker, collecting cash from various traders and palming it into a leather satchel tied round his waist, but totally out of sight unless you were looking for it. He would wander off to a vehicle somewhere where younger, fitter members of the family would be waiting with a cash box, make a deposit, maybe get some change. To look at him, flat cap with holes in, filthy tweed overcoat, his face unshaven and unsmiling, you wouldn't think he had several thousand pounds strapped above his groin.

'Bloody hell, that's what I call getting your figure back quick.'

I stopped in my tracks at that, thinking it must be some sort of market code as it had come from behind one of the stalls.

'Had it in the back of the cab did she?'

I focussed on the mass of foliage on the stall nearest and realised there was somebody there wearing green overalls, which was very effective camouflage, and they were talking to me.

'Oh, hello,' I said, recognising the woman from the transit van who had blocked our life-saving dash to Brick Lane.

'You got her to the hospital on time, then?' she said, grinning at Amy. 'Must say she's looking well.'

Amy, who was holding my hand, began to squeeze.

'You told her I was having your baby?' she hissed from the corner of her mouth.

'Yeah, we made it. Mother and baby doing fine. It wasn't... it was—'

'Some other woman, yeah I know, tell me about it,' said the chirpy florist. 'Men, eh?' she said to Amy.

'Too right,' said Amy. 'What a waste of space.'

'I promised you some fresh, didn't I? For the mum.'

'No, honestly—' I started, but she was having none of it.

'Frankie!' she yelled to the next stallholder, though he was only an arm's length away. 'Give us one of your hospital specials. That's a B not a D.'

Amy squeezed my hand again.

'B for Birth, D for Death. Same basic bunch of flowers, I think, but one has lilies.'

Frankie handed her a wrapped bouquet over a stack of trays of plug plants which could have doubled as the last redoubt at Rorke's Drift.

'There you go,' the florist said to me, handing over the bouquet. 'Special price, ten quid to you.'

It was wiser not to argue, so I groped for my wallet and handed over a note.

'Thanks, love, they're great,' I said to her, but she was on to her next victim.

I turned towards Amy and presented the bouquet to her formally.

'And they said romance was dead,' she sighed.

I transferred my wallet to my inside pocket – you can never be too careful in a street market – and in doing so, I glanced down the street the way we had come. And there among the sea of happy gardening faces was one I recognised.

'What exactly am I supposed to do with these?' Amy was asking me.

'Sling 'em,' I said. 'Thalia's here.'

A moment ago it had been a chocolate-box scene, a riot of colours and textures. Impossibly balanced piles of plant trays, buckets of cut flowers in bloom, mini-forests of shrubs and staked climbing plants. Happy Sunday shoppers arguing about price and best practice. Cheerful Cockney wideboys selling wheelbarrows to people with twelfth-floor flats in high-rises.

And now it was a funnel, a gorge, a ravine, jammed end-to-end with people moving so slowly I wanted to scream. There was no way out to the sides because of the stalls. We just had to plough on through it.

'Come on, run!' I shouted in Amy's face.

'No, wait. We can—'

'No we can't. Run!'

I grabbed her by the wrist and began to pull her after me, using my left shoulder to push startled plant hunters out of the way.

The first victim was a middle-aged woman who cannoned into a stack of begonias in trays.

'Oi!'

'Watch it, pillock!'

'Leave it out!'

The next was a huge man carrying a bright yellow plastic bag of peat-free compost. It might have been peat-free but it still felt like a bag of bricks to me as I bounced off it, losing my grip on Amy in the process.

For a second I thought I had lost her completely. I even had a flash vision of her being rolled along Columbia Road under the feet of the shoppers like the obligatory sacrificial cowboy in the stampede scene of a thousand clichéd westerns. In fact she was just the other side of an upright fuscia being carried by a woman who could have been anyone's grandmother.

'Angel! Stop and talk to her!' Amy yelled.

'No! Don't!'

I remembered Stokoe acting out how she must have come up behind The Sarge in his flat, the description of her zapping the policeman down in Deal, how cool she had been in the days before The Sarge's body was found. How she must have stalked us from Stuart Street.

'Don't you push my nan,' growled a voice.

It was the huge bloke carrying the compost under one arm, the other, as thick as a cow's thigh, was straight-arming me in the chest. I felt as if I was being poked with a steel girder and the jostling crowds behind me seemed intent on pushing me on to it.

'No trouble, mate, no trouble.'

'Too fucking right, squire. You behave.'

'Amy!'

The natural momentum of the crowd was pushing us apart. Amy had stopped dead in her tracks and I tried to sidestep a couple who were struggling with a large pot plant trained up a cone-shaped frame that looked like a cross between a pagoda and a V1 launch pad.

I failed. They dropped the plant pot, I put my foot through the wire frame thing and I went down on to my hands and knees. Almost immediately somebody – and I swear it was the little old granny with the fuscia – stepped on my right hand. I yelped and tried to stand up but promptly fell over again, the green cone contraption now wrapped around both feet.

All around me people were shouting: 'Bloody hooligan', 'Stroll on', and 'Look out, he's pissed', and at least two of them landed well-placed kicks in passing. If these were peaceful organic gardeners pottering about on a Sunday morning, God knew what they must be like when the blood lust was raised at a main event such as the Chelsea Flower Show.

Then I was finally on my feet, and hands were tugging at my jacket and words such as 'damages' and 'pay for all this' were flying.

I couldn't see Amy or Thalia anywhere, there were simply too many people too close. Then there was a middle-aged man right in my face, waving an empty flower pot.

'I paid £9.50 for this—'

'Thanks.'

I grabbed it, dropped it upside-down on the road and hopped on to it, putting a hand on the man's shoulder for balance.

Across the bobbling sea of heads I spotted them, twenty, perhaps twenty-five metres away, floating towards the end of the street to my left. Amy was walking backwards, talking animatedly, trying to keep some breathing space between herself and Thalia who was advancing on her like an automaton.

'Do you bleedin' well—'

I pulled out my wallet and ripped some notes from it, not counting, just thrusting them at the man before pushing him out of the way and diving back into the crowd.

I knew I couldn't get to them in a straight line; a zigzag diagonal approach was the best I could manage, reaching out over the shoulders of the market goers as if trying to haul myself in on an invisible rope.

Through a gap in the crowd I caught sight of Thalia full-length for the first time. She was wearing a short black dress which was torn at one shoulder and at the hem so the lining hung down. The dress, her legs and her hair were streaked with dried brown mud. She looked as if she had climbed out of a grave and she was clutching something to her chest, something that looked like a rolled up blanket.

'Amy! Get away from her!'

Amy ignored me, perhaps she hadn't heard. Thalia had, though, and she turned to glare at me.

I was still stuck in a morass of oblivious humanity, but on seeing Thalia's face – mud-streaked, lips curled back in a rigid smile, her eyes shining and totally vacant – I was suddenly not all that keen to get too close.

Amy must have been waiting for the diversion. As soon as Thalia looked towards me, Amy swung the bouquet of flowers she was still holding and whacked her in the face.

She didn't wait for a second swing, she turned and began to run, but Thalia reacted quicker, lunging after her.

Another three faltering paces and I was behind her just as she was behind Amy. And suddenly the crowd was melting away from us and people were screaming.

I stumbled over something which sent me careering towards the last few stalls on the far side of the road. It was a filthy, dirt-encrusted blanket, the thing Thalia had been clutching like a baby. But it was what she had been carrying in it that had got the civilians screaming and anxious to give us enough room to get on with it.

Crazily, I noticed that Thalia was barefoot. I don't know why that bothered me as I should have been concentrating on the long-bladed knife with the white handle she was wielding at waist height. It wasn't a carving knife, it was more like a short Roman sword, the blade a good half a metre long. I just knew it would fit the hole in Vince Sargeant's head and I remembered that of all the things Stokoe and Sell had told us to draw us into their web, not once had they mentioned the murder weapon. That was because they didn't have it. Thalia had taken it with her and buried it in some back garden down in Kent.

The blade flashed in the sunlight as she swung the knife up and out to her left. A woman screamed and jumped to avoid it, piling into me, her head catching me under the chin and snapping my jaw up, rattling my teeth.

As I spun the woman out of the way, the blade started its return arc and I could do nothing except try and keep my balance as Amy screamed and went down and rolled over into the road.

My shoulder hit something soft but unyielding. It was a stack of plastic bags of compost, each about a metre long and half a metre wide, like solid, shiny pillows, and printed with instructions for planting tomatoes. I grabbed the stack to steady myself.

Amy rolled over twice, clutching the back of her right thigh. I could see where the material of her new jeans had been slashed; see the material darkening with a bloodstain.

I saw Thalia trip over Amy's flailing legs and almost fall, but, instead, she jumped over Amy, landed in the road, and turned, reversing the knife in her hand to aim a downward, stabbing, fatal, blow.

She was solid gone now, no pulling back. Her eyes blazed and I knew if I looked at them, I would be powerless to help.

My hands closed around the top grow-bag on the stack I had fallen against. I gripped the corners of the end nearest to me and I pulled and swung it as I jumped towards them.

The compost bag swept over Amy's head and smashed into Thalia's left shoulder, exploding and showering the three of us with fine black material.

Thalia dropped the knife as she staggered backwards under the force of the blow and then there was stuff – compost – in my eyes and I never did see clearly what happened, although I heard most of it even above the screaming and the swearing and the shouting.

There was no avoiding the awful, inevitable sound of brakes squealing in protest as they were jammed on. That unmistakable thud which always seems to come after a dreaded split second of silence, although that is probably just the brain being over dramatic in retrospect.

I could feel Amy scrabbling at my legs and I sank down on my knees next to her, rubbing filth and fine black dust out of my eyes. I fumbled an arm around her and she rocked against me, sobbing and howling 'Oh God, oh God… '

My eyes cleared, but I almost wished they hadn't.

A white Volvo estate car loaded with plants had reversed into the road. The woman driver, leaning out of her window, was shouting,

'I never saw her! I couldn't see… '

Thalia was lying ten feet away, face down, her head bent at an unnatural angle to her neck against the kerbside.

'Jesus Christ!'

'Get the fucking kids away!'

'Get an ambulance.'

'Somebody—'

I pulled Amy's head to my chest. Pairs of legs formed a forest around us.

'Do you know who she was, mate?' said a voice.

'Her name's Thalia,' I said, shaking my head.

'Tragic, mate, tragic. What sort of name's that, then? Swedish was she?'

'It's Greek, actually,' I said as we heard the first siren.

34.

Then

'What an animal. You're magnificent,' said Thalia.

She clicked her fingers above his nose and Springsteen reared up and butted her hand, staying there on his hind legs, nuzzling his way into her affections. I had seen him bring down birds in flight like that.

'What a handsome lad. What a beast.'

Springsteen was on his back now, letting her rifle the hair on his belly. He made no attempt to move, resist or draw blood. Maybe she'd drugged him. I was beginning to think she had drugged me.

'Just what are you doing here?' I asked, the words slurring.

She frowned at me.

'I thought we were going to see that off.'

I was holding the bottle of lemon flavoured vodka she had bought in the last bar we had hit together; the last of about seven. That had been somewhere in the City and it had seemed logical to get a real cab home, dropping me off first in Hackney before taking her on. Somehow she had ended up at Stuart Street.

'Oh, yeah,' I said, remembering. 'I'll get some glasses and some ice.'

When I returned from the kitchen and handed her a tumbler of vodka and ice, she was standing legs apart, bending right over at the waist, so that Springsteen could playfully bat at her dangling hair with his paws. He kept his claws sheathed and I feared he was losing his touch.

We sipped our drinks standing there facing each other. She was wearing a black TALtop and a very short hound's-tooth check skirt. Her high heels put her well over six foot so she looked down at me.

'Cheers.'

We chinked glasses and drank, keeping eye contact for far too long.

I broke the spell by flopping backwards to sit on the sofa. I stretched my legs out in front of me, aiming a pointless kick at Springsteen, and balanced my glass on my chest.

'What's the matter?' she asked with a smile. 'Tired?'

'Knackered. Where did I leave Armstrong?'

'Soho Square,' she said. Then: 'I think.'

'Which pub was that?'

'The third one. Maybe the fourth.'

'You're a bad influence.'

'I hope so,' she said, holding her drink in her left hand, pressing the glass against her cheek.

'Why? What have I ever done to you?'

She made an 'O' with her mouth in mock surprise.

'Insulted me, cut me to the quick, given me an inferiority complex. Nothing much.'

'Whadderyermean?' I slurred.

'Hold this.' She handed me her glass so I could drink two-fisted. But the thought was a fleeting one.

'I just couldn't believe you chose Amy's legs over mine, you know. It's been preying on my mind ever since.'

She snaked a hand to the side of her skirt and pulled a zip. The skirt dropped to her ankles and she stepped out of it towards me. Her thick, black shiny tights disappeared into the TALtop, making her legs go on forever.

'I thought I'd catch you on the rebound, get you drunk and then ask for a second opinion.'

She stood there for a minute, hands on hips, looking down at me, smiling.

'Well?' she said.

I just sat there like an idiot. A drink in each hand and a raging thirst.

She turned one foot to the right, altered the angle of her knees, slightly rotated her hips. Then she put her right foot between my outstretched legs and gently kicked them wider apart with her high heel.

'I can see I'm going to have to bribe the judge,' she said, sinking to her knees and reaching for me.

That was when I noticed she was left-handed.

35.

Much Later

'Have you lost weight, or have you just got a suit that fits?'
'Hello there, Duncan, there's a pint on the bar for you,' I said to him. Then to the others, 'It's nice to see them out in the community, isn't it?'

The pub was filling up, so I was glad we had started early enough to commandeer one of the round tables in the corner. The pub was called The Bank because it used to be a bank. The service had, however, improved beyond all measure.

Fenella and Lisabeth had, to my surprise, been the first to arrive, although they had waited outside on the pavement until I had spotted them as I was paying off my taxi.

'I told you no one would recognise you in a suit,' Fenella said.

'Yeah, I was sort of relying on that.'

Inverness Doogie and Miranda were there, so was our revered landlord Naseem Naseem (revered because his rents never caught up with inflation, due to a shoddy calculator someone had given him two Christmases ago). Mr Goodson, from Flat One, had promised to look in if he had the time.

Bunny and Dodd, two musicians I had played with in the past were there, along with three musicians I had never seen before. It might have been the chance of a free drink that attracted them, but from the way they were clustering around Roshan Ara, I suspected it wasn't just that.

'They wouldn't take any money,' said Duncan the Drunken placing two pints of bitter on the table. 'So I got in an extra.'

'That's OK, Dunc, I'm running a tab.'

Duncan looked suitably impressed and demolished most of one of the pints immediately.

'So, where's the little woman, then?' he asked, and once again I marvelled at how long he had lasted down in London.

Though why stop at London? Duncan must be the only male in the country, if not Europe, who still refers to his wife as 'the little woman'.

'Amy?' I said. 'She's away for a business meeting.'

I didn't bother to add 'in Milan,' as that would have been too pushy.

'Doreen's not coming either,' he said reaching for the second pint. He held it up in a toast to me. 'Happy Birthday. No prisoners.'

'Oh Angel, I almost forgot,' Fenella announced with about as much sincerity as an accountant saying your tax returns shouldn't take a minute.

She rummaged in a shoulder bag as big as a sack and produced a folded copy of the *Evening Standard* open at the Horoscopes column.

'Look at that. Isn't it spooky?' she giggled. I read:

LIBRA (23 Sept-22 Oct) If today is the birthday simply follow these Rules Of Life: Remember all your friends; buy them lots to eat and drink, not forgetting the vegetarians. Be kind to animals, especially cats.

'Thank you, Fenella, that was sweet.'

I leaned over the table full of drinks and pecked her cheek. Lisabeth glared at me but allowed it.

Duncan had picked up the paper.

'That is fucking weird, man, cos, like, it is your—'

'Relax, Duncan. There's a printer down in Southwark does you a fake page to insert into the paper. It's a sort of personalised birthday card.'

The idea sank in.

'So, like, if you had a secretary who followed the stars, you could plant one saying it was about time she shagged the boss?'

'Got it in one, Dunc.'

'Sounds a bloody good business to be in,' he said.

It beats what he used to do, I thought.

'So, how's the fashion business? Got you out of Hackney, didn't it, so there is that? But you've kept the flat on, I hear?'

'You heard right, Dunc. And business is good, I have to say that.'

Duncan stared into his glass.

'Shaky business, fashion. I'll stick to cars.'

'Good call, Duncan. Wise move.'

'I wouldn't fit in that sort of world. All those women getting their kit off, poncing around for the photographers… '

'It's not that cushy a number, Dunc. I've been off sick quite a bit while we've been doing the latest promotion. The doctors have diagnosed RGS.'

He leaned in, confidentially. 'Sounds bad. What is it?'

'Repetitive Groin Strain.'

Roshan Ara called me from across the table.

'Angel, look along the bar.'

I did as she suggested. It was a long bar and waiting to be served in various groupings were ten women. All were wearing TAL tops in one or other colour or style.

I made a circle with my thumb and forefinger and waved to Roshan who gave me a thumbs-up sign.

'What happened about the takeover of the company, Angel?' asked Fenella, who had been following my gaze.

'TAL sold out, Fenella, it didn't get taken over. There's a difference.'

'Oh,' she said, feeling rebuked. 'So what does TAL stand for now then?'

'That Angel Look,' I said.

The Do-Not Press
Fiercely Independent Publishing

Keep in touch with what's happening at the cutting edge of independent British publishing.

Join The Do-Not Press Information Service and receive advance information of all our new titles, as well as news of events and launches in your area, and the occasional free gift and special offer.

Simply send your name and address to:
The Do-Not Press (Dept. TAL)
PO Box 4215
London
SE23 2QD

There is no obligation to purchase and no salesman will call.